HOME FREE

Dan Wakefield

A DELL BOOK

Published by
DELL PUBLISHING CO., INC.
1 Dag Hammarskjold Plaza
New York, N.Y. 10017

Dell ® TM 681510, Dell Publishing Co., Inc.

ISBN: 0-440-13699-7

Reprinted by arrangement with
Delacorte Press/Seymour Lawrence
Printed in the United States of America
First Dell printing—May 1978

CALIFORNIA DREAMING ...
ON SUCH A WINTRY DAY

Once he stopped for a drink at the bar of The Pier and so took longer than usual getting home and Stella's eyes were snappish.

"You don't go getting ideas when you're there in town, do you?"

"No," he said. "None at all."

Which was true.

It was still true the day he disappeared from her for good.

It wasn't *his* idea.

He was walking down the street when he noticed a car, cruising slowly. . . . The car pulled up beside him and stopped. It was Barnes. Driving the car. He rolled down the window and Gene peered in. . . .

"Hey, where ya goin'?" he said.

"L.A. Wanna come?"

Gene opened the door and got in.

"Let's go," he said.

"Where do we go to get your stuff?"

"I've got my stuff," Gene said.

"Where?"

"On. It's all I need. In fact, when we get to L.A. I won't even need the coat."

For The Dove,
who saw me through it

Once there was a way to get back homeward.
—JOHN LENNON AND PAUL MCCARTNEY,
"Golden Slumbers"

Freedom's just another word for nothin'
left to lose.
—KRIS KRISTOFFERSON,
"Me and Bobby McGee"

He was there because he had promised.

Besides, he had no particular reason or urge to be anywhere else.

The promise was not that he would go to college at the University of Illinois at Champaign-Urbana but that he would get a college degree, in any thing, in any place. That's all his father had asked when he gave him the money to do it. There wasn't even a time limit on it though maybe that was assumed, that he'd do it in the four years it took most everyone else. He had meant to, but being booted out of one place and dropping out of another had set him back, and then he had to take time off to make some bread when he'd gone through what the old man had given him. That made the promise even heavier: he had taken the money and he'd damn well get the degree, no matter how long it took.

Ages it already seemed like.

He was scratching a mosquito bite and waiting for the instructor to show for this section of a gut course called in the catalog Survey of American Colonial History and known among students as George Washington One. He was idly looking over the class to see if he could spot some

serious, plain-looking chick he could hit on later for
class notes, when he suddenly saw her come into the room.

Not the serious, plain-looking chick.

This was something else.

She was wearing a short white dress, a thin gold chain
at the waist, the rest of her dark, intense, feline; black
hair fell with long luster down her back, dark eyes were
topped by large brows and cupped beneath with deep
half-moons, the eyes large and quick, giving the catlike
suggestion to her face. Gene moved up out of the scrunch
he had settled into in his chair, hoping she'd sit beside or
near him but instead she went to the desk at the front
of the room and with a graceful movement perched on the
edge of it, her long legs, richly tanned, dangling.

There were nervous giggles. No one knew if this was
the teacher or some kind of kooky chick trying for attention. She pulled out a cigarette and four jocks jumped to
light it. More giggles. Gene didn't move. The class bell
rang and he didn't mind it, even though at this advanced
stage in what was finally a seven-year and four-college
trip to the big B.A. that special sound usually worked on
his nerves like a dental drill.

"I'm Louise Fern," she said, "and this is History one
oh three. Usually it's a gut course. This time it won't be."

There were no more giggles.

At the end of the hour she was crowded by students,
wanting attention, asking unnecessary questions.

Gene waited. He wasn't afraid of waiting. He wasn't a
jock but women liked him, liked his lean concave posture,
head bent for listening, even then somehow seeming taller
than his medium height.

He knew all the moves, but he wasn't thinking of
games now. This was a new experience. Just when he
hoped he had had them all. But this was decidedly
different. It was like he had tunnel vision and Louise Fern
was standing at the end of the tunnel. Filling it up.

He waited till just the two of them were left in the room.

"I'm going to buy you a drink," he said evenly.

She looked at him sharp, then shrugged.

"Well, if I have no choice," she said.

"You don't," he said smiling.

Neither do I, he thought.

He took her for the drink, then he took her back to her apartment, then he took her to bed. The next morning he said he intended to stay.

"We'll see," she said.

He stayed the rest of the academic year, hardly leaving except to shop for groceries, buy booze, score grass, and go to her lectures.

In bed, biting and tickling and pinching, they kidded about her being an Older Woman and him an Innocent Young Student. She was twenty-seven, he twenty-three. Sometimes they played teacher-student games. Like she would be the stern, spinsterish teacher and he would be the hood she had flunked in her course who had come to force his cruel lust upon her.

They got into each other's heads as well as bodies.

He saw how history was for her, how she got high on it. When she talked about The Closing of the Frontier, or The Rise of the Railroads, her voice took on a whole other quality, a husky intensity. He read everything she told him to, stuff that especially turned her on and then they'd discuss it. He could see it, in her, but he couldn't feel it in himself like that. He had never been able to get off on a subject, there were some he dug more than others, that was all.

She asked if there hadn't been anything else, aside from

academic subjects, that really turned him on, like playing some kind of music or sports.

"Running," he said.

He told her how it gave him a clean feeling, both in his head and his body. He imagined when he ran that the wind was really going through his head, clearing it out, blowing away the accumulated cobwebs of old tangled memories, blowing away the bilge of bad dreams, trash of turmoil, dumpings of dead arguments, dumb deeds. Clean. He went out for track in high school but was cut because he lacked the competitive spirit, a failing the coach said probably meant he was a fairy. He didn't care about winning, he didn't want ribbons, just the feeling that came from the running.

Lou said she could dig, it sounded like what good dope did sometimes.

They liked doing grass and hash but they didn't drop acid. Lou didn't want to mess with her head since she liked it the way it was; Gene didn't go for the idea of something "expanding" his mind, he wanted to turn the sucker down.

He said it showed they agreed on the basics.

He had to move out a few days when her parents came to visit. They were hard-shell Baptists from Arkansas and they assumed their baby daughter, special as the youngest of four, would remain a virgin until she was married. They didn't even know she smoked cigarettes much less dope. Before their visits she eliminated the deep orange nicotine stains from her fingers by scrubbing them over and over with lemon juice.

Gene got to meet them on the ruse he was one of her students dropping over to get an assignment he'd missed.

She asked him to stay and have macaroons and lemonade with them. Not looking at Lou he said to her parents, "Your daughter has taught me more than any teacher I ever had."

"No, no," said Lou, choking on her lemonade.

"Louise has always been modest," her father said proudly.

"She never tells us," her mother said wistfully, "of her accomplishments."

Sitting stiff in his chair Gene feared he might fart or say "Fuck!" so excused himself after the one macaroon.

When they'd gone and Gene could come back Lou got some specially good hash and they fucked and talked all night. She asked if his parents would visit or he visit them and he said how his mother had died his first year of high school and Dad, retired and tired, lived with Gene's much older married sister and her family in Chicago and frankly Gene couldn't face him again till he had the degree.

"Your albatross," Lou said.

"A real bummer."

Mostly they were high, sometimes just on each other. What the counselors always told Gene he lacked was not intelligence but motivation. Now he had it. Her. She shared his bent for daring, difference, doing things your own way, any way but dull.

The song they played all the time, kind of like their personal anthem, was "The Harper Valley P.T.A." It had come out right when they met, September of '68, and it matched their mood. The sultry singsong of Jeannie C. Riley telling how all the respectable folk of this little town were hypocrites living wild behind the proper front they put up. It was their kind of song, A Fuck You kind of song, and they liked to think of it as saying "Fuck You" in particular to Champaign-Urbana, Illinois, and what they regarded as its monster-sized, tiny-minded university.

Everything wasn't all fun and games, though. One night lying in bed after love he asked her how come she never got married, she must have got asked a lot. She said in a flat, toneless voice she'd got asked a lot and said no a lot. Then she raised up on an elbow and fixing her eyes on him so he couldn't look away, so he couldn't forget, she laid on him her feelings about "The Horse-Carriage-Love-Marriage Syndrome."

"People mistakenly think those things go together but they don't have to go together at all. Not even horses and carriages much less loves and marriages. There are plenty of horses that aren't tied to carriages and that's the kind *I'd* be if I were a horse. Untied. Not pulling a big load of people behind me like a woman drags a family all her life. If I were a horse they wouldn't even get a bridle on me. They call that 'breaking' a horse. Well no one will ever break *me*."

Gene gently put his hand on her arm.

"No one here's tryin, babe."

"You promise?"

He did.

It was the first time he'd ever had to promise a woman *not* to marry her in order to stay with her.

Something new.

There always was with Lou.

Like the time in the spring when she came home with a small jar of supermarket red caviar and a bottle of New York State champagne to celebrate her getting a two-year appointment in the History Department at Northeastern University in Boston beginning next fall.

"Far out," he said. "I can learn to do baked beans."

"Oh," said Lou, not heavy just curious-sounding, "you coming, too?"

The thought of not living with her made him feel

dizzy, like looking down from some incredible height onto nothing at all below.

He realized she was his life, in a way that he'd never really had one before.

But he couldn't tell her that.

"Boston's got lots of colleges," he said. "I might as well finish up there as anywhere else."

"I can't promise anything," Lou said. "About us, I mean."

"Who can promise anything?"

"Just so it's understood. We're both free."

He patted her hand.

"Hey, roomie, I know how ya feel."

She smiled.

"OK, roomie," she said.

Gene popped the champagne and put on Jeannie C. Riley singing "The Harper Valley P.T.A."

I

Rents were sky-high in Boston but they found a one-bedroom apartment whose drawbacks in comfort were balanced by economy. It was on Carver Street, which ran for just a block down from the Trailways station out to Boylston across from the Boston Common. It looked almost like an alley, and winos were fond of using its entryways for shelter during their deadened sleep. Gene and Lou learned to step through without disturbing them.

Other people might have been freaked by the blaring announcements of bus departures and the neon throb of a parking lot sign pulsing in their living room window, but Gene had lived for a year with Lou in her apartment that was over a chiropractic clinic on the highway heading into Urbana across from an all-night diner whose wagon wheel symbol glowed in the dark and attracted all kinds of last-minute, tire-skidding customers. They figured that must have been practice for the place by the bus station.

The important thing was this was *their* place, for in Urbana Gene had just lived at Lou's. He wanted to make it nice, their nest, so he stripped off the dank, dark wallpaper, painted white, decorated with plants and posters. Philodendron, Swedish ivy, asparagus fern. See Madrid, Ski Sugarbush, Stop the War.

Now they could get it on.

Their lives.

Gene had never really thought that way before, he had just sort of let things happen. Now he was anxious to please, wanting to make sure Boston would be a good trip for them. Since Lou didn't go for pledges or promises, much less marital contracts, Gene just figured he would see that everything was so cool she would have no reason to split, it would just be the natural thing to keep on together.

Before he could look for a college in Boston to cop the last twelve credits he needed he had to get some bread together. When Lou started teaching at Northeastern Gene got a job tending bar at The Crossroads over on Newbury Street off Mass Ave, working the eleven-to-seven shift. That left a hunk of the mornings free and he promised himself he was not just going to lie around doing some kind of dope and listening to records, he was going to make some use of his time. What he was going to do was, for one thing, get into cooking.

He liked to cook because you had to concentrate and your mind couldn't drift into thinking of other shit. Cooking kind of affected his head like a mild sort of dope. He was damn good with any type of eggs and tough on stew but he wanted to get into serious recipes, work up a regular repertoire. He went out and bought himself a paperback James Beard cookbook and a stockpile of gourmet devices from whisk to garlic press.

They had to eat late, of course, but Gene made what preparation he could in the morning so when he blew in after work he was ready to roll. Lou really seemed to dig it, she liked good food but cooking to her was a hassle, a distraction that fucked up her head from work she was doing, like lecture preparation, thesis research, the kind of things that didn't mix with trying to remember how many cups of this and dashes of that. So she sat reading and thinking and having a martini or so in the living room while Gene did his thing in the kitchen. It suited them both. That's what he wanted.

But the night he made his most ambitious meal, a surprise he'd been preparing to spring from the time he first saw it in James Beard, she wasn't there.

Roast beef and Yorkshire pudding!

He had the day off and had got this incredible dinner on. Always before, she was home when he got in from work a little past seven, so he planned the meal for then, timing everything so the roast would be rare the way she liked it, the pudding a risen prize.

Now it was eight. The pudding had fallen. The beef was well past well.

Where?

There, now.

She came in laughing, high.

With this guy.

Barnes, his name was.

From what Gene could gather out of the excited garble of her talk she had picked him up or let him pick her up (although she didn't say it that way) at Waldenbooks on Boylston Street. His pitch was he was a writer and wanted to buy his book for her, he liked to think people like her would read it. (She fell for *that*?) Then to celebrate the fact she was going to read it he offered to buy her a drink at Gatsby's bar across from the Statler and after the second drink she said for Godsake you'll never make a profit like this, buying your book for people and then buying them drinks, she said he had to come back and have a few drinks with her and her roommate.

Gene could tell she hadn't bothered to mention she roomed with a guy.

This Barnes was one big disappointed dude. Tall and

slightly stooped, head pulled in as if afraid of a swat, long sallow face that was winsome before he laid eyes on the roomie and now was decidedly woeful.

Lou very merrily told poor Barnes to make himself at home and handed the book he wrote to Gene while she went to make her martinis that usually tended to put everyone at ease, consisting as they did of a tall glass full of gin, an ice cube, and two portions of vermouth applied with an old Murine dropper.

"Wow!" she called from the kitchen. "What smells good?"

"It might have been dinner," Gene said.

She didn't seem to hear.

Gene held Barnes's book in his hand. A paperback. The cover had a picture of a sexy blonde, hair strewn around her and skirt uplifted. Over the body in dripping red letters were the words *Death of a Deb*.

"Good title, man," Gene said.

What could you say?

"They changed it," said Barnes.

"To what?" asked Lou, coming in with drinks.

"To that," he said, pointing at the book. "My title was *Coming Out to Die*."

"Can they do that?" Lou asked.

He coughed, nodding accusingly at the book.

"They did," he said.

"Listen, everybody," Gene said, "I hate to interrupt the fun and all, but is anyone going to be interested in having any dinner before the evening is out?"

"Thanks, but I'll just finish my drink," said Barnes.

"No, no, I'm sure there's plenty," Lou said. "Isn't there, Gene? If there isn't, we'll just divide what we have. Share and share alike, right?"

Gene took a big slug of his martini.

"Right on, sister. Anything you say."

"Listen," said Barnes. "I oughta go."

"No! You haven't got your profits back," Lou said. "What is it they call them?"

"Royalties."

"See? You're way behind. Still in the red. The dinner'll put you ahead."

Rather than listen to more of this bull Gene plunked an extra plate on the table and brought out the shriveled roast and the fallen pudding.

"Wow," said Lou, "a real roast! What's that other thing?"

"It used to be Yorkshire pudding," said Gene.

"You cook a lot?" Barnes asked.

If this was one of those guys who thought men who liked to cook were fags, he was going to get a cold Yorkshire pudding in his mug.

"Whenever I can," Gene said. "I happen to dig it."

"Wish I could do it," said Barnes. "Tired of Van Camp and his goddam pork and beans."

Lou complained the roast wasn't rare.

"It was about an hour ago," Gene said, "while you were farting around at Gatsby's."

"What does that mean, 'farting around'?" said Lou, putting her knife and fork down.

"Hey," Barnes said, "I like it this way. No shit. This is great."

"It means whatever you think it means," Gene said.

"Can't stand rare myself," said Barnes. "The more done the better. Well is well with me."

"I don't call having a drink with a friend 'farting around,'" said Lou.

"Oh, I didn't realize you and he were old friends."

"I didn't say 'old' I said 'friends.'"

"Well," said Barnes, wolfing down a last hunk of burned beef and jumping up from the table, "I really gotta be going now. Hope you'll both come over sometime. I'm on the Hill. Name's in the book. I'll open a

can of beans or something. Anyway, drinks. Really. Anytime."

He made his escape, leaving Gene and Lou at battle
stations.

"That was some hospitality," she said.

"I'm supposed to feed every pickup you drag home?"

"I didn't drag him anywhere and he wasn't a pickup."

"What was he then?"

"A friend, goddam it. Or might have been. Don't you
understand about that? Just because we locked ourselves
up and didn't see anyone in Urbana doesn't mean I'm
going to do that here. We *need* friends. People. Otherwise we'll smother each other."

She persuaded him she wasn't out to make the guy nor
did she have any such ideas or why the hell would she
have brought him home anyway?

He took a deep breath and said he was sorry he'd
thought such things.

She apologized about being late and not calling.

He said he guessed she was right about having friends.

She said then why not start with Barnes?

Gene thought that sort of brought things right back to
his feeling she picked the guy up or let him pick her up
because she had some kind of thing for him.

He didn't say that, though.

He said "Why not?"

━━━━━━━━━━━

Gene had to admit that in one way Barnes was the
perfect choice for a friend.

If anyone needed one more than they did, he did.

Living all alone in this dramatic duplex pad, high
long windows looking on rooftops, spires and chimneys
clustered around like a lump of London, the Charles
River glinting down in the distance.

The sleek low Scandinavian furniture looked out of place.

So did Barnes.

He seemed to be sort of lurking there.

On both sides of the fireplace boxes were stacked used grocery and liquor boxes full of books.

"Why don't you unpack them?" Lou asked, looking at titles.

"Sure, man," Gene said, "I'll build you some shelves." What were friends for?

Barnes looked embarrassed, scratched his head.

"I like it this way," he said. "When you put up your books on the shelf it seems permanent. This way I feel I'm free to pick up and go."

"Maybe sometime you'll feel free to stay," Lou said.

"Maybe. Sometime."

Lou said they liked his book, which was true. It was funny. Not the murder, the people and what they said.

Barnes brightened, brought out a better bottle of brandy.

It was somewhere toward the end of that one he told them how he went a year to something called The Iowa Writers Workshop to learn how to write The Great American Novel but had to drop out and make some bread doing newspaper work. When he finally got to the novel he didn't care anymore if it was great or even American he just wanted out of the newspaper business, he had OD'd on asking people questions all the time. A "real writer" he knew in Denver sent Barnes's book to his literary agent who sold it as a paperback original mystery with a big enough advance so Barnes could split and have enough time to live while he wrote another one. When he got the check he went straight to the airport, looked at the list of departing flights on the first TV monitor he came to, and picked one.

"Why Boston?" Lou asked.

"It sounded old. That's how I felt."

He said he was thirty-four then but that was six
months ago so he must be thirty-four and a half, and
felt he was going on forty.

"Don't sweat it," Lou said. "Two years I'll be thirty."

Gene couldn't tell if that was consolation or kind of a
come-on.

Barnes didn't even seem to hear. He was lying on the
floor propped against his couch, belting the brandy, when
suddenly he sat up straight, stuck his arm in the air, and
said, "I will never again ask anyone what he has for
breakfast or thinks of the President or does in his spare
time."

Then he slumped, as if shot, inert on the floor.

Snore.

They arranged him on the coach, brought blankets from
the bedroom, tucked him in, turned off lights, tiptoed out.

Gene figured they had a friend. He was glad, since
Lou wanted some.

It was cool with Gene that Lou didn't take him to faculty affairs or bring home academic colleagues. She decided and he agreed it was best to keep her two lives separate, home and work, since her living with a guy who was not only four years younger but naked of any degree would not do much for her own image. Besides, she said after teaching and going to committee meetings all day she was tired of talking academic.

Students and their parties were a different ball game. Lou was the kind of teacher they liked to invite and she liked to go. These were not finicky faculty cocktail sherries but casual sprawls, everything comfortable. She didn't mind taking Gene, either, all she had to do was say "This is my friend, Gene" and that was the introduction, no need for name-rank-social-serial number, where are you from or going.

They took along Barnes to a student party over on Phillips Street, the back side of Beacon Hill where students and dropouts and rundowns lived alongside Chinese laundries, secondhand TV sales-repair stores. Mellow old Mamas and Papas music was asking you to "Look Out Any Window," the crowded living room fragrant with grass and sweet wine. Barnes was disappointed he didn't bring

booze but found a nice bubble-gum-popping girl named
Nell who dredged him up some old Mr. Boston Lemon
Flavored gin from out of the depths of the kitchen.

A scruffy-looking wild kid staring at Lou all night got
fortified enough on wine and grass to float up to her and
declare his undying love and she smiled and introduced
Gene and said they could all be friends. He ended up on
their couch the next morning, pledging his loyalty to both,
saying his regard for Lou was unsullied by vile thoughts of
sex.

Gene appreciated the purity.

The party was good for everyone. The bubble-gum girl
who got Barnes his booze was a social work student and
evidently his case appealed to her. Barnes not only had
friends, now he had a lover.

The kid on the couch, known only as Thomas, like
Fabian was just Fabian, arrived outside the window Monday morning blowing a horn that sounded like a sick
moose. He was driving a converted milk truck painted red
white and blue that said "Amalgamated Enterprises," and
below that, "Let's Make a Deal." Thomas said it was his
"company truck," his business being buying, selling, and
trading such a wide variety of goods as furniture, record
albums, dope, kitchenware, TVs, stereo components, and
pills, mostly uppers and downers with a scattering of anti-
biotics and antihistamines thrown in. In his spare time he
went to college, or rather colleges, sitting in on lecture
courses at Northeastern, Harvard, BU, and MIT.

"You mean you're not registered anywhere?" Lou said.

Thomas looked shocked.

"Then you have to pay!"

He expressed his pure devotion to Lou by tooting outside their window every M-W-F and driving her to North-eastern.

If Thomas wasn't such an all-around scruffy-looking general fuckup, Gene might have been a little jealous.

What the hell, you couldn't knock free transportation.

━━━━━━━━

Gene didn't feel left out or anything because Lou had the world of her work at Northeastern completely separate from him, shit, he had his own little world tending bar at The Crossroads.

Afternoons there were cool and dim, restful. Gene dug it most when the old guys got it on arguing about the baseball players of the past, it wasn't really arguing it was just to say the names: Rizzuto and Marion, Musial and Bauer, Lemon and Ford. The names were like a litany and when they got it going Gene loved to listen, the litany lulled him, too, helped turn down his own mind.

The peace of the place was always shattered when Flash came in, topping everyone else's stories, especially about sports or sex, telling again how he might have made it in the pros but at 6'2" he was too short for *forward* in the NBA. Telling again how in college he ran the 100 in 10.4, which was lightning in '61 and had earned him the name Flash.

He usually came in around the happy hour but one day he showed a little after three, wearing instead of his usual splashy threads a grungy old sweatshirt and jeans. Instead of one of the frothy blended drinks he usually had he ordered a double dry martini straight up with an extra olive.

"This is a good time to drink," Flash said. "Between lunch and the cocktail hour you have a kind of dip in there, that's when you need a little something to pick you up."

Like all good bartenders Gene agreed with the customer, and by the second drink Flash was pouring out his troubles to him. Or trouble. There was one biggie, which was that Flash owned—had owned—a travel agency, and the business had just gone bankrupt.

"That's rough, man," Gene said.

"Hell, ya can't let that stuff get ya down," Flash said. "When ya get off here? I'll take you over to Dorchester, we'll hit a couple spots I know, scare up some action."

"Sorry, man," Gene said, "I'm cookin tonight for me and my woman," but when he saw Flash's face fall he added, "You come, too. There's plenty. Stew."

"Oh, thanks, ole buddy, but no thanks, I'm on a diet. Strictly vitamins."

"Pills?"

"Nah. In the booze. Plenty of vitamins in booze. You know, it's made out of potatoes and grain and shit like that. They boil it down, so you're actually gettin the essence."

"That's all? The vitamins in the booze?"

"And the olives. Fuckin olives can keep you goin for weeks. Shit. You take those wops up in those hills over there, they raise whole families on olives. Maybe a little spaghetti thrown in, but that's no vitamins."

"Tonight, you're gettin some stew in you."

"Well, hell—"

Flash was revived, not by the stew but the sight of Lou, which inspired him to "spruce up a bit" in their bathroom, taking a shower and applying every talcum, lotion, and ointment he could find to drown the stench of his moldy clothes.

Over stew he regaled them with tales of bankruptcy, making it seem the most glamorous trip in the world.

Flash had put all his hopes as well as capital in buying up a block of three thousand tickets to the Rolling Stones concert at Shea Stadium, and putting together a package tour that would hopefully lure every hip kid in New England.

"Sounds good," Lou said. "How'd you blow it?"

"Details. I got bogged down in details. Like the box lunches for the bus ride. Christ, but I had that organized. Made a deal with a guy runs a super mar-kette in Revere for three-day-old Wonder bread. A pal in the North End promised sixty salamis in return for using my passport for a quick little business trip he had to make to Panama. Pickles? Beautiful. Chick I knew was doing PR for a local pickle company—but shit, there I go getting bogged down in details again."

The detail Flash failed to notice until it was too late was that the Stones were also booked in Boston and Providence on the same concert tour where they played Shea Stadium. So not too many fans fought to pay extra to see them in New York when they could see them at home.

"Did any—uh—go on your tour?" Lou asked.

"Ninety-four," Flash said, shaking his head. "Shit, they must have been some kind of misfits. I didn't have the heart to go to the station and see em. Jesus. Ninety-four losers in one place."

"What about you?" asked Lou.

"Me? Hell, I'm the comeback kid. I got friends. You got friends you can always bounce back. Look at Gene here takin his bankrupt buddy home for a hearty stew. Bankrolls you can always get. What counts in the long fuckin haul is *friends*."

Gene guessed they had another one.

When he thought about it Gene was kind of proud about bringing Flash home, he figured it showed he wasn't uptight anymore about Lou liking men who were just their friends. He saw she was just more comfortable with men, there wasn't any sex angle to it, that's just the way she was. The concept of "meeting with the Sisters" was catching on big in Boston, but to Lou the idea was as foreign as the

old-fashioned custom of "getting together with the girls."
She wasn't against it or anything, it just didn't happen to
be her scene. She tended to clam up around women, unless
they were in the company of their own man.

A few days later Flash fell by The Crossroads, dressed
to kill. He had just got some kind of temporary loan and
was going out to find himself a date and celebrate.

"You hit the dating bars?" Gene asked.

Flash drew back, offended.

"Those meat racks?" he said. "Wouldn't go near em."

"Where then?"

"The source, man, the airport."

"Bar?"

"Incoming flights. You wait till the passengers are off,
go up to a stewardess coming out and say you expected a
certain girl on this flight, you had a whole evening planned
around her coming, and she didn't show—well, hell, take
it from there."

"You just go up to any airline?"

"I personally prefer Delta and Allegheny. You get a
more outgoing, positive type. But to each his own. Who
knows? You might dig Eastern. Go out to Logan, give it a
try."

"Nah, I'm all tied up, man."

"Well, sure, that Lou is somethin else, but you ought
to share the wealth."

"Huh?"

"What I mean is, socialize a little. Like I was thinkin,
I got this girl flies in from Atlanta every week or so, a real
peach. Thought we could make it a foursome."

"The four of us go out, you mean? Have dinner?"

"Uh, well, sure, that might be good, sort of as an ice-
breaker. But what I had in mind was then when we all get
to know each other we could trade off. Me with Lou and
you with this delectable, exquisite peach. Then back
again. You dig? Sort of a round-robinish sort of thing."

Gene thanked Flash but said he and Lou weren't into

that kind of scene. He tried to make it sound casual, just something they didn't enjoy, like watching "The Brady Bunch" or eating Armenian food.

Back of the counter, his legs were trembling.

Finally Flash believed there was no way to get the round robin on.

He shook his head.

"You and your middle-class hang-ups," he said.

When Gene got home that night he discovered he didn't quite have it together enough to laugh and tell Lou about Flash's proposition for getting on a round-robinish sort of thing.

On the other hand, he didn't get bugged at her because he knew Flash wanted to ball her.

He figured all together it was some kind of progress.

Lou was right that you shouldn't just shut yourself off from people. Hell, it felt good to know they'd brought Barnes and Nell together, and besides that it was a trip to figure out how it happened, how it worked.

Lou said the differences did it—not just the fifteen years difference in age, but their personalities. Nell was the kind who wanted to Help people, for Barnes the word Help was a personal plea. See? They fit. She as his personal social worker, him as her one-man emotional slum.

Besides, it was good to have another couple like that to boogie with. Like Gene and Lou would have just sat back and missed the best two ticket-bought nights of their lives if it hadn't been for Barnes and Nell.

And the coke.

Barnes went down to New York to see the literary agent who sold his mystery and told him about a new one he had in mind, setting the story at Harvard, he would hang around there awhile and take notes. The agent was so turned on by it that Barnes before coming back saw a friend of a friend and bought $100 worth of coke to celebrate the triumph of the book he had just thought of trying to write.

It came in a tinfoil package, astonishingly small.

"Don't anyone sneeze for Chrissake," Barnes said as Nell tamped a little mound of it out on her tortoiseshell hand mirror. On Barnes's instructions she separated the mound out into slim lines with a razor blade, while he rolled tight a ten-dollar bill for sniffing it up.

"Bill should be a hundred," he apologized, "if you do it right."

"We're just folks," said Gene.

They sniffed, in turn, sitting back awhile and waiting for it to happen, coming on suddenly giggly, funny, everything anyone else said was funny to the rest, and Nell asked who was best, Joni or Janis. Gene said each was best of who she was. Lou asked why. Nell said both were coming to Boston to give a concert and who should they hear? Everyone yelled and argued, happy high confusion till Barnes said the solution: "Both." Clapping, cheers, cheer, till down again, a drag, the trouble with coke was being over so soon and then you wanted more to get back up; product with built-in sales pitch.

But even after being down from the coke Barnes said they all had agreed, all had to see both Joni and Janis, he'd get tickets if Gene made stew.

Dinner and the theater!

None of the four of them ever forgot. The stew maybe, the concerts not.

Joni all light, on a bright stage, nice light airy fluffy feeling, the feeling you got from hearing her "Clouds." The audience buoyed, buoyant, bouncy, behind her, with her, all the way, wanting to show, make her know, how they loved her—once she forgot the words to a song and everywhere were smiles, sighs of sympathy, a feeling through the hall that everyone wanted to run to the stage and feed her some special warm homemade chicken soup. Sad songs she sang them, yes, too, but sweet, sincere, soulful, soft as a breeze. Yes, yes, yes, Joni! This was the bright warm milk of the world.

Janis all dark on the stage before a spot struck sudden

on her, she in a deep purple satin outfit, cut sexy-crazy, sight of her set off screams and some fans scrambled out of their seats to run down the aisle and get near the stage get near Janis, source of that painful power pulsing out through the wiry little body, the sing-shout plea to "Take a little bit a my heart now, bay-bee . . ." and they would if they could in a way they did, the hungry audience hot and mean in a heavy atmosphere of smoke from joints the management gave up trying to stop, the smoke thick, everywhere, electric roar of the band a blare but her voice going over it, beyond it, guts wrenching but making it music. This was what it was to be alone in the dark and not be afraid to be afraid.

After the Joni Mitchell concert they all went to Barnes's, built a fire, drank wine, played her records.

After the Janis Joplin concert they just went home, not saying anything.

But that brought them closer, too, knowing they all understood things they didn't have to say.

For the first time Gene could remember he really had it together, doing things he usually didn't but wished he had later, living and loving and having friends. He had the nice sense he and Lou were settling—*in* but not *down.* Settling down sounded stodgy, settling in sounded warm.

He didn't even mind the holidays coming, he figured he might even send a few cards.

Greetings.

They were for him, but not from Santa.

Uncle Sam.

He had got the message before but always been safe with a student deferment. At the rate he was going through college—colleges—he figured there was no way the war would still be on when he graduated. But it seemed like they couldn't turn it off. It was part of life now like college and marriage and kids and career and retirement. They had quietly added Vietnam to the list. Like adding a new sand trap to the course just in case it was getting too easy.

Mainly he had tried to forget the whole thing.

But it had not forgot *him.*

"There's got to be a way," Lou said when he showed it to her, "out of it."

"There is," Gene said. "Canada. Jail. I can take my choice."

Lou shook her head. She said there had to be others, at least another.

She went out and got a copy of the *Cambridge Phoenix*. That was a weekly paper that had stuff in it for students and hippies like the regular dailies mainly had stuff for housewives and guys who sold insurance and followed the Red Sox. The *Phoenix* had classified ads for everything from secondhand stereo bargains to getting laid, from how to get abortions to help for kicking heroin. They had a whole column just for draft counseling, and Lou and Gene went over the list and picked out what sounded best.

——————

At the Draft Counseling Service in the basement of the Arlington Street Church, Gene talked with a hip-looking young lawyer, or maybe he was still just a law student, who had muttonchop sideburns and wore a corduroy suit with a sweater underneath the jacket. He looked like one of the young lawyers on a TV series who shun the offers of big corporate firms to help the oppressed and live on containers of black coffee and takeout sandwiches. He said to call him Pete.

"Tell me, Gene," Pete said, tapping his pencil, "do you have any strong religious background?"

"I was baptized," Gene said, "a Methodist."

He thought of how church was as a kid, the men sitting stiffly in their best suits, the women wearing hats that seemed precariously perched on their heads with the aid of pins, everyone vaguely itching, mouthing holy hymns, fighting temptations to doze through the preacher's drone; time sticking in the slow thick syrup of Sunday. None of it fed him, nothing was filled.

"No," Gene said. "It wasn't—it isn't enough."

"Have you had any mental or emotional problems—ones that required professional help—a psychologist or psychiatrist."

"A couple," Gene said.

Pete picked up his pencil, hopefully.

"How many is that? Two? Or more than two?"

Gene figured.

"Three," he said.

"What was the problem?"

"They didn't know."

He smiled, thinking of the Dylan song that said, *My best friend the doctor won't even tell me what I got . . .*

"Why did you seek this professional help?"

"They told me. The schools. I was breaking their rules."

"Which ones? Serious?"

"Not attending classes. Booze in the room. Dope."

"Hard stuff?"

Gene shook his head.

"Just weed," he said.

"The doctors—what did they tell you?"

Gene pressed his temples, remembering rooms, licenses framed on the wall and Sister Corita prints with lively colors and quotations from famous people endorsing life; testimonials from statesmen and philosophers assuring that things weren't as bad as they seemed. Gene's favorite was the quote from e. e. cummings, "damn everything but the circus." In front of it, at a desk in one of those rooms, sat a sad-eyed, gentle woman who looked as if it had been a long time since she'd been to any circus. The third time he saw her she said, kindly and sadly, that there wasn't any magic in her field, that she didn't know how to instill motivation into anyone and she hoped sometime he would find something that would move him to use his potential. He appreciated that she hadn't handed him a lot of crap, given him lectures like the men shrinks had whom he'd

seen at other schools. Both those dudes sat there and told
him like they were laying some heavy information on him
that he used dope and alcohol as an escape.

What the hell else did you use them for?

Pete reviewed Gene's case and determined that he
lacked any of the mental or physical defects that would
have saved him from military service.

Shit. He was even deficient in having deficiencies. His
physical was less than two weeks off.

Lou called a conference. She didn't say that, she just
asked everyone to meet at Barnes's place.

"What good'll it do?" Gene asked.

"Ideas," she said. "Somebody might have one. Maybe
if we all keep talking and thinking about it, concentrate
on it, somebody'll just come up with something."

Lou was like the chairman. She wouldn't even let
Thomas pass around joints or Flash make a batch of rusty
nails, though each of them complained she was stifling
their inspiration.

"Later for that," Lou said. "First we try to think."

They were allowed to sip wine and smoke regular cigarettes.

Gene told about the draft counseling guy, and how he
didn't think the stuff that Gene had or had done would
get him out.

"Not even three different shrinks?" Barnes asked.

"That's nothing anymore," said Lou. "It's probably the
national average."

"Fuckin wine," said Flash. "How do people drink the
stuff?"

"Quiet," said Lou. "So what do we do?"

"It's easy," said Thomas.

There were general groans.

"Go on," said Lou.

"We make Gene crazy," Thomas said.

"How?"

"Start about a week before the physical. Feed him some acid, uppers and downers, hash, grass, any kind of dope, booze, no food but some garlic maybe, no shave or bath, by the time he gets there he's crazy. Besides, they won't be able to stand the smell."

"No," said Nell.

"I've seen it!" said Thomas. "I helped guys through it, helped em do it."

"When?" Nell asked.

"Last year sometime."

"Yeh, but now they know," Nell said. "This guy at Northeastern showed up like that, dropped acid and all, this army doctor just smiled and told him, 'Have a good trip, it's the last one you'll take till we ship you to Nam'."

"Maybe it wasn't good acid," said Thomas.

"No," Nell insisted, "they know now."

"It figures," said Lou.

"Maybe they know everything now," said Gene. "Maybe there ain't no way."

"Well, if they get your ass," said Flash, "try to sign up for radio school. Learn a fuckin trade."

"No!" Lou shouted.

Barnes was pacing, scratching his head.

"If there was just one of those little things, that Gene had . . ."

"What little things?" asked Lou.

"You know. Like bee stings."

"What about them?" Gene asked.

"They can keep you out. If you're allergic to em."

"You're shittin me," Gene said.

"No. I knew a guy once. Why?"

"I think I am. Allergic. Or was anyway. As a kid. I got real sick once after a bee stung me, had to go to the doctor."

"*What* doctor?" Barnes asked.

"Family."

"Yeh, but *who*, his *name!*"

"Dr. Gardner. Why?"

Barnes lifted his body about an inch off the floor. For him, that was a leap.

"Write him! Call! Good old Dr. Gardner. Get him to give you a letter about it. Get on the phone! Get ahold of the guy, *now!*"

"Can't," Gene said.

"*Why?*"

"He's dead."

"You know for sure? Maybe he's not. Maybe he's just old."

Gene shook his head.

"Died of a heart attack at a high-school football game."

"You *sure?*" Barnes said. "You really remember?"

Gene nodded, holding his head.

"We lost, seven to six. Missed the extra point. That's what did him in."

"That'd be somethin," Thomas said, "if you had to go to war cause the guy missed the extra point."

"Shut up," Lou said.

"Hell," said Flash, talking out of the side of his mouth now. "What's wrong with all of ya? All we need here's a letter from a doctor, right?"

"Sure but the doctor's dead."

"Doesn't have to be *that* doctor," Flash said. "*I* know a doctor."

"Yeh," said Gene, "but will he give me a letter that—"

Flash waved away the question.

"The stuff this doctor gives me, a letter's nothin."

"Listen," said Lou, "does this sound real? Like it really can work?"

"Yeh," Barnes said, "but there might be a hitch."

Thomas rasped a laugh.

"Even I coulda told ya that."

"Knock it off," said Lou, looking intently to Barnes.

"The guy I know, who got out because of the bee sting business, when he went for his physical he had a letter from his doctor but then they gave him a test."

"Shit," Gene said, "they put him in a room with bees?"

"No, no. They gave some kind of serum, see, and they give you this shot of it, and if you're allergic, the place where they stuck you swells up and gets red. Then they know you got it."

"Christ," said Gene. "What if I haven't got it anymore? What if they stick me and nothin happens?"

It was quiet.

"You make it happen," Thomas said.

"How?"

"Don't you know?" said Thomas, smiling. He was the center of attention now.

"Goddam, Thomas," said Lou, "if you know something say it."

"It's not so much what I know it's *who* I know."

"*Who then?*" Lou yelled.

"A chemist. Well anyway, chemistry *student*, I guess, since he hasn't graduated yet. I met him at MIT when I took the aviation course."

"So what can he do?" asked Lou.

"Make a serum. If *they* got a serum that can tell if you're allergic to bee stings, he's got one you can take beforehand to make sure the other one shows you're allergic."

"He's *got* this stuff?" Gene asked.

"Well, I don't know if he's actually *got* this particular stuff. He might, though, cause he's into the antiwar thing. But if he hasn't got it he can make it."

"Shit," said Flash, "this kid can just make up a serum like we need?"

"This kid, as you call him, in his own kid laboratory, has produced among other things the finest acid on the East Coast. Some people say it's better than Owsley's stuff out

West. Among other things. This'll be a challenge to him, like a little puzzle. And if he can't come up with the stuff, he'll tell me."

Lou looked to Barnes, maybe because he was oldest, or used to be a reporter or something.

He shrugged.

"It's worth a try," he said. "It might work."

"OK," said Lou. "Flash gets the letter, Thomas gets the serum."

The letter came first. Flash produced it the following day.

A few days later Thomas came by. He didn't have the serum. He had an idea, though.

"Even if we get the serum," he said, "you ought to have a little extra insurance."

"Life?" Gene asked. "In case the fuckin serum poisons my ass?"

Thomas thought just for good measure Gene ought to show he was crazy, maybe not completely crazy but a little off. He thought it would do the trick if the day of the physical they painted on Gene's chest in big red letters, "What About the Bees?"

Gene and Lou looked at each other. They didn't think so. Still, sometimes the crazy stuff helped. They'd think about it.

More important, when the hell was the serum coming through?

"Stay cool," said Thomas, "he's working on it."

"He'd better hurry," Gene said.

There were only three days to go.

━━━━━━━━━━

Thomas brought it, the night before. The serum. It was in a little vial, precious looking, like it contained radium or something.

"Shit, man," Gene said, "I gotta shoot it up?"

Thomas cackled.

"Nah," he said. "Just swallow it."

"When?"

"Just beforehand."

"That's what he said?"

"Who?"

"The chemistry guy. The guy that made it."

"Sure. Just swallow it, he said. Beforehand."

Lou sighed.

"OK, man," Gene said.

"Are you going to paint it on your chest?"

"What?"

"You know, 'What About the Bees?' "

They hadn't for sure decided, but they didn't think so. Thomas was disappointed.

In the end, they agreed on doing it straight. They figured the place would be full of kids with all kinds of shit painted all over them.

Gene wore a tie.

"Bee stings," the sergeant said contemptuously when Gene showed the letter. "Where you're goin, you won't have to kill any bees."

"No, sir," Gene answered.

He called everyone sir.

The sergeant handed him back the letter and said, "OK, go down that hall, turn right, room thirty-two. Give this letter to one of the doctors."

"Yes, sir."

"Hey, kid," the sergeant called after him, "keep your prick in your pants so it don't get stung."

The whole thing obviously pissed off the sergeant something awful.

"Yes, sir," Gene said, not changing his expression.

After the hall turned Gene ducked quickly into a men's room, went into a stall, closed the door, and pulled from

his left-hand pocket the little brown bag with the vial in
it. His hands were shaking. He put the bag back in his
pocket and started to unscrew the top of the vial. Shit. It
was stuck. It was on too tight. He closed his eyes and
twisted so hard he saw purple spots, and it suddenly came
loose. Jesus. He put the cap in his pocket and swallowed
the stuff, drank it down straight.

It tasted sort of like gin. Maybe it was. Maybe that's
all it was. Well, whatever, it was too late now. It was all
he had.

The doctor had a mustache. Gene thought he looked like
a Frenchman he'd seen in a movie. Gene felt like *he* was
in a movie. The doctor read the letter, then went back to
his bag and took something out. A needle but not like a
regular hypodermic needle. Smaller.

He stuck it in the back of Gene's right hand.

It left a tiny mark, just a dot, like a pinprick.

"The reaction should show in three to five minutes,"
the doctor said.

"Yes, sir."

"You may sit down."

He motioned to a folding chair.

"Yes, sir."

Gene sat down.

He stared at his arm. The little tiny prick-mark.

Shit. He'd forgot to bring a watch. He looked up at a
clock on the wall. He couldn't figure how many seconds
must have passed before he looked. Fifteen, maybe,
Twenty. He looked back down at his forearm. It was white.
Well, nothing could happen for three minutes anyway.

What if it didn't?

He stared at the arm, trying to think the reaction out,
pulling with his mind, Come on you sombitch you serum
goddam you work oh shit you motherfucker do your thing
get red get welt get weird get something anything. . . .

The arm was pure white, the dot from the needle perfectly calm.

He wanted to tear at it, rip at it, then he thought. He thought of something to try to do.

When it seemed four minutes had passed and his arm was still pristine, Gene said, "Excuse me, sir, may I go to the men's room?"

"Hmm? Oh. Certainly."

The doctor seemed distracted.

Gene went as quickly as he could move without breaking into a run of panic, and got himself into one of the stalls. There were several army guys pissing in the latrine. He took down his pants, sat on the toilet, and made grunting noises. At the same time he took the fingernail of his left index finger and he dug it into the flesh of the pinpoint on his right hand, he scratched it as hard and as deep as he could possibly do it, till he managed to raise a redness, a scratchy redness. He gave it one more last dig and then hurried back. He held the hand out to the doctor.

"Hmmm," the doctor said glancing at it, "positive."

Positive. Was that it? Was that the magic word, the combination of syllables that set him free?

The doctor was signing something.

Gene put his hand in his pocket, fearing the irritation he'd made on the flesh might disappear too fast or something.

The doctor signed a paper, told Gene to give it to the sergeant.

"Yes, sir," Gene said.

Was this it, his ticket to freedom?

He knew it was when the sergeant got red in the face and said, "OK, move your ass out of here."

"Yes, sir," Gene said.

Air. He stopped and leaned against the building. Then he walked fast, went in the first bar he came to, and asked for a glass of beer. It was hard to get it up to his mouth, the way his hands were going.

He went home and grabbed a hold of Lou, hard, and told her he was free.

She screamed, jumped, threw things.

"It worked!" she yelled. "Goddam Thomas's serum really worked!"

Then Gene started laughing, whooping, bending over, hooting, hysterical.

"What?" Lou asked. "What happened?"

"Nothing!"

After he got himself calm he told her exactly how it went. She was pale, trembly.

They vowed they would never tell the true story, especially to Thomas.

The only thing that mattered was Gene was free.

They had the celebration at Barnes's place.

Gene made stew.

He remembered how his first college shrink had asked him what he believed in and got pissed off wher Gene said "Stew." Well, he would answer the same thing now but add to it "living with Lou." No matter how it looked on some kind of psychiatric rundown Gene knew those were two real actual things he believed in and that wasn't bad. It was probably more than most people had.

The night of the party was the first big serious snow of the winter but that didn't matter. Gene and Lou put the stuff for the stew in knapsacks and set out into the storm, letting it kiss their cheeks red, laughing as legs sunk deep in drifts, passing the slick cars, stalling and sliding and stealthily slipping through streets, headlights laying pale slats on the night-fallen snow. The Gene-Lou party pressed on, nipping sometimes from a canteen of brandy. Getting the serum through! The others got there, too.

Thomas brought some extra-good grass and a guy who was crashing with him in Cambridge who was AWOL from the Green Berets on his way to Toronto. He called himself Moon. On the way they'd stopped and cut down a tree to chop for firewood.

Gene and Lou both hugged Thomas and thanked him
for supplying the serum that set Gene free, though pri-
vately they prayed he was not in charge of getting the ex-
Green Beret across the border.

Barnes had set in a case of gallon jugs of Cribari and
Nell had enough Bazooka bubble gum to seal the whole
building. Flash called to say he would be a little late due
to weather conditions at Logan, but to keep the faith.
Gene began building the stew while Lou put music on.

Flash blew in with a Braniff stewardess who looked
like Sophia Loren but talked with an Alabama accent. Her
name was Belinda June Lee and at first she was nervous
about getting into what looked to her like some kind of
beatnik hippie maybe even Commie sort of scene but
Flash had brought the makings for rusty nails, his new favorite drink, and after one the way Flash made it she
kicked off her shoes and said she thought this party was
real down home.

"Belinda June's something else, man," Gene said to
Flash when he came to mix more drinks in the kitchen.

"That's the kind I was talkin about when I mentioned
that round-robinish sort of thing," Flash said from the corner of his mouth. "Could you dig it?"

"Just not my scene, man."

Flash sighed.

"You and your goddam middle-class hang-ups."

Lou announced the stew was ready for anyone anytime
they wanted it.

Moon asked what kind of stew it was and Lou stood up
on the couch and announced, "This can only be called
a *magic* stew. It will cure an ungodly collection of ail-
ments of mind and body—warts, dandruff, schizophrenia,
just to name a few. It is a stew of inspiration, healing, re-
juvenation. Love. Oh, yeh. It tastes good, too."

There were cheers when Lou stepped down but Belinda
June cried, "Good God, what's *in* it?"

Belinda June feared the "magic" of the stew might come

from having what she called "L, S and D" in it, but Flash reassured her with another rusty nail and a quick consumption of his own first bowl without any adverse effects.

Everyone ate, delighting in it, delighted, not just by the taste and warmth and seasoning, not just by the stew that filled their stomachs, but fed as well by the feeling of it, partaking of it, a family for a while, together, out of the cold, warm inside, feasting, with friends, with food and fire and music.

"Listen!"

Gene jumped up like a sinner at a tent meeting, raising his arm like he wanted to repent.

He just wanted all his friends to hear the song they just had heard, only not just listen to it, *hear* it, the way he had heard it just then.

"Here Comes the Sun," on the Beatles' *Abbey Road*.

He played it again and they listened, trying to hear the way that he had, and mostly they did.

The song said how it had been a long and lonely winter—not the real one, the one that was blowing with fury outside. It meant the winter inside you, the daily freeze you lived with usually. *That* was the ice that was slowly melting. There, inside, was where it had been so long since it was clear. But now, little darlins, look and see the smiles upon your faces. That long freeze is over and it's *all right*, cause—hear it now, listen, look, see it and feel it—

Here comes the sun

They got up and danced to it, everyone, partners and not, in couples and circles, over and on the furniture, alone in a corner or strutting in the center, a trio linking, parting, everyone part of it, getting inside the music, getting the music inside of them.

Later, long shadows fallen from the walls, dancers turned travelers, bundled and wrapped against the outside cold, Gene and Lou found themselves loosely curled on the couch and when they started to rise and unravel

Barnes said no, stay, he was going to Nell's, and he spread a bright blanket over them.

Snapping of cinders the only sound left now they held, huddled, snuggled.

"Sometimes it feels safe," Lou said.

"Right," Gene whispered. "*All right.*"

Slowly, gently, nothing to hurry, they helped one another out of clothes, stretching and pulling in concert, comfort, comfortable, close, cold then cuddling warm with each other, finding themselves, fitting, fondling, fond, found, they came together.

Later, no clocktime counted just later, after, warm and tangled, sounds of snowplow opened eyes a moment into windows washed pale blue, dawn lit.

Here comes the sun

That season of bitter wintercold was one they would always remember as a time of special warmth. Walking through icy snowcrunch to the high-beamed apartment on Beacon Hill where Barnes held perpetual open house and everyone helped keep the fire going; sometimes they toasted marshmallows on it or hot dogs, sometimes they just stared into it, watching the pictures it made, the dances and the tongues, the burning villages and bright sacrificial offerings to gods, the flare of celebration, smoke of dreams. You could get high just by watching it intently, but to help there was Barnes's booze and Lou and Gene's jugs of Cribari and Thomas's grass and sometimes hash and coke and pills and Flash's sweet mixtures for him and whatever stewardess he had at the time. The one with him New Year's Eve said they ought to have a special toast for the new decade, but Lou said no, that was too long. They drank to who and what was there, then, that was plenty: the friends, loves, fires.

Even in spring they went to Barnes's and built fires, best on rainy days when they threw up the windows, scenting and accenting their highs with the heady blend of woodheat and showersmell. Sometimes they fell asleep by the

fire, waking at dawn to the last snap of cinders, winking
out of final flames, ashes blown gently over brows in dusty
blessing.

━━━━━━━━━━━━━━━━━

It seemed like the mood of that time would be on them
always and in it Lou didn't even mind making plans with
Gene about the future. No promises, of course; they both
were still free as always but there wasn't any reason not to
make a few practical plans.

Lou would go stay with her parents for the summer and
finish her thesis for the Ph.D. That's how she'd done her
M.A. thesis, going back to live where she couldn't drink or
smoke but knew her parents would feed and take care of
her needs so all she had to do was hunker down and do the
work without distraction. With some juggling of dates and
addresses that made him a state resident Gene got accepted
at U Mass Boston to finish up the final dozen credits he
needed, half in the summer session, half in the fall, a light
enough load so he could hold down the job at The Crossroads as well.

He sent his dad a postcard with a picture of *Old Iron-
sides*, and wrote, "Going for last 12 credits, bring you
degree in person next Feb. Love, Gene."

He got back a plain card, the kind without any picture
on it, that said, "Don't give up the ship. Love, Dad."

Shit, the old man had a right to pull his leg a little.

He promised himself when he got the degree and took
it out to Dad in person he would also stay awhile, take the
old man to a ball game, take him out fishing like the old
man had taken him so many times growing up.

He wondered where the hell you went fishing in Chicago.

Gene and Lou weren't the only ones making plans. The
spirit that started with "Here Comes the Sun" seemed to

be like a contact high, lifting and energizing all of them, moving them out of old ruts, picking up promises dropped.

Barnes had really started hanging out at Harvard and making notes for his new mystery. He wasn't just pissing his time away in the Harvard Square coffeehouses either, he was catching some lectures, sitting in on seminars, going for beers with students and faculty. He had even come up with a title for the book: *Congealed in Crimson*. He said that's what the place did to people's brains. From his personal contact with Harvard he had come to hate it but he said that was good as far as hyping up the old inspiration. He had rented a one-room cottage on Cape Cod for the summer because he learned that's what writers who lived in Boston were supposed to do and he was trying to get things right.

He wanted Nell to come and stay in the one-room cottage with him, knowing of course he'd have everything taken care of that way but she had already got a social work gig in Appalachia for the summer, taking on a larger if less compact depressed area than Barnes. He moaned and grumbled but Nell said she knew he could do it he had done it before and besides, she'd be back from the field in September and ready to resume operations as his own special caseworker.

Flash was going up to make a pile selling aluminum siding in the boondocks of New Hampshire, Maine, and Vermont. It turned out this was the secret of his seemingly miraculous ability to put all he had in some crazy scheme, blow the whole thing, and be back on the scene again a few months later with a bankroll to launch still another grand venture. He would go up and live on a couch in the game room of his sister-in-law in Nashua, New Hampshire, and with this low-overhead base of operation blitz the boonies with his high-powered sales of aluminum and vinyl house siding. He was a natural salesman and always did well enough to come back and launch a new scheme designed to make him a tycoon in whatever new

enterprise caught his fancy. Who knew what next? Maybe
solar energy, he mentioned reading an article . . .

The only one who didn't have any plans for the summer
was Thomas, who didn't want any. When Gene thought
of getting through the summer alone and Thomas the only
friend left in the city he got real down, so he tried not to
think about it. The summer was still a month off and he
might as well groove on the time he had with Lou till she
went off to Arkansas.

━━━━━━━━━

Ever since Gene's narrow escape from the draft Lou
had gotten into doing antiwar stuff, she said that whole
number they went through had really brought it home to
her: how it felt to face going off to fight and maybe die for
what you thought was wrong.

Gene believed all that in his head but as much as he
thought the war sucked he couldn't get into working
against it. He felt kind of silly and phony doing political
stuff, like he was out of place or something. He knew all
the people his age were supposed to be political but he
rarely ran into them personally. He had known this couple
once, though, who were real radicals. Patrick and Lau-
rinda. They went all over the country organizing against
the war, living off donations they got passing a tin can
around. Then they happened to hear one of these kid
maharishis and decided what they'd been doing was just
an ego trip. They ended up in Vancouver, making cheese.
Gene ran into a guy who had been there and seen them.
He said they were fine, but awfully quiet and subdued,
which was probably because of their deep religious experience.

"This cheese they make," Gene had asked. "Is it any
good?"

"Damn good. People like it."

"Well, good for them. You know?"

That was how he felt about it.

Lou didn't press him to do any antiwar things with her until it came to Tricky Dick invading Cambodia, and that really pissed her off. Most of the universities in Boston were going to strike and a big protest march was scheduled that Lou said Gene really had to go along with her on.

It turned out to be a beautiful early May day and the whole thing had a kind of holiday spirit. Flags whipped in the wind, like clean washing. The air was crisp, the sky unblemished. As the marchers went down Beacon Street people waved from the sidewalk and some joined in. Dogs and children would follow for a while, then drop away, and others sprang up to tag along. A chant would rise from a few, and then rise and spread, sweeping the march: "Hell, no, we won't go!" Lou took Gene's hand and squeezed. Gene squeezed back. Another chant rose, insistent, pressing: "Peace *now*, peace *now*, peace *now* . . ." It was hard to believe such a march would not end it. Stop the bombing, stop the war, stop the slaughter. So many people, good people, marching in concert, in common cause. Gene looked back and saw the ranks filling Beacon Street all the way up past Charles to the top of the Hill and the State Capitol building. Its gold dome shimmered, radiant with history and promise.

Gene felt a tingle, found himself thinking: *Here comes the sun.*

When summer came and Lou left, Thomas fell by and he and Gene smoked a joint, mostly in silence. With Lou not there, they didn't have much to say to each other. After the joint Thomas said he had a big deal he had to bring off next morning, he'd better split. Gene wished him luck.

Gene had forgot what a drag it was living alone. He ate out of cans because it was quicker, sometimes forgot to eat at all. Had a pickle and a beer. Whenever he was in the apartment he kept the radio tuned to a twenty-four-hour news station. He wanted only words, not music. The repetitive babble helped stuff the empty space in his head like wads of cotton.

Reminders of her stung him, unexpected. Reaching in the closet for a shirt and feeling the touch of her winter dresses made him swallow. Her new issue of *Harper's Bazaar* arrived in the mail, not knowing the difference. He slipped it out of sight in a pile of other magazines.

He was working the night shift at The Crossroads which was better than anyplace else he knew but in spite of the mechanically frozen air the job seemed stickier, more closed in. The drunks were sloppier, the old guys morose.

He hung in there, though, hitting the books, making

every class, meeting all assignments no matter how chicken-shit. He didn't just want to squeak through it, he wanted to do it right, make her proud of him.

———

There were showers in the afternoon, and at night the wet grass of Fenway was essence of green in the flood-lights. Flash had called to say he was coming down from his sales job in New Hampshire with a couple of tickets for the Yankee game if Gene could get off. He traded a shift with Kevin, the other bartender, and sat with Flash above the left-field wall, where you could almost reach down and tap Tommy Harper on the shoulder when the Sox were in the field. At matchbox-size Fenway you could still feel part of it, not just a dot in some impersonal super-stadium. Balancing a tall waxy cup of beer and a hot dog and booing the Yankees, Gene felt fresh and like a kid, the summer's oppression uplifted with an evening breeze and the world clean and sharp and as ordered as the diamond set solid and neat in the deep green firmament. They had more beer and bags of peanuts, and the Yankees failed to spoil Gene's evening, though they beat the Sox 7–3 and Flash kept mumbling, "Fuckin Yankees. Got nothin. Fuckin Bobby Murcer. Some excuse for a superfuckinstar." Gene agreed with everything—"Right on, shee-it, man, way to go"—and did not care that Yaz fanned twice and failed to get a hit or that the efforts of the Boston bullpen were puny at best. He soaked in the rhythms, the patterns, the tides of sound; ritual of pitcher, motion and delivery, bat unleashed and cracked against ball that shot up arching in graceful trajectory, base runners going, sliding, exploding dust; infielders pivoting, ball thrown across like a taut line to pop in a waiting glove. Connections. Measurements. Meaning. Full.

After the final out Gene and Flash hit a couple bars, then stopped and shared a joint on a bench on Commonwealth Avenue beneath some stone Revolutionary soldier.

"Watchin that ball game," Flash said, "it kinda got me down."

"You mean the Sox blowing it?"

"Nah. They haven't got a chance in hell this year."

"So?"

"Just watchin those jokers. That Yankee infield. Shit. They're not so hot. When you're a kid, even in college, you think the pros are some kind of supermen. Hell, they're just ball players, some better, some worse. I never even tried. I could have had a shot. At least a tryout. Our college coach had connections in the Lakers organization."

"I thought you were too short," Gene said.

"For forward. Maybe I coulda switched to guard. I wasn't much of a shot, but I had speed, and best of all, I could go to my left. That's important."

"Yeh, man."

"Not many guys can go to their left."

"I know."

"Shit. I mighta caught on. I'm not sayin I'd have been another Jerry West, but I might have played a few years in the NBA. Got me some good business contacts, bought into some kind of franchise operation. Look at The Hawk. At least he has his fuckin Sub Shop."

"Yeh."

They were quiet for a while, and then Flash said he'd better hit the road. Gene clapped him on the back and thanked him for the ball game.

"Forget it," Flash said.

He started off and then stopped a moment, under the streetlight. He turned to Gene and said:

"I wasn't shittin ya, man. I really could go to my left."

"I dig," Gene said.

Flash nodded. Then he turned and walked on.

On weekends the city seemed like an empty echo chamber. Evidently everyone was either out sailing in the fleet of small boats that choked the Charles in a bobbing white traffic jam, or were hidden inside hooked up to TV and air conditioning. In Back Bay the streets were nearly deserted, the trees motionless, the sky hot and blank.

After hitting the books all day since a breakfast of cold beer and some deli potato salad one late July afternoon Gene went aimlessly roaming around, looking in windows, studying marquees of movies he didn't feel like seeing, lists of exotic ice-cream flavors he didn't want to try.

He stopped at a little outdoor café that was open on Newbury Street, and ordered an iced coffee. There were a few little round tables with old-fashioned drugstore chairs around them arranged under an awning. Maybe it was like Paris. He doubted it. There were two older women with hats at one of the tables, and at another one a guy with a beard and sandals eating some elaborate ice-cream concoction and reading a paperback. *Moby Dick.* Heavy. That was one result of Gene's long rambling education. He may not have read all the shit but he'd heard of it.

A girl in a flowered dress sat at a table a little in front of him and ordered a chocolate sundae. She carried a straw purse and a copy of the *Evening Globe* and a map of the city. Tourist. She put the purse and the *Globe* on a chair next to her and fanned herself with the map. Her medium-length black hair was mussy from the heat and every once in a while she brushed it back with one hand. She wasn't any doll but she wasn't bad either. Plain and pleasant-looking. And bored.

Gene thought about it. He hadn't been laid since Lou left, almost a couple of months ago. She wouldn't be back for almost another month. The best part about the girl in the flowered dress was that she was a tourist. No matter what happened he would probably never see her again. There was a smudge of chocolate above her upper lip. Idly, her tongue licked over it.

It had been a long time since Gene had tried to pick up a girl. He remembered the main thing was to start talking. It didn't much matter what you said. He wiped his mind clean, like a blackboard, and smiled. He began to speak.

The girl spoke back, and more words went back and forth between them and Gene heard his voice suggesting they try to find someplace cool.

When they got there he admitted his apartment wasn't very cool, but the beer in the refrigerator was.

"OK," she said.

He popped two cans, gave one to her, and said, "I'll bet you're from Baltimore."

"No."

"Well—then let's pretend you are."

"All right," she said.

He didn't want to know anything about her. They talked about the heat some more and then Gene turned on the radio so they didn't have to think of any more shit to say.

After the second beer he kissed her and they moved to the bedroom. They undressed and made love—remotely, distant, dreamlike. When it was over they dressed and had another beer. When the "girl from Baltimore" finished hers she said she'd better be going. Gene said OK, and walked her down to the street and said good-bye. She gave him a little wave and went away, with her straw purse and map of the city. She forgot the *Globe*.

Gene went back and turned the radio off. It was the first time he'd balled another woman since he'd been with Lou. It wasn't even like the same act had been performed. This had been empty and flat, like a stale beer. He didn't want to do it anymore with anyone else. He'd rather jerk off remembering Lou.

The end of August brought an unexpected cool spell and Gene got stoned by himself and went out to sit on a bench in the Common, savoring the nippy breeze, knowing it meant he'd be seeing Lou soon. Going back to that stale apartment seemed like a bummer. He curled up under a tree and closed his eyes. He blinked awake to brightness, opening to a soft lemon light pouring down through the leaves. The fresh breeze stirred around him, cool and soothing. He stretched, smiled, thinking of the music, hearing it in his head, feeling all it meant:

Here comes the sun

II

When Lou got back to Boston Gene had a surprise for
her. He had got them a new apartment, nothing grand
but at least a little more spacious and gracious than the
funky pad behind the Trailways station. It was a long
thin floor-through on Marlborough Street near Mass Ave,
a bargain because of being corroded with archaeological
layers of grime and needing repairs, but boasting big
windows onto the street and a carved marble fireplace that
didn't function but looked very fine. For a six-pack
Thomas helped scrub the place down and Gene applied
plaster and paint, hung bright yellow curtains, added to
former furniture an old leather couch from an office sale.
For a housewarming present Thomas produced a brand-
new queen-size Beautyrest mattress. He said not to mention to Lou it was hot.

To crown the whole enterprise Gene rigged a thrift
shop chandelier from the living room ceiling.

"It's *royal*," said Lou.

"For you," he said, adding to please her, "Me, too."

Next stop the queen-size mattress with madras spread
in the bedroom where they forgot the Almadén Chablis on
ice and the supermarket red caviar and the Reese's Peanut
Butter Cups. They were hungry first for each other and

they filled themselves up in the shadowed room, to the
tune of random sounds of a warm September afternoon:
roller skates on concrete, the play-by-play of a Red Sox
game on a neighbor's radio, sparrow chatter.

Later, their own purring.

There was mellow Donovan music playing when Lou
got home from her faculty meeting, and the place was
bright and warm, welcoming. She unloaded her books
and briefcase on the couch and sniffed the good scents
coming out of the kitchen.

"Hey—what's cookin?"

"Surprise!"

"What kind?"

"Bouillabaisse. With lobster even. The works."

"Wow!"

"If the phone rings don't answer. Door either. This is
just you and me, babe."

"What happened?"

Gene came out of the kitchen grinning, wiping his hands
on a dish towel.

"Grades came in the mail today. From summer."

"You passed!"

"*Passed?* That's an insult. Pulled down six hours of A."

"Far out!"

They toasted with Rhine Garten Chablis, sitting on the
floor. They hadn't got used to the new couch yet, except as
a place for piling stuff.

"If I keep on truckin, I'll finish in February. Finally."

"It's great, babe. Really."

"It's a load off."

"Your father—he'll be so pleased."

"Too late for that. Relieved, maybe."

"Maybe you should call him?"

"No. Not till it's over. Not till I've got it right here in my hand with my name on it. I've talked big before."

She leaned over and kissed him.

"He'll really be glad. And me, too. For you."

Gene filled their cups again, smiling as he raised his.

"No more something, no more books, no more teacher's dirty looks. What the 'something'?"

"Hmm?"

Lou looked preoccupied and distant.

"Hey," Gene said, "where are you?"

"Huh? Oh. Just thinking."

"Of?"

She took out a cigarette, lit it, tilted her head back, blew a long slow stream of smoke at the ceiling.

"Have you thought about what you'll do?"

"When?"

"When you get your degree."

"I dunno. Maybe have a blast. Not just booze, though. Food and all. Maybe bouillabaisse. A whole fuckin *vat* of bouillabaisse. Keep the mother on for days, keep addin to it, a goddam *marathon* bouillabaisse for—"

"*Fuck* the bouillabaisse!"

Gene's head jerked back as if he'd been hit without warning.

"What the goddam hell? You don't like bouillabaisse all the sudden? Fuck it, I'll take the whole thing I made for tonight and dump it in—"

"Goddam it I'm not talking about *bouillabaisse*, for the love of fucking Christ."

"Well, begging your goddam pardon, what the fuck *are* you talking about?"

"I'm talking about what I asked you, which was what are you going to do when you graduate?"

"What do you mean by 'going to do'?"

"I mean what anyone means when they ask anyone what they're going to do when they graduate. I mean what *work* are you going to do?"

"Why the hell you so uptight about my working all the sudden? Haven't I worked ever since we been here?"

"I don't mean those kind of jobs."

"Oh, you mean 'those kind of jobs' that helped feed us and sent me back to school aren't good enough anymore?"

"They're perfectly fine when you're going to school."

"And when you get out they're not good enough?"

"No, as a matter of fact, they're not."

"Why the fuck?"

She took a deep breath and spread her hands on her skirt, steadying.

"Gene. Please. Listen."

"I am."

"OK. What do you want? For your life?"

"This. I don't mean arguing. I mean living with you. That's what I want."

"That's not enough," she said fiercely.

"Isn't that for me to decide?"

"Not if you refuse to be adult about it."

"Oh. I'm not being a good grown-up citizen. I guess I should go out and hustle my ass into the IBM training program."

"I didn't say that."

"That's how it sounds."

"Forget it, then."

"I'll sure as hell try to."

Lou got up and walked to the window.

She sighed and said, "I'm sorry, Gene. I didn't mean a scene."

He went to her, touched her.

"Me, too," he said, "either."

They kissed, tentative, and tried to change the subject. But it stayed there, in the room with them, invisible and real.

Something else hanging over me, Gene thought.

He began to suspect there always would be. You got rid of one, the next dude popped right in to take its place.

At dinner Lou said the bouillabaisse was especially good. Gene said he'd used a new recipe, one with fennel seed in it. There was silence again. They could hear each other eating.

Gene hadn't been the only one who had got it on in the summer. While he was pulling down his six hours of A, Lou was wrapping up her doctoral thesis. Nell not only did her social work thing in Appalachia, she came back looking healthy and tan. Barnes emerged from his one-room Cape Cod cottage more sallow than ever but he had his new mystery finished. Thomas hadn't done anything, but he hadn't tried.

But the one who came off the season like a real champ was Flash.

After his summer of low-overhead living and high-volume sales in the boondocks he returned to Boston in triumph, renting a bachelor's pad with ocean view in the swinging new Harbor Towers apartment complex, and business space in a fashionable row of newly renovated offices on the Wharf.

The first official undertaking of Flash's new business was a party to launch it.

Gene said he and Lou would be honored to attend, but just out of curiosity, what was the business?

"Professional sports," Flash said.

"Any special one?"

"Very special. It's new."

"You mean you made it up?"

"No, no, what kinda crap is that? This is an established, historically traditional sport. I meant new in the pro field. This is a sport with class. Background. Originated in Scotland, old buddy, the country that gave us golf. Which happens to be the most popular sport in the English-speaking world."

"So what's this one?"

A pause. Flash pronounced the word with as much drama as anyone could drag out of two syllables.

"*Curling*," he said.

"Curling?"

"It'll soon be a household word."

"I think I heard of it. Where a guy tries to keep running on top of a log without falling in the water?"

"No, no, dummy that's *birling*. Log birling. That's an individual competition."

"What's curling?"

"A team sport. Played on ice. You mainly need brooms and what they call the 'stone.' Equipment costs will be low, which of course is a plus factor in establishing franchises for the league."

"There's a league already?"

"The North American Curling League. I am league president, as well as owner of the Boston franchise."

"Far out," Gene said.

He meant it. When Lou got home she said she'd never heard of curling and Gene said maybe it only existed in Flash's head. Lou decided to look it up in the old *World Book Encyclopedia* Thomas had given them and damned if it wasn't there. Curling. It had four-man teams that slid or "curled" a heavy stone or iron to a mark called a "Tee" on an ice rink. The rink was supposed to be 138 feet long and 14 feet wide. There were rules and regulations, the whole bit. It even started in Scotland.

Lou said she thought it sounded kind of dull.

Gene was just amazed it existed.

The party in Flash's new office looked like a combination
of the Miss Universe Contest and the annual convention
of the Massachusetts Elks club. The former group were
personal friends of Flash, the latter potential investors.
The only furniture in the office was what proved to be a
Ping-Pong table covered with a bedspread on which were
set two giant punch bowls. Behind it were a pair of tan
blonde beauties wearing red miniskirts, white blouses,
high-heeled black boots, and identical sashes of red silk
emblazoned with the gold letters N E A E A. On the
walls were a map of the United States with a red pin
stuck into Boston, and a gold-framed black and white
photo of Flash in a basketball uniform, frozen in the
act of a jump shot.

Flash pushed his way through the crowd to greet Gene
and Lou. He was wearing jodhpurs and riding boots, a
gold-colored sport coat with brown leather vest, a white
silk shirt, and an ascot.

"Some threads!" said Lou.

"New image," Flash explained. "Gentleman sportsman."

He went on to inform them that the N E A E A on
the sashes of the punch servers stood for "New England
Athletic and Entertainment Association." That was the
parent corporation which operated the North American
Curling League. The N E A E A was sort of an um-
brella, Flash said, under which he could move in many
directions, both sports- and entertainment-wise.

"Don't forget the Rolling Stones," said Lou, intending
a gentle warning.

"By no means," Flash said. "They still have a following."

He had to excuse himself to mingle with potential investors, but asked Gene and Lou to join him and some of
his new associates for dinner.

Barnes bumbled into them, looking embarrassed. He
was all spruced up, his eyes nervous.

"Where's Nell?" Lou asked him.

"Fine," said Barnes.

"I didn't say how, I said where."

"Home, I guess; I just thought I'd drop by for a sec."

"Sure," said Lou.

Barnes wasn't asked to the dinner, Flash figuring rightly he was on the make and might take away from the influence he wanted to reserve for his first investor. That was Stan Plumley, a balding guy wearing a maroon double-knit with pink shirt and white tie. He sold auto insurance in Bangor, Maine, and Flash had sold him aluminum siding for his house last summer. More recently, Flash had sold him the North American Curling League franchise for his community. Flash had seated Plumley between Sissy and Sue, the two punch servers at the party.

Flash had taken them all to Bob Lee's Islander, a Polynesian place in Chinatown that rewarded patrons with leis around the neck and served exotic drinks. When Plumley went to the men's room, Gene asked if he had actually paid five grand for the Bangor, Maine, franchise in the North American Curling League.

"Certainly," Flash said. "He is pledged to raise that amount. Thus far he has made an initial investment of a hundred and seventy-five dollars of his own cash moneys, as a show of good faith, and will proceed to collect the balance from among the leading businessmen of his community."

"The other four thousand, eight hundred and twenty-five dollars," said Lou.

Gene poked her under the table.

"We at N E A E A feel," Flash said, "that funding of a franchise should be as widely distributed as possible, so as to insure broad-based community support."

When Plumley returned from the men's room, Flash proposed a toast to the new Bangor franchise.

"Let us raise our glasses," he said, "to the Bangor—"

"What?" asked Plumley.

"Exactly," said Flash, lowering his glass and looking thoughtful. "We have to think of a name. My own club

is the Boston Brooms. That would have gone well with
Bangor, too. Brooms. But that's water over the dam.
What would sound good with Bangor?"

"Battleships?" suggested Lou.

Gene poked her under the table again.

"The Bangor Battleships," Flash said reflectively. He
shook his head. "A bit cumbersome," he said.

"Can it be a color of sox?" asked Sissy. "I mean like
the Red Sox or White Sox?"

"How about the Bangor Blue Sox?" Lou said. "It'll be
so cold, even if they don't have sox their legs will be blue."

She poked Gene under the table before he could do it
to her.

"We haven't yet finalized the standard uniform," Flash
said, "so I don't know if sox will be a prominent part of
the gear."

"Blazers," said Plumley.

"I doubt the teams will wear blazers, Stan," Flash
said, "except perhaps for road trips. I like to see a club
in matching slacks and blazers, carrying their equipment
bags, as they debark from plane or bus."

"Not wear em!" Plumley shouted. "Call em that!"

Flash looked momentarily puzzled but Sue clapped her
hands and said, "Of course! The Bangor Blazers!"

"Oh, yeh, terrific," Flash said.

Sissy and Sue each gave Stan a little kiss on the cheek.
He grinned, high on rum and attention.

"To the Bangor Blazers!" Flash shouted, raising his
glass.

They all drank.

Drunk, back home, Gene was giggling and shaking his
head.

"Fuckin Flash," he said. "Fuckin *curling*. Crazy. Lose
all his bread again. Always gotta try some impossible
goddam business."

"Not so bad," Lou said. "Better'n not ever tryin. Least
he tries. Some people don' even try."

"You talkin about me?"

"Nobody. Talkin bout nothin."

Through his drunken haze Gene knew it was best to shut up and go to bed.

Barnes's big news brought everyone together.

An actual Hollywood movie producer with credits and credentials was going to make Barnes's mystery a movie. Not the new one, *The Crimson Corpse* (they had changed the title), but good old *Death of a Deb.*

Fuckin Barnes. Wearing a pair of those gold prism glasses that you get in head shops. His eyes looked jumpy and small behind them, perverted pinballs. But below, his jaw was set in a solid grin, a jagged curved jack-o'-lantern.

"Rich!" said Nell, popping her pink bubble. "Tell em, man."

Barnes said the deal was a hundred grand. Ten grand for a year's option, ninety more if the movie got made.

Squeals, whistles, shouts.

Somehow everyone, Barnes included, thought of "his movie money" as the hundred grand he might get instead of the ten he was sure to get.

They all had their own idea about how he should spend it.

"A nightclub," Gene said. "How about starting a nightclub? Barnes's Blue Heaven, man. You could sit in a corner chain-smoking, doin a Bogart number."

Thomas suggested a scientific approach to the dog tracks.

Nell was for a bank. Putting the money there.

Flash groaned.

"No vision," he said. "None of you. Don't you know your Prophets? 'Where there is no vision, the people perish.'"

"Yeh," said Barnes, "but look what happens when there's too much."

"If you are making snide reference to the North American Curling League," Flash said, "it is still a viable entity with enormous growth potential."

There were groans and hisses.

Nell started more brandy around, Thomas was a regular joint-rolling assembly line. It seemed like money, even the thought of it, got everyone high and then wanting to get higher. Maybe that's how it was when you had your bull markets.

Lou said if she had the bread she'd buy land.

"Land," said Barnes. "Yeh, I like it. I mean I like the idea of buying it, owning it. Something real. You can use it, walk around on it. *Land*. Sure. But what the hell would I do with it then? After I walked around on it?"

"Besides," Nell said, "Barnes hates to walk. If it's more than a block he takes a cab."

"He could buy his own cab to have on the land," said Thomas, "so he wouldn't have to walk."

"Really," Barnes said. "What would I do with land?"

"Build a house on it," Lou said. "Or buy some land with one on it already."

"But I'd end up not really living in it," Barnes said. "I'd say I would, and I'd mean to, but after a week or so I'd get bored and want to go back to the city. Some city or other. See. I really don't think I could live anywhere."

"None of us live anywhere," Gene said. "Not really. Not like people used to do."

"But Barnes wouldn't have to be there all the time," Lou said, "like living there permanent. When he got tired of living in the house he could loan it out to friends. There's always people looking for a place to be for a while. Then later on Barnes could come back to it, maybe he'd want to stay there awhile with some other people there, too."

"Ugh," Thomas snorted, "it's getting to sound like another one of those hippie communes. Everyone on downers and baking bread and babies crawling around in the cow dung. I've been to em. And then the people all end up getting pissed at each other anyway."

"No, not a commune," Lou said. "That's where the people go planning to stay there and so pretty soon they all feel stuck. Like being trapped. This kind of thing I'm talking about would be a place where anyone could go when they want and leave when they want. Including Barnes. He wouldn't be stuck there, but it would give him a base."

"Give him a *place*," said Gene.

"Like home," Lou said.

Barnes leaned forward, intent.

"Yeh," he said. "I'd call it that."

"Call *what* that?" Thomas asked.

"The house and land he's going to buy," said Lou, warming to the idea, feeling it begin to catch and move around the room with the smoke and brandy, people imperceptibly lifting with it.

Barnes sprang out of his chair and then began to move, slowly, like he was stalking something.

"I'd call the place 'Home,'" he said, "because nobody has one anymore. At least none of us, people like us. I mean, we all have our little apartments—or big ones, it doesn't matter what size they are, it's all the same. *Com*-partments they are actually, like on a train. They might as well *be* on a train. They're just places where we put our books and clothes and records and our grown-up toys and our bodies for a while. A place to lie down. We're all in these little cubicles alone or maybe with someone else—a roommate or lover—but even with two or even three or four it's still the same principle—we move on and find other compartments in other cities, like switching trains, but still moving all the time, going back and forth and never anyplace where we can fall back to and say, 'Now I'm Home.' And feel it's true."

Barnes took off his prism glasses and didn't look demented anymore, just intent. The room was quiet, caught up in it.

"Home," Gene said softly. "I hadn't thought about it for a while."

"Nobody has," said Flash.

"Hey!" Nell said. "It wouldn't just have to be for us, either. People we meet who need to be Home for a while. And don't have one."

"You can't get all of Appalachia up there," Thomas said, "or all the orphans in Massachusetts."

"No, man," Nell said, "just a few people, that we'd meet anyway, in our lives, and like them."

"Mmmmm," Barnes purred, nodding, rocking gently back and forth, moving into it, the dream, saying, "You go there when you want to go there, that's why it's Home. But no one cries when you leave, no one gets pissed and calls you a black-sheep bastard."

"Sheep," Lou said. "Let's have a flock. At Home."

It seemed like it existed now.

"Possibly," Barnes said, "but first we got to have a St. Bernard. With a flask of brandy around its neck. And the flask will say 'Home' on it."

"How about nobody's name on the mailbox," Flash said. "It could just say 'Home.' If a person happened to be in a position of wishing to avoid collection agencies, he could hide out at 'Home' and no one could find him. Some

dude comes sniffin around, you point to the mailbox and
tell him that's you. Mr. Home. Hell, there's something *to*
this thing."

"You got it," Barnes said, granting the wish. "The
mailbox will just say 'Home.'"

"And anytime we're there," said Gene, "any of us,
we'll all be 'Home.' Our name. The Home family."

"At the family Home," said Lou.

"Beautiful," Barnes said.

Shouts, whistles, people putting on records, making
a fire, rolling more joints, celebrating the founding of
Home.

Gene took a hit of the joint he forgot he was holding
and passed it to Lou.

He really was getting into this thing, in his head. Home.
In a way they really were a family, that's how families
happened now, friends who got together not because
they were born under the same roof out of the same
people but because they *wanted* to be under the same
roof with the people they liked to be with. Not all the
time, Lou was right, everyone would end up hating it
then and each other, but knowing you had it, a place,
go to on weekends, holidays, whole summers. Maybe if
it really happened he could work it so *that* was his job,
running the place, sort of like the manager. Hell, people
got degrees in hotel management, it must be an all right
thing to do, this would be something like that really. If
Lou had a Tuesday-Thursday schedule maybe they could
commute, you wouldn't have to be on the spot all the
time but just on a regular basis to keep an eye on things,
keep things going. People, animals, being outdoors, fixing
things. He was made for it. What was wrong with doing
that for your life? Look at Thoreau. When he made his
pitch to Lou he'd throw in Thoreau and the Cornell
School of Hotel Management. How respectable could you
get for Chrissake? He leaned back on the floor, closing
his eyes, smiling.

Later Lou bent over him and asked, "Where are you?"
"Home," he said.

━━━━━━━━

Barnes sent in for catalogs of land for sale and everyone
feasted on them free. Houses with acres with running
brooks, ocean-front footage, forests of pine, mountains
with views, valleys with shady dells, trout-lined lakes,
ultimate privacy, perfect seclusion. Peace for sale. Pick
your own kingdom.

The day they went looking for Home was wind-whipped
and rainy, the sky sulky gray. That didn't help. Neither
did northern Maine, site of the best bargains. The land
was scratchy poor, brambled, and brown. Weathered old
houses leaned and pitched, dilapidated. Mongrels curled
in boarded doors of deserted gas stations, paint-peeled
and pump-falling. Roadsides were weighted with the
molding iron architecture of automobile graveyards. Towns
looked random and bleak, fields dead and barren.

"So this is Home," Thomas said, rasping out his laugh.
Barnes sucked on a silver flask of brandy.

"Hey," said Gene, "we haven't seen any *places* yet.
Wait till we see the places."

The first place was a small house buried back in the
hills on dirt roads, left by a widow who went to live with
a sister in Philadelphia. The realtor couldn't find the key
but showed them the view through the windows. Dusty
curtains. Fang-baring dogs let up a bloodcurdling yelp
and the group automatically huddled together.

"Bowker boys," the realtor explained. "Live down the
road. They're no good and their dogs're just like em.
Mean as sin."

The next place was gutted by fire, a window-broken
shell on a dismal hump of weedy ground. With ten plus
acres, a bargain at forty-two-five, the man said.

There was also an immobile home on concrete blocks with a splendid view of a billboard advertising Mail Pouch Tobacco.

There was a modern, split-level, suburban-mold home with two-car garage, stuck abstractly in a hillside.

As Thomas observed, it was not for them, it was more of a house for "regular people."

There was a falling-down barn with five acres a farmer was tired of trying to till anymore, complete with outhouse and chicken coop.

There wasn't any Home.

"Oh, well, easy come easy go," Thomas said as they headed back south toward Boston.

"Shitman, we just begun," said Gene.

"Sure," said Lou.

"Wait and see, man," Nell said to Barnes, and gave him a reassuring squeeze on the arm.

Barnes was glum, silent.

Rain pummeled the windshield.

Gene and Lou were sitting around in bathrobes, drinking coffee, sharing a joint, reading the Sunday papers. It seemed like they didn't talk as much anymore. They were doing what they intended to do, they had a much nicer place to live, and yet something always seemed a little bit off lately. Sometimes Gene wished they had stayed in the funky pad behind the Trailways station. He thought of it fondly, the spirit of the place. Or maybe it wouldn't make a difference.

Maybe it would help if they talked more.

Maybe that's why he went and told her his dream.

"Had the damndest dream," he said. "You know how some are so real you wake up believing them?"

"Mmmm," she said, idly looking at department store ads. "What was it?"

"I dreamed we had a baby," Gene said. "A girl. We were trying to think up a name and—"

Lou let the page she was holding fall.

"I don't want to hear about it," she said.

"My dream?"

"I don't want to hear about having babies. We discussed that a long time ago. We agreed about that way back in Urbana."

"We did?"

"You're goddam right we did."

"I thought we agreed about marriage. Not doing it. That doesn't have anything to do with having kids. People have kids all the time now without getting married."

"*Kids!* Now there's more than one? How many do you have in mind? Cheaper by the dozen? The little old woman who lived in a shoe?"

"I just said 'kids' in general. I only meant one."

"Then you meant one too many!"

"Babe, it was just a dream. I was telling you a dream I had."

"Some dream. I can see it now. Snot and cereal."

"It wasn't that way."

"But that's the way it is. In real life. Not in dreams."

"OK, OK, sorry I mentioned it."

"So am I," she said.

She got dressed and went out for a walk.

━━━━━━━━━

A few weeks after the trip to find Home the first snow fell.

Back when summer was over and everyone had got together again they all had agreed to gather at Barnes's place to celebrate the first snow, whenever it was. That was the time they had the great bash last year, with the magic stew and all, the first big snow, so it seemed like a good idea to do it again.

The snow came early, and didn't seem the same.

Instead of just being beautiful it seemed to be causing a hassle for everyone.

Barnes and Nell had dinner at Felicia's in the North End, and as if it wasn't bad enough having to stand on the stairs forty minutes to wait for a table, when they got out they couldn't find any cabs because of the snow and had to walk back home. Barnes was grumpy, blowing his nose a lot and drinking straight bourbon to try to kill the cold he was getting. Nell was mute, not even doing her bubble gum.

Lou had been late getting home and Gene hadn't cooked, not knowing whether she'd want anything, so they just started drinking as soon as she showed and Gene got out a can of sardines and a discolored hunk of cheddar and some Triscuits. That was dinner. By the time they got to Barnes's they were already sort of smashed.

Flash came late, cursing the snow because Logan was closed and his scheduled Braniff baby would probably land in Detroit tonight instead of his bed.

Thomas's milk truck had skidded on the ice while he was trailing a beautiful girl and he not only busted a fender against a fireplug, he lost track of the girl. Probably never find her again, lost, gone forever, probably she was the one he'd always been looking for.

"Where's the music?" Gene asked.

"Not on," said Barnes. "Nell?"

She sighed, stood up, and stacked on a random bunch of records, not bothering to see what they were.

Thomas rolled a couple of joints and started them around the room.

"Why don't we do something?" Barnes said.

"About what?" asked Lou.

"Not *about* anything. To have something to do."

"If we made a fire," said Thomas, "we could be sitting by the fire. That'd be doing something."

"Only one log left," Barnes said. "And the Sunday *Times.*"

"Magi-logs," Thomas said. "Someone could go out and buy a couple magi-logs."

"Who?" asked Barnes.

"Anyone," Thomas said.

No one did.

Flash took a big toke off a joint and said, "They'll ruin everything."

"Who?" asked Lou.

"Fuckin new basketball league. ABA."

"What's wrong with em?" Gene asked.

"Playin the game with a goddam beach ball."

"They do?"

"Might as well. It looks like it. Goddam basketball painted red white and blue. Jazzy new uniforms, all kinda colors. Pretty soon it won't be a sport it'll be a fuckin circus."

"It's progress," Barnes said.

"Progress, my ass. Won't have athletes anymore. Have clowns. That's what the public wants. Let em have it. To hell with tradition. Look at the hard time curling is having. You know why?"

"People lack vision," said Barnes.

"Besides that. It's a traditional sport. Centuries old. People don't dig that now, they wanna go see some clowns throwing a beach ball around."

"If this was Home," Thomas said, "the St. Bernard could come around and give us a hit from the brandy keg."

"There's some in the kitchen," Nell said.

"That's not the same," Thomas said, "as having the St. Bernard bring the keg around."

"Well, I'm no St. Bernard," Nell said.

"Jesus, Nell," Barnes said, "just cause you're pissed at me you don't have to take it out on everybody."

"OK, Mr. Good Humor Man."

"Hey, Barnes," Gene said, hoping to head off him and Nell, "you looked anymore?"

"For what?"

"Home."

"Yeh."

"Where?"

"Vermont."

"What happened?"

"Nothin."

"How?"

"I believed an ad in the paper. Said 'castle on lake.' Went up to see it. What the hell. Forty grand for a castle on lake."

"What was it?"

"Cinder-block house on swamp."

Lou got up and made a mean batch of martinis.

Gene drank one out of a highball glass, full.

"Where's the sun?" Thomas asked.

"Gone down, man," Gene said. "Winter now. Dude goes down early."

"I mean the music. *That* sun."

Gene crawled over to the records and put on *Abbey Road*. They listened, in silence, to "Here Comes the Sun." No one got up to dance. The song seemed out of place, like playing "Jingle Bells" at the beach.

When it was over Gene took it off and piled on four other sides, the first ones on the stack.

Thomas made a fire with the one log and the Sunday *Times*.

Gene scooted over to where Lou was lying and looking at the ceiling.

"What you see, babe?"

"Shadows."

"Oh."

He lay down to look at them himself, wondering if he could find some message in the way they waved and flickered, the rhythm of their dance. He didn't know what

Lou saw in them and wasn't sure he wanted to know. She
was several inches and several worlds away from him. He
could feel the huge distance between them, the empty
gap.

"Hey, play it again," said Barnes.

"What?" Gene asked.

"Whatever it was."

Gene went back and put the last song on again. It
was "Helplessly Hoping" on the *Marrakesh Express* of
Crosby, Stills and Nash. They had all heard it hundreds
of times, it was one of their standards, but it never fit
before, as it fit now the feeling of the room, the people
in it.

Is that hello or the sound of good bye-eye-yi

He looked at Lou when the song said:

We are fo-or each other.

Still?

He was hoping.

Helpless to do much else.

In the shadows on the ceiling—he could see, with the
music—her Harlequin hovering.

Him.

Everyone seemed to get silent drunk, sullen drunk.

"Shit," said Lou. "I'm outa cigarettes."

"Got a Kent," said Barnes.

Lou shook her head, irritated.

"Luckies," she said. "I'll go get some."

Flash stood up and stretched.

"I'll come," he said. "Need the air."

Flash and Lou went out to get the cigarettes. They
were gone for over an hour.

"What took so long?" Gene asked her.

Lou shrugged.

"Stopped for a beer."

When Gene finished writing what he knew was finally his final Final Exam he went over to the Captains Bar in the Statler and ordered a vodka martini on the rocks. It was not quite 11:00 A.M. and the only other customer was a white-haired gent at the bar with a glass of beer. Gene settled himself at one of the little tables along the wall and a waitress who was wearing a miniskirted sailor suit with black net stockings and bowling shoes brought him the drink and a little bowl of peanuts. It was dark and quiet and anonymous. Gene especially liked hotel bars for drinking alone because they gave him the illusion he was not in any particular place, he was simply in a hotel, which might be anyplace, and no one was likely to find you or know where you were. It was like getting out of town for a while without really having to leave.

He took a sip of the drink, saluting himself in silence, having to smile in spite of it all at the irony of such solitary celebration on this long-anticipated occasion. He had thought when he finally if ever finished his marathon college career he would throw the biggest bash of his history, and that would be pretty damn big. He would buy enough booze and dope to last a week, build a giant stew that would never stop, and go among the guests

wearing nothing but his academic robe, bestowing bless-
ings and bounty. Best of all Lou would be proudly beside
him, her faith in him justified, her passion intensified.
She, clad only in her own academic gown, would stroll
with him, hand in hand, and occasionally after spreading
their benevolence over the party they would quietly go to
the bedroom and close the door, slip off their robes that
would fall in a black swirl to the floor, and, supremely
naked, make educated love.

Instead, he was hiding out in a hotel bar, putting off
the subject of what should have been his triumph in
getting a degree he didn't want because other people's
hearts would break if he didn't have it, because the mention of it to Lou would immediately raise the now more
painful subject expressed in the single nagging sentence:
"What are you going to do?"

When you grow up?

He guessed he was grown. He could still remember
how adults always asked him as a kid, as they asked all
kids:

"What are you going to be when you grow up?"

"I'm going to be a fireman."

Gene fixed on that because he found it made them
happiest.

"Fireman."

It was what they expected you to say. It was cute. It
proved their adult superiority because they knew you
wouldn't be really, you were just a kid and didn't know
any better and thought it was exciting to answer alarms
and ride in a bright red truck with a siren and slide down
a pole.

"Did you hear that? He's going to be a fireman!"

Ooh, ahh, chuckle, inneeee sweeet?

Other kids didn't ask. Just grown-ups. Other kids might
say what *they* were going to be, but they were too polite
to ask *you*, you could say or not.

All were taught to chant the list of job opportunities:

Rich man, poor man, beggar man, thief;
Doctor, lawyer, Indian chief.

Gene found none of the above appealing. He liked the
idea of being an Indian, but didn't aspire to Chief. Indian
or Fire. Lack of responsibility. No ambition. Direction-
less. Boat without a rudder, ship upon the sand.

Maybe if things had worked differently he'd have gone
on working in his dad's grocery, from part-time as a kid
to full time as a man, having a kid of his own to work
part-time and then passing on the store to him, and him
to his kid, just like some kind of natural cycle, like birds
migrating, knowing what to do and where to go without
having to ask or think about it.

He had liked the store, the clean smell of it, aromas
of vegetables, everything fresh, the real touch of fuzzy-
skinned green beans, slick limes, soft green foliage crown
of a bunch of radishes, hard golden teeth of the smiling
corn. Now all that was wrapped and sanitized and sealed,
laid out under the antiseptic supermarket aura that was
neither night nor day, the droning fluorescent neutrality.

His father saw it coming, so Gene as a kid knew the
store would no longer be there when he grew up.

"The chains are coming," his father prophesied so often
at supper while his mother listened with gloomy respect.
"They will kill off the little man, the independent. The
little man believed because he wanted to believe that
people in a hurry might switch to the chains but the
faithful old customers wouldn't desert us, prefer to spend
a little more and get personal service, friendly attention,
a better cut of meat, but that was a pipe dream. The
chains are getting stronger and soon will squeeze the rest
of us out."

As a little kid Gene pictured these giant chains, link
upon gargantuan link, slinking and clanking through the
streets, wrapping themselves around the little men, squeez-

ing them till they were limp, their poor pink tongues hanging out in deathly surrender.

When his father's prophecy was filled by one of the chains putting up a giant store three blocks away, he sold his own place at a loss and took a job as a butcher at the chain store, working invisible behind the walls, not seeing or being seen by the customers.

So instead of a grocery store he got from his father the money to get a degree. His father, solemn, said he had saved it just for that purpose, that even though he couldn't pass on the store he could give him this opportunity which counted for more. He believed in the college degree with the fervor and faith of those who never had one, imagining the possession of it opened all doors, solved all material problems. If you had it, his father explained, you could write your own ticket.

To where?

Hell, at least one power the goddam degree had was making his daddy happy knowing he had it.

After another vodka martini he decided to call. Give the old man the pleasure of knowing. No sense to wait for the actual piece of paper, he would send that along when it came.

He paid his check and got a couple of bucks worth of change and went to one of the public phones in the corridor leading to the lobby. He got his married sister's number from Chicago information and plinked in the coins.

"Hey," he said when she answered, "this is Gene. In Boston."

Maybe she'd forgot. Who or where he was.

"The old man around?" he asked.

"You don't know, do you?"

It was not a question but an accusation. Her voice like a knife.

"How the hell should I know?"

"You're his son, that's all."

He was sure as hell not going to feed more money in just to get a lecture on how he should keep in touch, be a better son.

"Look," he said, "just tell him I finished up my credits. I'll get the degree. Tell him I'll write the details."

"Don't bother. He's dead."

"What?"

"December. We tried to find you."

He realized the phone was in Lou's name, he had never put his address on the postcards he sent when he moved, when he reported he was going back to school. He didn't even say which one.

The operator told him to deposit twenty cents for another three minutes.

"I'm sorry," he said, and put the receiver back in its cradle.

A man in the phone stall next to his was saying with frantic urgency, "I tell you, I got to have it *now*, not a *month* from now."

Gene walked toward the glass doors at the end of the corridor. He watched the calves of a woman walking ahead of him, wearing a swell-looking fur coat. They were muscular legs like dancers have, the calves knotting as the step went down, then loosening as it lifted. He followed her awhile, absorbed. Concentrating on the calves. He went into a luncheonette and ordered a cup of coffee and French fries. He hadn't eaten all day. He ate the French fries slowly, separately, purposefully. The coffee burned his tongue. He blew on it, staring at the tiny flecks on the black surface. He wondered why there were always those tiny flecks in luncheonette coffee. Maybe it was his fault. Dandruff maybe. After a while he drank it.

He did not remember going back to the apartment. He remembered sitting there on the living room floor with a big glass and a bottle of gin, wearing just his ratty bath-

robe. He remembered he had vomited. He remembered
Lou coming in sometime after dark and saying, "My God,
you look like you've seen a ghost." He remembered saying,
"Yes."

The collar pinched his neck. He had not worn a tie for over a year. His one standard "grown-up" suit felt itchy and cumbersome. He had bought it on sale when he first came to Boston at one of those "plain pipe rack" stores, and he didn't mind that it was really too big. He liked the feeling he was hiding out in it. The vest added to the sense of protection and disguise.

"Tell me, Mr. Barret," said the rotund man behind the personnel desk, speaking through a fixed and professional smile, "why did you choose to come to Boston to complete your education?"

"Because my old lady got a job here."

"Your mother is employed in Boston?"

"Oh. No, sir. My—uh—girlfriend."

"Your *girlfriend* found employment in Boston and so you left your former college and followed her here?"

"Yes, sir."

The smile that was not a smile leaned forward.

"Come, come now, Mr. Barret, we have to do better than *that*."

"We do?"

"Oh, indeed."

"Why?"

Fat fingers laced together, chin rested on them, smile drawn above.

"Because rational decision-making is a key part of the maturation process."

"What's a better reason for coming to a place than to live with the person you love?"

Palms raised upward, nothing to hide. Smile still painted in place.

"If you don't know, Mr. Barret, I doubt I could explain."

"Right."

Firm handshake.

At the door, Gene turned, said through his own smile:

"Incidentally, sir, with all due respect, you're the slimiest cocksucker I've come across yet."

Mouth open.

Out.

Coffee break.

A railroad car luncheonette on Cambridge Street near Government Center was nearly deserted, there was counter room for unfurling the employment section of the *Globe*. Gene studied the columns, pencil poised to ring any reasonable possibility for the "real work" he was pledged to do. For Lou. For himself, too. He said. Or she said.

The headings themselves, the boldface-type descriptions over the details of what was being offered gave him a dry, aching feel:

Commodity Options, Full Charge Bookkeeper, Shipping Dept. Helper, Offset Feeders and Tenders, Layout Person, Printed Circuit Board Assembler.

But he made himself look below the titles, read the real nature of what was available:

"CLERK: Conscientious person to learn computer billing."

The thought of a lifetime lurched ahead of him, sick on the roller coaster.

"PURCHASING AGENT: Ambitious, systematic individual for supervis. capac. Prefer background in fence, hardware."

No chance there, no background whatsoever in fence, hardware.

"EARN REAL MONEY" caught his eye, wondering if it meant the other ads were just come-ons for funny money. Monopoly money. But he realized it only meant this promised *more* money. Real meant a lot. All you had to do was "Learn to sell and install aluminum and vinyl siding. Perfect opportunity to become your own person in one of today's fastest-growing fields."

The chance to "become your own person" appealed but shit, siding was Flash's field, and he wasn't about to go up to the boondocks and try to muscle Flash out of siding sales, aluminum *or* vinyl. Let em send some innocent up there.

The ads he liked the ring of he knew would not pass as appropriate or serious or worthy for a man of his degree. A shame, for he liked the offer to

"DRIVE DANDY DAN ICE CREAM TRUCK on established routes."

The idea of driving a Dandy Dan Ice Cream Truck was a gas in itself, but to think you wouldn't be driving it just anywhere, not into untried or hostile territory but on *established routes*, that was a real zinger. That meant the kids would be waiting for you, they'd hear that "Dandy Dan" jingling bell theme music coming and they'd be out on the sidewalk with their little fists full of change, faces all rosy with eager little smiles.

He could see Lou's rosy face and its eager little smile when he drove home his first night in the Dandy Dan Ice Cream Truck, and stepped out in his red-and-white jump-suit uniform with "Gene" written in scroll over his pocket and the black-billed white cap perched rakishly on his head.

No thanks.

The only other one that really caught his fancy was "ORGANIST, must be able to entertain a mature crowd."

Far out. Could it be for one of the strip joints in the Combat Zone, someone who had to pound that organ so wild that it kept the "mature crowd" from rioting till the next act came on? Or maybe this was for the job of organist at Fenway Park, who had to play the "Fight" music at just the right time, trill to the homers, hit loud chords of inspiration when the Red Sox came to the plate, and all the time keep the "mature crowd" in hand and off the field with martial music drowning out the ugly decision of an umpire?

Now this was a job with thrills and challenge, and one he could wear a suit to work in, too, satisfying both his own sense of restlessness and Lou's sense of propriety.

But shit. He didn't play the organ.

Gene was jostled as people sat down on each side of him. It was nearly noon and the place was filling up. He folded in his *Globe*, looked up at the menu of the day, and ordered a Pepsi and a meatball sub.

"Don't be discouraged," Lou told him after the first week of trying.

━━━━━━━━━━

Gene wished to hell he had Flash's knack for inventing jobs, even though they didn't last long.

Flash fell by one night full of enthusiasm for his new career. He was decked out in white bell-bottom trousers, brown suede boots, a red silk shirt, and two strands of love beads.

He was a rock impresario.

Well, not quite an impresario. Not yet. That would come later, staging mammoth concerts and so on. Right now he was simply the manager of a new rock group.

"Which one?" asked Gene.

"Rasputin and the Schemers."

"Far out," said Lou. "Historic yet. How'd they get the name?"

"Dude on bass went to college," Flash explained. "He's like the leader. Rasputin. Grew himself a little goatee, to throw a little evil in the image. Then there's a brother and sister, they're like the Schemers part. Chick plays organ, he does guitar."

"What're they into?" Gene asked.

"Just grass and pills. No hard stuff. I laid that down heavy, one of my conditions for takin em on. No hard stuff."

"I mean what kinda music," Gene said.

"Oh, Christ, you know, the regular shit you hear. Like everyone else. It all sounds the same to me. They're no worse than the other ones. The difference is, they got me to handle em."

Flash had heard the group at a small bar in Somerville, got to rapping with them, kind of started improvising what he could do for em. That was their first gig, the one in Somerville. They lived around there and the bartender fixed it up for em. But shit, they had no future. Nothing lined up. What they needed was professional help, guidance. Flash offered them a package. He would act as their road manager, publicist, promoter, business agent, all rolled into one, for an even fifty percent of the take.

"Fifty might seem a lot," Flash admitted, "unless you take into consideration I'm doing three or four different jobs for em."

"You got em any gigs yet?" Gene asked.

"Hell, I'm mappin out a whole tour, puttin it all together."

"Where?" Lou asked

"Startin at this roadhouse I know just over the New Hampshire border, in Hudson. Near Nashua. We'll go west into Vermont, then cross into northern New Hampshire, hit Bangor over in Maine and work our way down from there."

"You really got it lined up?" Gene asked.

"Mostly, yeh, I just went up there, got commitments for most of the route."

"How?" asked Lou.

"Shit, that's where I sell siding. The boonies. I know all the little roadhouses, drink with the goddam managers. I told em this group was hot, they would pack in the customers. How the hell do they know? How the hell do I? I figure you put 'ROCK GROUP' in big letters after their name, who knows the difference? Then if they do pack em in, we get some good figures under our belt we can come back to Boston, build from strength."

"Sounds great," said Gene.

"Thank God I had the foresight not to put all my eggs into sports when I founded the N E A E A."

"How do you mean?" asked Gene.

"You recall, the parent organization of the North American Curling League is the New England Athletic *and Entertainment* Association. In my management of Rasputin, I can use the same stationery. It comes under entertainment. Foresight. Somehow I knew, I sensed that sports was on the way out. Circuses, that's what it is now. Besides, it doesn't fit in with the spirit of the times. The spirit of the times is not competitive. Age of Aquarius and all. Spirit of harmony, love, expressed through music. Competition is out. Professional sports will soon be laughed off the fields and out of the stadiums. Who is a sure bet to fill Boston Garden on any given night—the Celtics or the Rolling Stones? Huh? Take your choice."

Flash's new career gave Gene inspiration. He knew he couldn't pull off a Flash number, but maybe if he quit just looking at the ads, gave himself some time to think . . .

The second week of his job hunting Gene got dressed every morning in his suit which Lou always touched up on the ironing board the night before to do her bit, show him

she wanted to help in his great career hunt; and after a
flurry of preparing eggs-toast-coffee and listening to the
news on the radio (a new habit which Gene felt lent his
job-hunting campaign a sense of being on top of things) he
strode off briskly to the corner of Mass Ave and Boylston
where he purchased a *Globe*, folded it neatly, and tucked
it under his arm the way the businessmen do, and with a
cheerful whistle proceeded to the Prudential Center, where
he spent the day.

He picked a comfortable chair in the Sheraton lobby
for reading the paper—sports, comics, maybe some columns opposite the editorial page. He didn't read the employment ads anymore. It had dawned on him they would
always be essentially the same. There was simply no job
he could stand that would also be approved by Lou. It
was a puzzle to which he knew there had to be a suitable
answer, one that was not to be found in the help wanted
columns. It was something he had to solve on his own. All
he needed was a little time and it would come to him.

The Pru was his headquarters. After the paper he rode
the elevator up to the Skywalk, where you had a pano-
ramic view of the whole city. Then he looked through the
wonderful shops in the complex, the Saks Fifth Avenue
and the Lord & Taylor, thinking which stuff would look
good on Lou, had coffee at the Pavilion coffee shop, got
a hamburger for lunch at Brighams, dropped into the
Mermaid bar to catch a few game shows on the tube, went
across the street to the Paperback Booksmith, and picked
out a mystery he'd take back and read in the Sheraton
lobby. Around four he'd hit the Mermaid again for a beer,
watch "Bonanza," and split just before the cocktail crowd.
He walked back home with his brisk pace, hurried inside,
threw off his coat and jacket, loosened his tie, and yanked
off his shoes.

"Wow. Now I know what they mean by pounding the
pavement."

"Don't worry," Lou said, "it'll happen."

It did.

At the end of the second week of his life at the Pru Gene figured he couldn't keep putting it off. He knew he could never stand sitting at a desk all day but that was the kind of job she wanted him to have, one where you had your name on the door and your Bigelow on the floor. But he figured maybe if he got the kind of job *he* liked at the kind of place *she* liked, she'd never know the difference. She told him there were lots of book publishers in Boston, and he could tell she thought that was good, a worthy thing to be into. As far as Gene could tell it would be just like any other kind of office job until it occurred to him if you published books you had to get them out to the stores. The books. You couldn't just leave them lying around. You would have to put them in boxes and someone would have to *move* those boxes.

When Gene came home one night and told Lou he had landed a job at the venerable firm of Adams House, Publishers, she was overjoyed. He said he was in the training program. That's why he had to buy a new suit.

Actually he was in the stockroom. But what the hell, he really did work for Adams House. He now had two suits and he alternated, wearing one of them to work every day. The other guys in the stockroom wore jeans and T-shirts and needled Gene about wearing a suit and tie. They called him "Diamond Gene."

But upstairs his attire and pleasant manner drew favorable attention.

A lady editor whom Gene often saw dozing at her desk commissioned him to bring her black coffee every day at eleven and three. Word of his courtesy and efficiency spread, and he was given the responsibility of escorting the aged editor Shepard Hoskins to and from lunch at the Ritz every day, a journey that entailed walking through the Boston Common and the Public Garden each way.

When Gene was handed this assignment, he naturally

wanted to know what to look out for. All he was told was
that Hoskins was too old to go by himself.

"Does he fall down?" Gene asked.

"No," the sleepy lady editor said, "he gets lost."

"Ah."

So every day Gene escorted Hoskins back and forth to
his lunch at the Ritz.

He was gaining responsibility.

Lou would be proud.

———

The weather that spring was raw and scratchy, conten-
tious and cold, smelling of mud and wounds.

No one made fires.

Now that he was a nine-to-fiver Gene didn't feel like
cooking much. Besides, he never knew when Lou might
show. The war was taking more of her time. It was also
making her thinner, more wan. What was her health till
the war was won? Or lost, whichever it was she wanted.
She missed meals entirely, forgetting insubstantial things,
living on cigarettes, peanut butter, and zeal.

One night he came home after work and found her
asleep, sprawled over test papers. He knew if he woke her
and tried to get her out for a meal she'd refuse so he
stealthily crept off and came back carrying a flat cardboard
box hot to hold and steamy with wonderful smells so
strong as to render a whole room woozy.

Gene sat the box down about a foot away from her,
opened the lid, releasing the full force of the fragrance.

She made a small moan, moved, sniffed, blinked, woke.

"My God," she said, "what's happening?"

"Pizza."

"With sausage-n-pepper?"

"With everything."

They devoured the gooey mass in earnest silence, slurping, stuffing, dripping, demolishing the great mixed wonderful mess including all crust, then picking at crumbs as they had a can of beer, burping and sipping, satisfied.

Warm and full, Gene suggested they get out of their goddam rut, go somewhere—maybe up to Maine this weekend. They could grab a bus, get off where it looked good, get them some fried clams, climb around the rocks, breathe some good fresh cold ocean air. Change of scene.

"Gene? I forgot."

"What?"

"A weekend meeting of all New England faculty-student peace planning committees at Providence. I'm supposed to go."

"Oh."

"I'm sorry."

"No. No need."

"Should have said."

He shrugged, so hard his shoulder wrenched.

She went back to her test papers.

He went to the kitchen and stuffed away the dead box of pizza, made himself a tall glass of gin with an ice cube. He spread out the *Globe* sports page on the floor and studied the NBA standings.

He heard Lou yawn, looked over to see her stretch, and said, "Hey, babe?"

"Hmmm?"

"Will you do me a favor?"

"What?"

"Will you promise that if you start makin it with any other guy you won't tell me? I mean, you know, I know you're free, we both are free, to do anything like that we want, but I just don't want to know about it."

She looked at him steadily and said, "OK, I promise."

Then she went back to her work.

She had promised, anyway.

Not that she wouldn't do it.

That she wouldn't tell him about it.

The weather went from raw and clammy to steamy hot. The gentle, breezy part of spring didn't happen that year. Gene was baking alive in his goddam suits and realized he'd have to hit Filene's basement and try and pick him up some kind of summerweight jacket.

All just part of the pressure of being a rising young professional man.

The hell of it was he was having to hold off the lady editor who liked him from pushing for the company to bring him up from the stockroom into some better job. It was hard to explain he didn't want the kind of jobs they considered "better." Just to ensure he stayed in the stockroom, he thought he might have to fuck up a little. Forget to bring the lady editor the coffee that kept her awake in the afternoon. Maybe let old Hoskins get lost in the Public Garden. Show a little irresponsibility.

One night he came home from work and found Lou there with a six-pack, some deli food, and a guy named Steven Alexander.

"Steven," Lou explained, "is active in the inter-University Peace Co-Ordinating Group."

"Oh," Gene said.

This time it was him and not the other guy who must

have looked unpleasantly shocked. He could feel the heat of his cheeks, and that made him more uncomfortable. He didn't know how he knew, he just knew.

Steven Alexander looked completely at ease. He was an instructor in mathematics at Boston University. Tall, with red hair in a brush cut and steel-rim glasses. Smooth, pale skin with freckles on his face and hands. He wore a light-weight cord summer suit of the type Gene had just decided he'd better try to buy before he baked to death. He wore a neat blue shirt and a black-and-white polka-dot bow tie. Though he was sitting on the floor along with Lou where she had spread out plates for the deli food, he did not look casual or mussed. He looked crisp.

"Please join us," he said to Gene, indicating the food. His voice was unbearably pleasant.

"In a sec," Gene said.

He took off the scratchy coat to his suit, went to the bathroom, and washed his hands and face. His shirt stuck to him. He didn't want to make a big production of changing his clothing. He just rolled up the sleeves of his shirt. He came out whistling, went to the kitchen, and cracked a can of beer. Pabst Blue Ribbon. That must be the beer of Steven Alexander. Lou didn't drink Pabst. Didn't used to, anyway.

He sat down on the floor and Lou said, "Corned beef's good."

She pushed the plate with corned beef toward him. He made the sandwich, careful to be sure it was a normal sandwich, neither scrimpy nor gigantic.

"Have a good day?" Lou asked.

"Super," Gene said.

"You look hot."

"It's a hot day."

"Yes, it is."

"We seemed to have missed spring," Steven Alexander said.

"Or it missed us," Lou said.

They laughed. Lou and Steven did. Gene smiled.

Lou finished her sandwich, wiped her hands, and went to the kitchen. She opened a beer for herself and asked Steven if he'd like another one. He said no thanks, he had to be getting along pretty soon.

"I mustn't forget," he said as he stood up, "those clippings about the deserters in Sweden you were going to loan me."

"Oh! Right."

Lou went to a pile of papers on the couch and extracted a couple of sheets of Xeroxed newspaper stories.

"Here," she said, handing them to him.

"I'll return them," Steven said, as he slipped them into his briefcase.

"No hurry."

"Good evening," Steven said to Gene, "it was nice to meet you."

"You, too," Gene said.

Lou walked with him to the door, and stood out in the hall with him for a moment or so. It was quiet and then Gene heard them exchange "Good night."

Lou came back in and started clearing stuff off the floor.

"I'm going to clean up," Lou called from the kitchen.

"Clean up what?"

"The kitchen. All this shit that's accumulating. Breakfast dishes."

"OK," he said.

The kitchen wasn't in any different shape than it usually was, and usually it was Gene who got around to cleaning it up when it started to get out of hand. He turned on the radio to a rock station, but it was hard to hear above the noise from the kitchen. It sounded like a minor war. Pans banged and clashed, plates and cups collided and pillars of suds billowed up like the clouds from explosions.

When it was over Lou emerged pale and bedraggled, pulling her dress over her head.

"I think I'll go to bed and read awhile," she said.

"It's awful early."

"I'm awful tired."

"He seems like a nice guy."

Lou looked blank a moment.

"Oh. Steven?"

"Yes."

"He is," she said, "he's a very nice person."

"You're fucking him, aren't you?"

"Why do you say that?"

"Because I believe it's true."

"Well, I guess you can believe what you want."

"What I want is for you to tell me if it's true."

"You told me once you didn't want me to tell you that. If it ever happened."

"Well now I do."

She got a cigarette, lit it, and sat down on the couch.

"OK," she said. "It's true."

"Congratulations," he said.

She stood up and yelled.

"Goddam it you asked me to tell and I told and you go and get smartass about it."

"OK. I'm sorry."

"We talked about this from the start. Remember? We agreed we'd both be free to—to do what we want."

"Yeh. I guess I just thought—I thought maybe we might not want to."

"Well, for a long time we didn't."

"I still don't."

"Then don't."

"It makes it different."

"Why? Why should it make anything different for us? I didn't say I loved the guy or anything. I wanted to make it with him, and he wanted to make it with me, and we did. That's all there is to it."

"And what if you both want to do it again?"

"Then we probably will."

"Do me one favor."

"Yes?"

"Don't do it here. I mean even if I'm not here or something. Do it at his place."

"OK."

"That's all."

"Good night, Gene."

"Good night."

Gene decided to take a lover. He didn't really want to, but he felt he should. Maybe it would help bring the balance back between him and Lou. Maybe if they both had other lovers it would somehow bring them closer again. If nothing else it might help make him forget about her fucking that Steven Alexander guy. He kept picturing Lou in bed with him, imagining her doing with him all the things she had done with Gene. It actually seemed . . . *obscene*. For the first time he understood what the word meant.

He thought about getting it on with Marcia, the lady editor at Adams House. He knew she liked him. She was thirty-something and divorced. She wasn't any beauty but she had a kind of drowsy appeal about her. The trouble was he liked her. They were sort of friends. If they had an affair they'd talk a lot and tell each other their troubles. He didn't want it like that. He wanted someone to fuck, and that's all. Someone who wanted the same thing.

He found her in accounting. Mitzi. She wore long false eyelashes and miniskirts and her ambition was to marry a doctor. She might have some jollies beforehand but she'd settle for nothing less when it came to tying the knot. Good. No one was fooling anyone. Gene was sympathetic to her dream.

"Maybe you should be a nurse," he said when they were

finishing their first drink, a martini for him and a tropical nights delight for her at Bob Lee's Islander. When Gene tried to think of someplace to take her that he thought she would dig, he remembered the dinner after Flash's party and it struck him as perfect. The semidarkness, the leis around the neck, the rum drinks with decorations. Hers had a little native canoe floating in it.

"Uggggggh," she said.

It was not a reaction to the drink, but to the thought of being a nurse.

"I can't stand sick people," she said.

"But you dig doctors."

"For husbands."

"Respectable?"

"Rich."

"Ah."

"Maybe not millionaires but steady rich. I don't go for these flashy types who are always messing with stocks and investments. I mean some of em are cute to date, but for a husband I want *regular* rich. No ups and downs."

"And till then?"

"Till then's *my* business."

"Maybe I can make some of it my business."

"You're cute," she said.

———————

It didn't help.

It gave him something to do, but it didn't make things any different with him and Lou.

"How come you're acting funny?" Lou asked.

"Acting funny how?"

"It seems like you keep staring at me."

"No," he said. "I wasn't."

But he was. It was after he'd been making it with Mitzi for about a week and he wondered if it was making

any difference. With him and Lou. He had no desire to
tell her about it, no wish for an excuse to go "Nah nah nah,
I can do it too!" He just wondered if there was any change
for the better in how things were between them. That's
why he'd been staring at her. Looking for something, some
sign, some emotional barometer that might show their private weather was improving.

But it seemed monotonously the same. Just like the
weather outside. Humid. Uncomfortable.

He and Lou had fucked the night she told him about
Steven Alexander and to his surprise it had been especially
good. Then afterward it seemed like it hadn't happened.
They had another good one the night after he'd first made
Mitzi, but then it was the same again. There didn't seem
to be any carry-over from their sex to the rest of their
lives. There used to be but there wasn't now.

Gene bought a little hash and decided he'd suggest they
get high on it and make love, thinking maybe something
profound would happen behind the hash, some insight or
mutual feeing that would carry over after the sex, after the
high.

He brought home the hash and a quart of deli potato
salad and the beer. They used to have that sometimes for
hot weather dinners, just potato salad and beer. He did
not get Pabst. He got Schlitz. That's what they used to
drink all the time.

He even put on *Abbey Road*. Shit, it couldn't hurt anything. Maybe it would help create the right mood. Gene
took a shower and put on some jeans and a clean sport
shirt.

Around nine o'clock he decided he'd better have some of
the potato salad. She hadn't said anything about coming
home any special time that evening, and sometimes she
didn't get home till ten or so. If Gene had wanted her to
get there early he should have said something. It was his
own fault.

Around ten thirty he went out and bought a jug of the

Rhine Garten. He left a note saying he'd be right back.
When he got back the note was still there. At midnight
when he took his glass to the kitchen he filled it with gin
instead of wine. He put an ice cube in it. A little before
three he decided he might as well smoke the hash. There
wasn't a hell of a lot anyway. It wasn't the best he ever
had. It was probably because of his not being in the right
mood. His fault, not the hash. His fault, not Lou. Every
fuckin thing was his fault. By four he knew she wasn't
coming back for the night. Once he'd have been scared
shitless because they always came home no matter what
and even after the thing with Steven Alexander it was like
an unspoken agreement that they not spend the night
away. Spending the night away was like flaunting it. Lou
had never done it before. Even though she may have made
it before she met Steven Alexander, with other guys, she
always came home, she always made it look good. Maybe
she *had* made it with a lot of other guys. Maybe even guys
Gene knew. That night when she and Flash went for
cigarettes. Times she met Barnes for drinks someplace. His
place maybe. Who knew?

Gene liked the gin better than the dope. Nothing
subtle. Just blasting right through ya. By dawn he had
finished the fifth and was back into the Rhine Garten,
which was all that was left. He had drunk the beer
much earlier. The only thing he hadn't polished off was
the goddam potato salad. He didn't feel like it. He had
wanted to have it with Lou. Tough shit. Wasn't that nice
and cute of him, thinkin up the little hot weather meal for
him and Lou? Shit. He took the carton of potato salad and
put it in the middle of the rug and stepped on it. It oozed
out over the rug and his foot. To hell with it. He got out
a couple of eggs from the fridge and threw them against
the wall in the kitchen. That made him laugh. "Scrambled," he said.

The key turned in the lock around eight. Gene was lying
on the couch. He had thrown all the stacks of papers and

books and magazines off it and they were scattered over the rug. A few papers were stuck in potato salad. Gene had taken off his sport shirt. He was just in his Levi's. He was hugging the jug of Rhine Garten to him, smiling.

"What . . . happened?" Lou said.

Gene laughed.

At least he'd got a rise out of her, a reaction, some kind of surprise, *something.*

"Have a good time?" he said. "Night on the town?"

"I didn't mean—" Lou said. "I fell asleep. I thought I'd just take a nap. I was tired. I—"

"Course ya were. Who wouldn't be tired after fuckin old crisp, efficient Steven Alexander all night? Tell me, is he crisp and efficient in bed? Methodical?"

"Shut up, Gene."

"Tell me, does he wear the bow tie? When he's fucking you?"

"Stop."

"Is it a turn-on? The bow tie."

"You drunken shit."

He jumped up, reeling, ran and grabbed her before she could move away and slapped her full force across the face. Her mouth opened. She dropped her purse.

As soon as he did it he was scared. Sorry.

He moved back, stumbling.

"Shit," he said. "I'm sorry. Please—"

"Get out," she whispered with terrible force. "Get out of here. You—you get your ass out. We're through."

He started crying. He bawled. He fell down on the floor and crawled. He pleaded, begged forgiveness, begged to stay, start again.

"It's done," she said.

She got some books and left.

And he knew she was gone. From him. Like she said. It was done.

He finished off the Rhine Garten, then he put on his new summer suit. He didn't shower or shave, he just put the suit on. He got some buttons scrambled but basically got the shirt on, and the tie. The coat was easy. He decided he should have a big breakfast to prepare him for the duties of the day ahead. He went to the Statler and had the "Hungry Pilgrim Breakfast," featuring cranberry juice, còdfish cakes, scrambled eggs, and baked beans. He topped that off with a hot cup of coffee, paid the check, and made it to the men's room barely in time to heave up the whole thing. Well, he'd had a hearty breakfast at least for a little while.

He sat in the Public Garden till a little after ten and then went to Adams House. Just for old-times sake he took Marcia a cup of coffee.

"What happened?" she asked him with a look of uncustomary alertness.

"I must resign my position," he said. "But you tell em. OK? Or don't tell em. They'll figure out. It'll just be our secret, you and me. Or I?"

Marcia helped him out of the office quietly, carefully, gave him two dollars and told him to promise her he'd take a cab and go home and sleep.

"Can't," he said. "Go home. No home. Can't go home to no home."

"Well—will you take the key to my apartment? Go there and sleep? I'll come at lunchtime and check on how you are."

"I'm fine," he said. "You're fine, too. Don worry bout a thing."

He waved, looking back over his shoulder.

"Be careful!" she called after him.

Suddenly he really was tired. He couldn't go home, no home, he didn't want to see friends, he didn't want to sleep on a park bench because some cop might mess with him, then he remembered how the winos used to sleep in the hallways of the buildings by their old apartment on Carver Street. It sounded like a terrific idea. He crashed in the hallway of the building they used to live in. Sentimental to the last. Tenants stepped over him. It seemed poetic justice.

He slept till around three in the afternoon, then got up and brushed himself off and went to the bar with the hillbilly music jukebox. He drank beer there till six, then went to Mitzi's place. Call upon his lover.

"Ohshit," she said when she saw him.

He collapsed in a chair, smiling.

"What do you want?" she asked. She didn't sit down.

"Drink," he said. "Martini maybe?"

"You've had too many."

"One more."

"Get out," she said.

"Why?"

"Because you stink."

He sniffed and grimaced, wiped his hand across his face and straightened up a little.

"Yeh," he said. "Guess you're right."

He swallowed, blinked, and stood up.

"Bye," he said.

"Do me a favor," Mitzi said.

"Sure, baby. Anything."

"Don't come back."

He nodded.

He didn't know how he got to The Crossroads. He didn't know the new bartender there, but some of the regulars recognized him, said Hi. He had four stingers before he felt the world tilt without warning and he fell off his stool. Two of the regulars were above him, and the bartender was wiping his face with a wet rag.

"You're givin a bad name to an honorable profession," the bartender said. But not like he was mad.

"Sorry," Gene said.

"These gentlemen say they will take you home. You live around here, don't you?"

"No. Used to."

"Where do you live now? What's the address?"

"Isn't one. I don't live anywhere."

The bartender sighed. One of the regulars said, "Call that guy Flash . . ."

That's the last thing Gene remembered.

He woke up and there they all were, floating above him. All but Lou.

There was Barnes and Nell, Thomas and Flash and a honey-blonde who must be Flash's latest stewardess.

Gene wondered, with faint curiosity, whether he had died. That would mean his friends had died, too. Everyone but Lou. She was still fucking that crisp-looking sonofabitch with the bow tie, back down on earth. But everyone else had died and gone to—Barnes's place? It looked like it. The high ceilings. Books still in the boxes. So that's what happened. You died and went to Barnes's place. Gene started to smile, but it hurt.

"He's alive," said Flash.

Gene winced and whispered, "No."

"You'll make it," Barnes said.

"Why?" Gene asked.

"Cause you're comin up to Maine with us."

"Home?"

"No. We didn't find it. This is just a trip."

"A trip," Gene repeated. "What kind?"

"Vacation," Flash said. "You're goin on vacation."

"Who?"

"You and Barnes and Nell. Me and Francie here got business in town."

"It's gonna be a good trip, man," Nell said. "We all need one."

"Yeh," Gene said. "Trip."

He closed his eyes, remember the music, the "Helplessly Hoping":

Did you trip at the sound of goodbye-eye-yi?

"Tripped," he said.

III

"I've done everything I know
To try and make you mine
And I think it's gonna hurt me
For a long long time . . ."

Linda Ronstadt was singing the words. Not in person of course. A new album. Volume turned up to the peak.

Gene was glad it was Linda Ronstadt, not someone soppy or sickly sweet. Strong. Gutsy. Belting it out.

Her voice didn't seem just to come from the house but out of the earth, over the water into the rickety little town and the scrubland and forest beyond it.

Something was cold against his hand and he opened it and fitted his fingers around another beer.

"Thanks," he said, not knowing to whom, and kept his eyes closed.

Everyone there seemed to know what he needed right now and didn't need.

He didn't need to talk.

Not yet.

The wind felt clean and the lapping sound of the water was reassuring. At high tide the water came right under the porch, and at low it faded way back out into the main

body of itself, leaving a stretch of brilliant green sea grass
and stones. It was a tidal river, fed by the sea. He hadn't
known they had them.

He was lying in a hammock on the porch of this house
perched over the tidal river and people were putting cold
cans of beer in his hands. The sun was warm on his face,
on his closed eyes.

He was in Maine.

His friends had brought him.

Yeh. Suited him fine.

Every so often he thought of Lou—not *thought of* exactly, but a picture of her, bright Kodachrome, would flash
in his mind, a shot of her caught while walking or smoking or laughing or asleep, frozen in the frame at some
familiar angle, and the sight of each such shot caused a
sudden pain, like a sharp little dental pic hitting a nerve.

He concentrated on keeping his mind blank, a clean
piece of slate. He focused on sipping the beer and hearing the record.

> "Gonna plant me a seed
> Grow me an ocean
> Cut me some trees
> Build me an island . . . "

Yeh.

You and me, Linda.

Gently rocking.

He fell in and out of sleep, letting things happen around
him. Footsteps. Voices. Barnes and Nell. Others. None. No
one. Nothing.

The next day he was ambulatory.

The house belonged—at least for the summer—to some
friends of Nell named Jerry and Monica who graduated
from Northeastern and after a year doing straight career-
type jobs in Boston decided they'd rather move to Maine
and take whatever work they could find and save up to

buy themselves some land. They knew they could never afford anything here around Damariscotta, it was on the coast and only a couple hours from Boston, but in terms of summer work it was swell. For managing a sandwich and soft drink concession up the beach they got a percentage of profits and this cabin-like sort of shack with the porch out over the tidal river rent free. Monica looked intense behind her granny glasses, brown hair pulled back tight and neat from a fair, nontannable face without makeup. She was sort of like the strategist. Jerry had curly blond hair and a big smile all the time and liked to putter around and fix things.

Monica was saying to Barnes that when they started looking in earnest for land they'd go up north and inland, that's where you still could find the good values.

"*You* can," Barnes said forlornly, "*I* couldn't. I'm the only guy in the country couldn't find some damn land bargain in Maine."

"Forget it, man," Nell said, giving him a solace squeeze.

It did seem kind of funny when you thought about it, though, not that Barnes couldn't find his land but that a guy like him had even looked for it. Suddenly it seemed like that's what everyone wanted, land, especially younger people like Jerry and Monica. It seemed like everyone suddenly discovered we were running out of it and wanted to get their own little piece before none was left, get their own parcel and put their name on a stick and plant it in the ground and then dig a hole you could hide in or put up a house you could live in or just stand there on it, knowing it was yours, your land, you were making your stand.

Monica offered to scramble Gene some eggs for breakfast but he thanked her no and had a glass of milk and said he sure did appreciate the hospitality and now that he'd had his breakfast if nobody minded he'd just get a can of beer and go back to the hammock.

Nobody bothered him till late in the day when Nell

brought him a mug of some kind of soup and said he had
to eat it.

He winced.

"C'mon, buddy, I can't."

"You *gotta*," Nell said in a fake-urgent whisper, her
eyes mischievous. "Monica made it for ya. It's got all
kinds of herbs and all. You know, like some kind of hippie
soup. It's real special."

Gene even grinned, and drank the stuff down. It tasted
like moldy figs. Maybe it was.

Everyone was gone awhile and then they all came back
and said Gene had to join them for a feast. They had a
tub of steamers and a couple dozen ears of corn and a
couple gallon jugs of Cribari rosé. Gene ate an ear of
corn and five or six steamers in order to satisfy Nell and
then settled down with a nice big kitchen glass full of
rosé.

Other people came. A couple cute chicks who ran a
natural food store. Two jock-looking guys wearing those
sweat shirts that say "Property of—" some-fucking-thing-
or-other, and a small, pretty girl with bangs they called
Pal. The two guys called each other Coach. Maybe they
were. Coaches.

The coaches brought some really dynamite grass that
even got Barnes high and started Gene giggling in spite
of his condition.

Nell put an arm around his shoulder, smiling at seeing
him smile, and said, "Hi, man."

"You're not kiddin, kid."

"About what?"

"Being high. Int that what you said? High?"

"Like 'hello,' I meant."

"Oh, *that* kind," Gene said and giggled again.

Barnes tilted toward them, grinning.

"What's goin on?" he said.

"Hello," said Gene. "Get it?"

"He means 'High,' " said Nell.

"Who isn't?" said Barnes, slumping to a seat on the floor.

One of the coaches had rolled another fat joint of the dynamite stuff—it looked like a sloppy white cigar—and it was going around.

"Here come de sun," said Gene.

They got stoned so good that Barnes said what a crime it was everyone couldn't get any damn drug they wanted right from the drugstore that's what a drugstore should be a store for drugs, like it used to be. He said in the good old days a hunnerd years ago that's the way it was, they had the coke in Coca-Cola and the cough syrups were loaded with all kinds of goodies, you could just go down to your friendly neighborhood drugstore and get you something to get you high.

Gene said maybe there still was dope in stuff you bought at the drugstore, stuff you never thought about because it just looked ordinary.

They raided the bathroom medicine cabinet and soon were spraying gums with some kind of throat spray they swore made you numb like coke and trying to snort Ben Gay, passing it around to all the others recommending it highly, by now they were all so high anyway it was hard to tell if anything else got em up even more but it was easy to think so and everyone was up for the scenic moonlight sail that Jerry suggested but when they all piled in his rowboat it tipped and spilled them out but luckily though all the people were high the tide was low so there were no fatalities. Just wet clothes, sore backs, bruised elbows and knees, heads beginning to swell and stomachs turned with all that had been inhaled and eaten and drunk and snorted, and somebody's lungs hooting at the moon in the time he was convinced of being a coyote. Back in the house the bodies draped out to dry themselves and after a few gulps and random giggles the mood turned quiet, contemplative, solemn, and the bigger of the two coaches, the one who rolled the joints, said "Sleep," and one by one without more talk, they laid down their heads and did.

━━━━━━━━━

Waking, it looked like a battlefield. This side must have lost. Bodies pretzel-bent haphazardly overlapping here and there not in lust just left there. A groan or sigh or snore or some odd move of stretching arm, leg shifting, showed they all weren't dead. Maybe just wounded. Or gassed. Some bodies gather and rise, squinting and blinking, sigh, disappear.

Somehow Jerry and Monica got it together to make it up the beach and get the concession going, and likewise the natural food store chicks in their own enterprise. Coach Billy, the big, sandy-haired coach with the bull neck and the pale blue eyes who seemed to be the *head* coach of the coach bunch got to his feet and then to the kitchen, popped a can of Bud, let out a cavernous belch, rubbed his iron potbelly, stared down at the fallen troops, and said, in so many words, to follow me, and stirring, straggling, stumbling, stunned, they did.

Stopped in town to pick up a couple of cases of Carlings, a couple of loaves of Wonder bread and two family-size jars of Skippy Peanut Butter in case anyone was up for lunch. Coach Billy insisted it was all on him, everything they ate or drank or smoked or snorted or chewed at The Broken Arms was on the house.

The house they called The Broken Arms was where Coach Billy, Coach Burt, and Pal all lived.

It was a bumpy ride back into scratchy scrubland mostly on an unpaved unmarked muddied and pitted and potholed poor excuse for a road. Visitors guaranteed to be shaken well on the journey. And again at first sight of the house.

Out of thick brush a clearing comes suddenly, blank, dusty, nothing growing, an emptiness like a hole in a picture and then set into it onto it a stark, stiff, naked frame box of a two-story house once white but colorless now, washed out, corroded, bleached, blanched, roof in places scalped of shingles and sagged in the center like an overridden mule, two of six square windows blinded by boards, the others open blank, a front porch with top tilted to one side favoring a lame pillar bolstered by unpainted two-by-fours, old-fashioned glider on it with rusty coils sticking down through stuffing, and littered around the blunt building a dead car on wheel-less rims, a rusted jack, deflated beach ball, playground swing, big red Harley-Davidson in running order and plumed with appropriate squirrel's tail, a bicycle not in running order stripped of all but a crippled frame, a metal beer keg, badminton net, two croquet clubs, old-fashioned round-topped refrigerator without a door. And out of some or all of this, skittering in and around it raising dust and yips comes a scraggy wire-haired terrier who also belongs here. They called him Coach.

"Hey," said Barnes, sensing he should say some salutary statement in behalf of his group, new visitors wanting to be appreciative, polite, "Hey," he said again before coming up with: "This is really something."

"We looked and looked," Pal said, pleased, "and finally found a place that had the two things Coach Billy really wanted."

"What?" asked Barnes, his mind boggling in the effort to imagine.

"Privacy and a front porch."

The Broken Arms had one kind of privacy but not another. It was sealed off from the world outside, but inside

its sagging walls you could hear any word or sound made
in any given room in it from any other given room. There
were five tiny rooms and a bathroom upstairs, and down,
one big one and the kitchen. Layers of different wallpaper
peeling and molting gave the interior a scrambled effect,
dim stripes and soiled flowers, patterns of stars and sailing
ships, repeated, running into one another. Pillows were
living room furniture, all shapes and colors and sizes so
you could stack them or strew them, sit or lie on them, or,
if the mood hit, throw and fight with them. After an afternoon of playing touch they came in and flopped on the
pillows and then Coach Burt teased Pal about missing a
sure touchdown pass cause of trying to catch like a girl and
she hit the target of his head from across the room with
a small green beanbag of a pillow and knocked off his
long-billed baseball cap and the whole room exploded with
pillows, everyone hurling and ducking and pouncing and
then they rained back down, subsided, sighs and huffings,
and Pal said she'd make a run into town for some clams
and there'd be spaghetti with clam sauce if anyone wanted
and everyone did, Barnes going with her and bringing back
wine, a case of Cribari rosé that by now he'd got used
to, and after the feast they smoked and everyone stayed:
sapped, zapped, crapped out on the pillows.

Late morning, finishing muddy black coffee and bowls
of Wheaties at the picnic table with benches that sat in
the kitchen, Barnes asked Gene to go for a walk. They
went along a narrow path in the scrubby woods and came
to a slow brown stream where they sat on a log. Barnes
tossed pebbles in the water, making little plinks. He said
he and Nell had to get back to Boston. He said Gene could
come and stay at his place awhile if he wanted.

"No, man. Thanks."

"Yeh, I think you're right. To keep away awhile."

"Got to."

"Wanna stay here?"

"Where?"

"The Arms."

"Christ. I can't just ask."

"They said it's OK. Already."

"Did *you* ask? *For* me?"

"No. They seemed to know."

Gene gave a quick cut laugh.

"I guess it shows," he said. "That I don't live anywhere."

Barnes shrugged.

"Who knows?"

Gene dug out a cigarette, lit it on the second trembling try, coughed. After a couple puffs he threw it in the stream and suddenly turned his face up to Barnes, the color of paste and panic.

"Hey, man," he said, "what am I gonna do?"

"You mean—this summer?"

"No, no. I mean, my *life*, man."

There were suddenly tears coming down. Barnes's mouth opened, then closed, then he put his arm around Gene and Gene buried his head against him, sobbing, all of it coming out now, racking and coughing and heaving, wrenching, gut-deep, spasms, sobbing not just for the loss of his love, his Lou, or his life, that dizzy dream, but for all life, the puniness of it, people going bravely ahead through the tangle of it, tearing and being torn, caring anyway, cursing and caring, brave pretending there being no certain still ending for them all, but sometimes, struck by it, seeing the dark ahead some had, like this, to wail against it, down from and out of the falling yawn of his limitless depths, the ache at the center, the nightmare side of the dream, the scream.

Barnes held onto him with both arms, like a child or a lover, murmuring as best he could sounds to comfort: "OK, man, yeh, it's OK, let it out, let it all out, go, let it go, it's all OK, yeh, go . . ."

Later, empty of it, dry and nose-blown and clean inside,

Gene sat up straight again, had a whole cigarette, and after clapped a hand on Barnes's knee and said, "You're good. Thanks."

Barnes said he and Nell'd be back up again to see Jerry and Monica, they could bring any of his stuff for him, just say what. And anything else he needed. That he and Nell could provide. They walked back along the trail through the often overgrowth, the sun hotter on them as they neared the house, sweat breaking, brambles scratching, swatting at occasional buzzing bugs, speaking no more, silence an understanding and a bond, stepping into the sudden circle of the house and the dust-grown yard, side by side, brothers. Before they left, Barnes gave him a biff on the arm and said, "Hang in, man." Nell gave him a package of Bazooka bubble gum and said, *"Practice!"*

As the car drew out of sight Gene stood, still looking at where it had been, arms hanging limp at his side, feet still, rooted, when Coach Billy's voice shot out like a crack, "Go out for one!" and he wheeled, already running toward the cocked aim of Coach's arm, running clear across the clearing, reaching, catching the shot spiral of the ball in his stomach, went backward with it, curled and clutching the catch, smiling as he fell. Welcomed.

The house made its own noises, apart from the people noises. As the days fell around him, Gene learned which noises were whose. His were close and few, lying on an old army cot in one of the small rooms upstairs, staring up at the ceiling stained by rain from a leak in the roof. Cots are quiet, like stiff boards. House creaks came at night mostly, slow, tired, like the haunting effects in old movies. So did the people-made creaks of the bedsprings come then, at night, and he learned to tell the difference between the ones made by Coach Burt with Pal and Coach Billy with

Pal. Coach Burt with Pal made quick high squeaky bouncy creaks like a singsong tune for kids skipping rope, and along with this came giggles and yelps, playful, nibbly, and then sudden cries of delighted shock. Coach Billy with Pal made steady, long rhythmic creaks, building, slightly faster, longer steady, like a march, methodical, and along with this were no other sounds except breathing, deep, matching the steady rhythm of the springs as the creak relentlessly rose in pace and ended with a deep cry like someone stabbed and then, the creaking dead, a long low fading moan. Later, steps, the chain of the toilet yanked, the swallowing whoosh of the flush. Morning, rattle and tinkle of cups and spoons, whistle alarm of water boiling, beginning of life again, repeating.

One night Gene and Pal were playing checkers and the two Coaches said they were turning in early and Gene said maybe he should, too, but they said no, you finish your game there. Gene lost his concentration and Pal won. He started to get up to go to bed and she put a hand on his wrist, sitting him down again.

"Would you like me," she said, "to come with you?"

"I guess I can't. Do that now. Yet. Thank you."

"Sure," she said.

She gave him a little kiss on the forehead, and went on up. Gene sat where he was for a long time, looking at the jumble of red-and-black squares on the checkerboard.

He figured out Pal was mostly Coach Billy's woman, but it was all right with him if she sometimes went to Coach Burt, after all he, too, was a friend, a part of the family. And both the Coaches had said it was fine with them if she went to Gene, in fact it might be the best thing any of them could do for him. If not, at least he'd know they all cared.

Pal was a nurse and worked in the pretty new hospital in Damariscotta. Coach Burt had a job at a summer camp teaching kids baseball and swimming and some basic track events like the high jump. He was good with kids, his

laugh, his line of patter. Coach Billy had a job lined up for
the fall coaching freshman football at a public high school.
He and Coach Burt kind of took turns doing paying jobs,
and Pal worked steady. Coach Billy was around the house
all day so he and Gene tossed the football and played a lot
of checkers, and sometimes sat on the porch and got
quietly high. Coach Billy was friendly but didn't talk much
and Gene never pressed him. Coach Billy mainly just liked
to sit on the porch, either playing checkers or getting high
or maybe just sitting, moving a little back and forth in the
rusty glider. He seemed like one of those people who has
either done something awful or had it done to him.

One afternoon he and Gene were sitting on the glider
with a can of beer and Coach Billy just started talking.
Gene hadn't asked him anything, he just started telling it,
slowly sipping his beer and talking in a quiet monotone,
looking straight ahead of him across the flat dusty ground
and into the bramble.

"I went to Wisconsin, on a football scholarship and I
was all gung ho about it. I did everything they told me.
I started as a running back my sophomore year and made
All Conference. My junior year I made second-string AP
all-America. I got married. To the Homecoming Queen.
I was still doing what they wanted me to. Then I saw
what was happening. I saw I was in a machine. I wanted
out, all the way out. I joined the Marines. I figured they'd
send me to Nam and they did. They told me to kill and
I did. Just point me to the ones you want dead and I'll
do it. I realized, shit, I had escaped one machine and put
myself into another machine. I just went along with it. I
did my time and I killed when they told me and then I got
out. Burt was in my unit over there and he talked about
going back to Maine where he grew up and just kind of
fooling around. That sounded right and I came with him.
I met Pal at the diner in town. We spent the day and
that night and I told her straight before anything happened I wasn't going to fall in love with her or anyone

or get married to her or anyone and she is free to stay and free to go but that's where it starts and ends. I will not get caught in any machine again, ever. You have to be careful, you have to be on guard, or sure as hell they'll get you in one of their machines. I've been in their football machine and their marriage machine and their war machine and that's it. They won't get me again, not in their full-time job machine or their settling-down-and-have-kids machine or anything else. Not even their Welfare machine. We all three put what we earn in the pot. Pal sees we have enough and looks after things. I have made myself unfit for all their machines. Even if they got me they would have to spit me out."

He had told it all in a steady, sure monotone, as flat as reading a stock market prices report. When he finished, he took the last sip of his beer, then folded the can double with his fist and tossed it out onto the dusty ground. Gene listened to a fly that was buzzing around him. He didn't say anything. What he thought was, *You are way out there, man. You are farther along than I am.*

"Fuck a duck," Coach Billy said. "Let's play some checkers."

Gene liked the Coaches and Pal but he really wasn't part of their family. They had their own thing going. And the house. The house had a spooky kind of vacancy about it, an essence of empty, wind whooshing through it, old boards groaning in the night. Sitting in the main room sharing a joint, no one talking, no sound but each person's suck of inhalation, Gene was suddenly swept with the feeling that the house was haunted and the people in it were the ghosts. Him, too.

He went into town and got a room and a job. The job was combination grill-man and waiter at Buster's, an old-fashioned hole in the wall with a six-stool counter and two small tables. It smelled of grease and summer, and Gene found it comforting. The room was down the street from Buster's. It had one twin bed with a large sag in the center, a rickety chest of drawers, and an old-fashioned washbasin. There was a bathroom down the hall with a tub on iron feet and a chain-flush toilet. The setup was fine. It was all he needed. Or wanted.

He went down to Boston to get his gear, throwing stuff as quick as he could into a streamer trunk and two battered suitcases. He had hoped to get it over with and go without running into Lou, but when he finished he stopped and rolled a joint, sitting on the trunk, and heard her steps and the sound of the key in the lock that felt like metal twisting in his skull.

At least she wasn't with a guy. Still, it hurt. The sight of her, making him want to melt. She was wearing a light yellow summer dress and sandals. Her hair was tied with a piece of yellow yarn. She closed the door and leaned against it.

"Hi," she said.

"Hi."

"You all packed?"

"Yeh."

"Kitchen stuff, too?"

"Keep it."

"But the stewpot, and—"

"Keep it. Please."

"OK. Gimme a hit?"

"Sorry. Sure."

He stood up and went to her and handed her the joint, trying not to touch her. He had the feeling if he touched her he'd burn. She closed her eyes and she took the drag. He forgot she always closed her eyes. All of a sudden he wanted her no matter what. He laid his hand on her cheek. She coughed, moved away, and handed him the joint back.

"No," she said.

"Please. Lou."

"Don't make it hard."

"Just this once. The last."

"No."

Pardon this interruption, but...
if you smoke and you're interested in tar levels
you may find the information on the back of this page worthwhile.

A comparison of 57 popular cigarette brands with Kent Golden Lights.

FILTER BRANDS (KING SIZE)

REGULAR	MG TAR	MG NIC	MENTHOL	MG TAR	MG NIC
Kent Golden Lights	8	0.6	Kent Golden Lights Menthol	8	0.7
Parliament	10	0.6	Kool Super Lights	9	0.8
Vantage	11	0.7	Multifilter Menthol	11	0.7
Marlboro Lights	12	0.7	Vantage Menthol	11	0.8
Doral	12	0.8	Salem Lights	11	0.8
Multifilter	12	0.8	Doral Menthol	11	0.8
Winston Lights	12	0.9	Belair	13	1.0
Raleigh Lights	14	1.0	Marlboro Menthol	14	0.8
Viceroy Extra Milds	14	1.0	Alpine	14	0.8
Viceroy	16	1.0	Kool Milds	14	0.9
Raleigh	16	1.1	Kool	17	1.3
Marlboro	17	1.0	Salem	18	1.2
Tareyton	17	1.2			
Lark	18	1.1			
Pall Mall Filters	18	1.2			
Camel Filters	18	1.2			
L & M	18	1.1			
Winston	19	1.2			

FTC Method

FILTER BRANDS (100's)

REGULAR	MG TAR	MG NIC	MENTHOL	MG TAR	MG NIC
Kent Golden Lights 100's	10	0.9	Kent Golden Lights 100's Menthol	10	0.9
Benson & Hedges 100's Lights	11	0.8	Benson & Hedges 100's Lights Menthol	11	0.8
Vantage 100's	11	0.9	Merit 100's Menthol	12	0.9
Merit 100's	12	0.9	Virginia Slims 100's Menthol	16	0.9
Parliament 100's	12	0.7	Pall Mall 100's Menthol	16	1.2
Eve 100's	16	1.0	Eve 100's Menthol	16	1.0
Virginia Slims 100's	16	0.9	Silva Thins Menthol	16	1.1
Tareyton 100's	16	1.2	Benson & Hedges 100's Menthol	17	1.0
Marlboro 100's	17	1.0	L & M 100's Menthol	18	1.1
Silva Thins	17	1.3	Kool 100's	18	1.3
Benson & Hedges 100's	17	1.0	Belair 100's	18	1.3
L & M 100's	17	1.1	Winston 100's Menthol	18	1.2
Raleigh 100's	17	1.2	Salem 100's	18	1.3
Viceroy 100's	18	1.3			
Lark 100's	18	1.1			
Pall Mall 100's	19	1.4			
Winston 100's	19	1.3			

FTC Meth

Kings only 8 mg tar

100's only 10 mg tar

Simply put, they're as low as you can go and still get good taste.

Of All Brands Sold: Lowest tar: 0.5 mg. "tar," 0.05 mg. nicotine;
Kent Golden Lights: Kings Regular 8 mg. "tar," 0.6 mg. nicotine;
Kings Menthol 8 mg. "tar," 0.7 mg. nicotine av. per cigarette,
FTC Report August 1977. **100's Regular and Menthol**—10 mg. "tar,"
0.9 mg. nicotine av. per cigarette by FTC Method.

"Please?"

"For God sake don't *beg!*"

She turned away from him, folding her arms as if closing the matter.

"OK," he said.

He picked up his suitcases.

"Barnes'll get the trunk," he said. "He'll get it to me."

She turned toward him.

"Gene," she said, "I wasn't being bitchy. It would have hurt. It would have hurt too much."

"Nothing hurts," he said, "if you can't feel anything."

"But you're not like that," she said.

"Maybe I can get to be."

She opened the door and he walked out, past her, careful not to brush against, the suitcase bumping his knee as he went down the stairs. At the bottom he heard the door close.

—————

He hung out at Jerry and Monica's a lot. He'd ask them to play the Linda record that he listened to when he first came.

Time washes clean, she told him.

He hoped so.

He walked, swam, fished, and did a lot of dope.

Still, he knew it would be a long, long time. To get Lou out of him. To be empty again.

On sweltering summer nights he lay on his bed in his undershorts, smoking. That reminded him of Lou, too. Not the smoking, the undershorts. He had worn the boxer kind all his life till he met her and she told him jockey shorts were much sexier. He had never thought of men's underwear being sexy, just necessary. He asked her what was sexy about jockey shorts and she explained they showed the bulge of the cock and that was a real turn-on.

The boxer shorts didn't show anything unless the guy had
an erection. It made sense to Gene and the next day he
went down to the Grand Union and bought four cello-
phaned three-packs of jockey shorts and had worn that
kind ever since.

He reached down and touched himself, thinking of Lou.
Then drew his hand back. The most depressing thing of
all was jerking off thinking of Lou. Realizing now the only
way he could have her was in memory. He slipped on some
jeans and a Maine state tourist office T-shirt that said
"LOVE ME," and his old moccasins, and walked down
to the pier. There was a couple holding hands, and a
bunch of high-school kids in a rowboat, diving off and
scrambling back in. Gene sat down at the end and let the
wave lap lull him. Occasionally, a foghorn hoot, low and
long, like a hurt cow.

I am here, he thought, on a pier in Damariscotta, Maine,
U.S.A., in the summer of my twenty-sixth year. In the year
of Our Lord 1970.

That much was clear. But there was one thing he didn't
know at all.

Why.

But it didn't seem to matter much.

One day Barnes showed up alone.

"Where's Nell?" Gene asked him.

"She left."

"Boston?"

"No. Me."

"Oh."

They went for a walk, out along the riverbank. After a
while they stopped and sat on some rocks. Barnes picked
a tall piece of sea grass and put it in his mouth.

"What happened?" Gene asked him.

"Nothin. That's the trouble. Nothin's been happening too long. I took her for granted. Didn't pay attention to her. Wasn't even fucking her much the last couple months. She knew I screwed around. She never complained. About anything. Then she just left. Couple days ago after she'd spent the night I woke up late and she was gone and so was the stuff she used to keep at my place—you know, a comb, a sweat shirt, toothbrush, odds and ends. I called her up and asked what was wrong and she said she just couldn't take it any longer. I couldn't argue, you know, cause I knew what she meant and she was right. It's just that I hadn't expected it. I figured I could keep on being a slob and have her around when I wanted her and not around if I didn't feel like it. But you can't do that to people."

"Did you love her?"

"How the hell do I know? I thought she was swell. I took her for granted. Now it's too late."

"Does it hurt bad?"

"Well, shit. I mean it wasn't some great world-smashing love affair or anything. I'm not going to bleed to death. I just feel lonesome right now. And stupid. If I'd paid a little more attention . . ."

He spit out the piece of grass.

"It's funny," he said. "It's like you and me did the wrong things, but the opposite wrong things. With our women."

"How?"

"I mean I didn't love mine enough and you loved yours too much."

"I don't see that, man. If you love someone, how can you love them too much?"

"It's hard to take. For the other person."

"Being loved?"

"Damn right."

"I thought it was supposed to be what everybody wants."

"It is *supposed* to be. But then when it happens a lot of people can't take it. It's hard. Especially when it's a lot."

"Why?"

"Listen. Have you ever had some chick fall madly in love with you? Want to be with you all the time, tell you all the time how terrific you are and how much she loves you, hang on every damn thing you say, look at you all the time with big lovesick eyes?"

Gene scratched at the back of his neck.

"Well, yeh. I guess I have. Had that happen to me."

"And how did you feel? The truth now. How did you really feel?"

"Shit, man."

"You felt like shit?"

"I felt like I was in jail."

"Exactly."

"It seems like you just can't win. If it's something to do with love."

"It ain't easy," Barnes said.

They walked back to the bar of The Pier and Barnes bought Gene and him some very dry martinis straight up. The liquid smooth and cool.

Gene had taken to hanging out after work at The Damariscotta Pier. It was a nice bar and restaurant with windows looking out over the tidal river. The tables were
filled with families and parties, couples and assortments of
summer people hunting up and down the coast like dogs
on the scent—of sea and the unmentioned magic powers
they presumed it contained, the allegedly healing ele-
ments of ocean, sun, gullsound. Attain a tan and with it
inner peace. You gotta believe.

Out the windows Gene could see the people clamber on
the rocks, taking each other's pictures. He had the feeling they were trying to prove they were alive, that they
could look at them later kept neatly in a book to prove that
they had lived, had once been in some particular place a
particular expression on the face. *So.* Snap.

Usually Gene sat at the bar part and drank beers and
looked, not for action but amusement. He didn't want to
get in the act, he just wanted to watch it. It was like some
uncut documentary film in which you only heard some of
the words; you had to guess a lot of what was happening
and who the characters were. Sort of like an Andy Warhol
thing. Very with-it.

One particular woman kept eyeing him.

He had seen her many times in The Pier, laughing too loud, always with a man, mostly a different man. She had a mane of wavy tangled dirty blond hair tied with a rubber band, she wore loose shift dresses of different solid colors—orange, blue, green—that came just to her knees, no stockings, and a pair of scuffed, run-down black high heel shoes that must have been ten years old. She was big, big all over, and the shift was like a tent to cover it, except for the calves, which were thinner than the rest of her, more proportioned, and were usually streaked with dust or dirt. Her blue eyes were dim, indifferent. The only part of her that sparkled was a large diamond wedding ring.

One night she stopped by where Gene was sitting at the bar, pinched the flesh of his arm, and looked at him as if she was considering cooking him.

"Come see me," she said.

When she'd left Gene said to the bartender, "Jesus, who was that?"

"Stella the Divorcée," the bartender said.

It was still that big a deal, being a divorcée in a small town in Maine. Like the scarlet fucking letter or something.

When Gene got off work a couple days later and was walking to his room a car honked. It was Stella the Divorcée, behind the wheel of a canary yellow Olds convertible.

Gene smiled and put his hands on the car.

"Hi," he said.

"You didn't come see me," she said.

"Not yet."

"Get in."

He did.

Why not?

Her house was off a dirt road way back in the woods, but it was one of those split-level modern jobs with picture window. The effect of house and setting was confusing, like someone had clipped a picture out of *Better Homes & Gardens* and pasted it onto a page from *Field and Stream*.

"You know what this is?" she asked pointing around her.

They were sitting in the living room, drinking Four Roses on ice.

"No," Gene said.

"This, my boy, is an actual, honest-to-God American Dream House. The genuine article. The one that begins with the little wifey-poo sitting home in the shabby rented job clipping out pictures and ideas from *House Beautiful*, and big hubby promises someday all that shall be hers and by God he delivers. He is a contractor and so he supervises the whole thing with little wifey-poo at his side, making sure all the little loving details are just so, and then while wifey-poo is safe at home scanning *Family Circle* for further helpful hints and finishing touches to make everything more perfect big hubby has to go to Boston on business in the conduct of which he comes across the cutest little nineteen-year-old clit you ever laid eyes on and after some months of guilt-ridden dalliance comes home crying to wifey-poo he can't live without her—not little loyal wifey-poo, he can live without *her* all right, he means little Miss Nineteen-Year-Old Clit."

She finished off her drink, went into the kitchen, and came back with the Four Roses bottle. She set it on the coffee table. Formalities, such as they were, were over.

"I'm sorry," said Gene.

"Ha! Forget it. I got me a deal, brother. I got me my little Dream House and I got me good alimony and I intend to see it keeps coming. I got me a little shop, driftwood crap for tourists, and it doesn't make money. It's not supposed to. All I have to do to keep it coming is not get married and I can't tell you how easy that is. At first I sat here in shock and soon found everyone thought cause I was

divorced I was laying every stud in the county so I
figured if they think so why not? And I eat and drink what
I want when I want to. No more counting calories, no
more pushing away from the table, no more Royal Canadian Air Force Exercises. What the fuck, I said one day
puffing and aching, let the fuckin Royal Canadian Air
Force do them. Why me? Yeh, you see little wifey-poo also
kept nice and slim for big hubby cause he liked it that
way, he liked the nice narrow little waist and the good
measurements. Well, little wifey-poo kept it that way, but
it wasn't enough. I could stay slim for him, but I couldn't
stay young for him. You can't starve and sit-up yourself
back to being nineteen, buster."

"No," said Gene.

She took another belt of the drink and laughed.

"The little clit won't stay that way either. She must be
up to twenty-five by now, and they've moved to Southern
California, land of the nubile beauties. Hubby'll never last
the course. He'll end up payin double and livin in a tent
on the beach humpin teenyboppers."

"Sounds like it," Gene said.

She lit a cigarette and turned to stare at him.

"You're pretty cool," she said. "I don't see you runnin
after all that little pink twat around The Pier."

"No," he said.

"You don't like it?"

He shrugged.

"Too much trouble," he said.

She threw back her head and laughed, hard and harsh.

"Too much trouble," she said. "I like that. I approve of
that."

She poured more of the whiskey into their glasses. Gene
was drinking his faster, too, now. For a while they just sat
there drinking the whiskey down, like they were ill and
they had to get a whole lot of this medicine in them. She
put her glass down and put a hand on his thigh and looked
him straight in the eyes.

"One thing I got going for *me*," she said, "is I'm no trouble at all."

"That's good," he said.

He did not find her attractive but found himself becoming oddly aroused by her, as if her bitterness and desire were a kind of stimulant. Also, she really wasn't so bad. She was fat, was all. Maybe that would be nice.

She mashed her cigarette out.

"Let's go," she said.

He followed her into the bedroom. She kicked off her heels and then before she pulled the shift up over her head she said:

"I want you to know what you're getting. You're not gettin nubile. You're not getting peach fuzz and hard little titties."

"I know," he said.

"Good."

The breasts, huge and pendulant, the stomach in folds, the thighs bruised and mammoth, she stood before him, smiling at his hard-on.

"Good," she said. "One thing you *are* gettin. You're getting *laid*."

And he did.

Again and again and again till he couldn't remember.

At some point she got another bottle and they kept it by the bed, not bothering with glasses.

Late afternoon the second day she grabbed his cock, which was hard still again and said, "You like it here?"

"Yeh."

"Let's keep this party goin."

"OK."

"Here. In my little ole Dream House."

"Sure. Got to go to work, though. Buster's."

"Buster's? Shit, that's no work. Besides, the season's almost done. He won't need you. He can get along. You work for me now. Keep me nice and cozy in the ole Dream House. Got any stuff in town?"

"Yeh. A room, near Buster's. I'll go get it."

She pressed her lips down over his cock and her teeth made a tiny little bite.

She looked up smiling.

"Oh, no you don't," she said. "You don't go marchin into town with all those pink little nubile twats twitchin at you. You might get other ideas, and Mama don't want that. Mama's gonna go in for ya and tell Buster you had to quit because of some awful emergency and then get your things and bring em right here. Mama's gonna get some gin for us this time just for a little change and you can lie right back here and play with yourself a little and think about what it's gonna be like when Mama comes back. But don't you *dare* get so heated up you spill any out because Mama will get real mad. She is greedy and she wants it *all* inside her."

She rubbed herself between the legs, grinning.

They lived like that. Days. A week. She let him go into town now on his own because she knew he'd have to come back. She let him drive the big yellow Olds in and get gas, and buy them the junk food she loved at the grocery and the booze they both needed at the liquor store. People looked at him funny now, amused or hostile, depending on whom. Mama made him tell her about it, laughed, slapped her thighs. She loved it. She loved that the fucking town all knew she was screwing herself silly with this cute little skinny young kid. One night she made him take a shower and put on his best outfit which was the summer cord suit and a tie and she put on a black satin shift and silver bracelets near up to her elbows and big silver earrings and they went and had dinner at The Pier Restaurant. She waved and called to people and laughed loud and every-one in the place was looking at em and Gene went along with it, smiling and graceful, somehow glad to help her say Fuck You to the world, or her tiny part of it. When they got back home she laughed and kissed him and took off everything but the silver bracelets and when they got into bed she whispered huskily, "Mama's real pleased with her young gentleman friend. He behaved real good, and Mama liked that a lot. Now cause he's been so good like that, Mama's gonna teach him some tricks."

And she did.

September was cold there, a chilly wind rattled the windows and seeped through cracks in doors and swept down the chimney with a shrill, chilling rush. They alternated drinking gin and Four Roses and stuffed down frozen pizzas with lukewarm centers, peanut-butter sandwiches on raisin bread, Hostess Twinkies, Sara Lee cheesecakes, cans of Chef Boy-ar-dee ravioli, pretzels, and potato chips . . . With their "meals" they drank Coke and after that they'd start passing a bottle between them and he would listen as her voice grew fuzzier, her laugh more scratchy and scary, her language more frequently punctuated with cocks and cunts and pricks and twats, until she would kick the empty bottle across the room and wrestle her clothes off, wanting him to give it to her on the floor, in the Dream House Picture Window Living Room, she would lie there heaving and waiting, waiting for him to smother as much as he could of her body, her thoughts, the sound of the wind and the echoes of other years, and he understood her need and covered her and filled her with all he could give, blotting out her hurt as best he could. Afterward they would lie there on the floor naked on the nap of the carpet, cold and not caring, not minding at all, being beyond that. No one mentioned the future because there didn't seem to be one.

Sometimes in town to get supplies Gene would walk along the sidewalk looking at the ordinary people, the ones who were doing something or going somewhere and he wondered whether he shouldn't think of such things, but when he tried to his mind would be like a blank movie screen and so he would just go on, back to the Dream House.

Once he stopped for a drink at the bar of The Pier and so took longer than usual getting home and Stella's eyes were snappish.

"You don't go getting ideas when you're there in town, do you?"

"No," he said. "None at all."

Which was true.

━━━━━━━━━━━

It was still true the day he disappeared from her for good.

It wasn't *his* idea.

He was walking down the street when he noticed a car cruising slowly, a head peering out.

A hand waved.

"Hey, Gene!"

He hadn't been called that for so long that for a moment he didn't connect the name with himself. He just stopped, not knowing why.

The car pulled up beside him and stopped.

It was Barnes. Driving the car. He rolled down the window and Gene peered in.

"Hey, man," Gene said. "Whattya doin here?"

Gene looked in the back of the car, which had suitcases and clothes bag piled up in it.

"Hey, where ya goin?" he said.

"L.A.? Wanna come?"

Gene opened the door and got in.

"Let's go," he said.

"Where do we go to get your stuff?"

"I've got my stuff," Gene said.

"Where?"

"On. It's all I need. In fact, when we get to L.A. I won't even need the coat."

"Guess I caught you at the right time," Barnes said.

"You could say that."

Barnes gave him a curious sidelong look.

"What the hell you been up to? Basic training?"

Gene smiled.

"You could say that."

Barnes pressed down on the gas. At the first chance, they turned west.

IV

The open road.

Roads, opening.

Closing behind you, people and places, left.

Others opening. With the road. The roads. Fast highways. Six lane. Super. You sailing. Smiling.

Roll down the window and let in the air. Tune in the radio, turn it up. Or off, talk. Tell about the time you, she, we . . . recall what happened when we all . . . remember? You know the words to the one about Laura—or is it Ora? Lee. Sing. Together, top of the lungs, or delicate, do the harmony, harmonize, sing-along, or sing alone, solo. Stretch, smelling fumes of gas getting pumped while the gallons and dollars and cents roll backward, up and out of sight, making a *ping* at regular intervals, take the key tied to the piece of wood marked *M* and take a pee, relieve yourself for the next stretch of road, guzzle a Coke that clunks down out of the body of the red robot, grab a Mounds Bar for munching through the journey's next leg, pause, while Gus is getting your change, feel the special freedom of standing still between motion, the rumble and whirr of it crisscrossing out there in front of you, long distance traffic wind blowing your hair a bit, the taste of dust and odor of gas a curiously nice intoxicant, subtly exciting; being on the road, on the move, on the go, going, no matter where, something filling in the act, in being in it.

Barnes wasn't in a big hurry and Gene was in less, so they didn't mind getting lost, swerving off the super-lane highways to bump down onto slim ribbons of blacktop or even long gashes of gravel in search of "real" places to eat, that is, no famous-name franchise food. They sought the sort of place Barnes categorized as "Your Quintessential Old-Fashioned Fly-Specked Diner," places with straightforward names like EAT, Jack and Fran's, LUNCH, Joe's Place, STEAKS, Main Street Restaurant, and FOOD. They hit the places with the old stained menus with a fresh sheet put in with a paper clip that said "Today" and had typed or more often written or printed words in ballpoint or pencil, the bill of fare, and anything described as "Special of the Day" they ordered, and any available pie guaranteed to be homemade on the premises they had for dessert.

After eating they'd make their way back to the superhighway, set the car in one of the slots headed west and as soon as it was dark Barnes started to look for potential motels, his taste there running to modern and efficient with TV in the room and preferably a nice dark bar on the premises though sometimes they'd just buy a fifth at a package store and drink in the room from the water glasses, watching TV or talking. When Gene joined the trip he had twenty-some-odd bucks in his pocket and wanted to put the little bit in the kitty for all the expenses and pay off what he owed Barnes later, he could keep a record, but Barnes said that would spoil the trip, take their minds off enjoying things, and since for Chrissake he was going out to L.A. to get paid $12,500 for rewriting a script of his mystery that the first guy they hired gave up on halfway through he could sure as hell foot the bill for Gene coming along. He couldn't have gone alone anyway, couldn't drive all that way by himself and if it weren't for Gene he'd have picked up some fuckin hitchhiker and with his luck it would have been some hippie slayer on the way to the Coast. The thought of Barnes driving by himself to L.A. and what might happen to him in fact made Gene feel not so guilty about the free ride, he accepted Barnes's assurance the small additional expense of having his companionship would be part of the "Business Expense" of his venture into Hollywood.

"Stick with me, kid," Barnes told him. "Once I get set up out there, I'll make you a star. Or anyway, maybe if they ever do the damn movie I could get you in as an extra."

Gene laughed.

"An extra. Shit, I'd be playing myself."

"Cheer up now, buddy. You're on your way to lotus land."

"That's one thing I haven't tried. Lotus."

"I got you out of there just in time, I think. Maine. That whole setup."

Gene had told him about it, all about the thing with Stella the Divorcée. Somehow it was easier to talk about personal shit in a moving car. You didn't feel called upon to look the other guy straight in the eye. In fact you shouldn't. If you're the one driving you're supposed to keep your eyes on the road, and if you're the one sitting next to him you're not supposed to distract him from taking *his* eyes off the road. So, sitting there with both people looking straight ahead, it was easier to say a lot. For both of them. Once when they were tooling through Illinois on some superjob of a highway Gene had the nerve to ask Barnes about something nagging at him for a long time. Not that it made much difference anymore, he just wanted to know.

"Can I ask you something, Barnes?"

"Sure."

"Did you ever fuck her?"

"Who?"

"Lou."

Barnes sort of shifted his body a little more forward over
the steering wheel.

"No," he said.

"Ever try?"

"Yes."

"Didn't make it?"

"No."

"She wouldn't?" Gene asked, surprised at how hopeful
he sounded, felt.

"No. I'm sorry. On all counts. She would, but I
couldn't."

"Why not, you suppose?"

Barnes took his right hand off the wheel for a moment
and scratched his ear.

"Cause you're my friend, I guess."

"But that didn't stop you from trying."

"I know. The only thing I can figure is, my prick has
more of a conscience than my goddam brain."

"Wow. The prick with a conscience."

"That's me, I guess."

"Don't sweat it, man."

"All the same, I'm sorry."

"Forget it. All that's gone."

Neither one said anything for the next few miles and
Gene turned the radio on. Got a kind of staticky call-in
show from Chicago.

At a small-town diner Gene bought a postcard to send
to Stella. On the part for the message he put, "Sorry had
to go. You were the greatest." He signed it "Love, Gene."
She never called him Gene but he didn't want to put anything she did call him on a postcard. The other side was a
color photograph of the Mississippi River. It was green.
Gene put a stamp on and slipped it in a mailbox, squeez-
ing his eyes shut, thinking to her in his head, *Be well.
Don't hurt too bad.* The metal flap of the box clanged
back. Shut.

Barnes said he'd like to stop off in Iowa City and see some old friends from his time at The Writers Workshop thing he had gone to there.

"Will they still be there?" Gene asked.

"Oh, yeh. Some will. Some always stay."

"How come?"

"It's that kind of place. You know how there's jocks who hang around their old colleges after they're through, just get some kind of job and stay on? Well, it's that way in Iowa City except instead of jocks it's poets. I can see it, too. It's an easy place to live. And there's always a party."

"Maybe we'll find one," Gene said.

Barnes laughed. He said the only way they would *not* find a party in Iowa City would be to lie on the floor of the car, roll up the windows, and lock the doors.

"No use to go to that trouble," Gene said.

━━━━━━

They found a party all right, but the trouble was they got there late. Not in the day—it was just around five in the afternoon—but in the week. The party had started Thursday night and now it was Sunday. That's why things were kind of a mess and the spirit had sort of gone out of it all. Parties often lasted three or four days, during which time a lot of people went back home to sack out or shower with someone they'd met at the party to do it in company with and then came back, bringing new supplies of booze and beer to replenish the stock but now the hard-core returnees were thinning out. One girl mentioned that tomorrow was Monday and she wanted to try to get back into going to classes.

"Monday, my ragged ass," said Gordo. "*Classes*. Shit. Not like in the old days, huh, Barnes? Youth is gettin soft now. Don't drink as much either. Too much sittin around

puffin the goddam weed. Lowers capacity, stomachs can't
hold it. We're breedin a race in which the human stomach
will someday be able to hold no more than a cocktail.
Alcohol will pass from the scene, markin the fuckin down-
fall of civilization."

Gordo then took a slug from the half-gallon jug of gin
that he held cocked on his right shoulder, drinking from it
like you do from a cider bottle. With his free hand he
rubbed his huge belly, approvingly, as if its size were proof
of its admirable capacity for alcohol. Gordo had a thick
black wiry beard and beady little eyes that seemed to have
no white part to them. Just little brown beads. When he
got his M.A. in writing he stopped writing, opened a combination greeting card and joke shop with dirty magazines
in the back, and settled down in Iowa City. If you could
call it that. At the age of thirty-four he was on his fifth wife.

This one was Melba, a roly-poly girl who Gene figured
couldn't be much past twenty. She had red hair, pink
cheeks, and big green eyes which she focused on Gordo
with obvious adoration, awaiting his commands. She never
had long to wait.

"Scare up some booze for these gennelmen," he told her,
and she scurried around among the bottles that were everywhere, trying to find some that hadn't been emptied. Evidently the jug of gin was Gordo's private stock. Melba
came up with an assortment of bottles from about a quarter
to a half full and placed them before Barnes and Gene.
They were supposed to pick one. Barnes selected a Sea-
grams VO, Gene took a Southern Comfort, just for the hell
of it. He'd never had the stuff, but if Janis Joplin dug it,
it must be somethin else.

It was. Somethin else.

Everyone swigged from the bottle, like Gordo did. All
the glasses were broken or dirty and there wasn't any need
to wash any yet since Gordo didn't use one.

Barnes had brought Gordo a copy of his paperback mystery, and Gordo held it awhile, like he was judging its

weight, then tossed it onto some magazine-and-bottle debris on the floor.

"Well, it don't look like the new *Ulysses*," he said.

"Gene," Barnes said, "I just want to explain something you might otherwise fail to understand. I told you Gordo's an old friend. There's some friends you've had so long you don't even have to like them anymore."

"I can dig it," Gene said.

"Goddam right," said Gordo. "What are friends for?"

He waved for his wife to come sit beside him so he could feel her up with his free hand.

"I can see you're really settled down this time, huh, Gordo?" Barnes said.

"Well if you mean by that am I re*stricted*, like a goddam dog on a leash, hell no. I just got me a nice little warm home base. This place has got too much young new slit comin in all the time for a man to sit back and restrict himself. But Melba here keeps me real busy, she got the hottest pants I come across yet. Hey, you guys had any dinner?"

"No," Barnes said. "I thought we'd fall by The Airliner and grab a tenderloin or something."

"Hell no, you won't, you're in my house you're gonna get fed. Melba honey, what you got good you can go whip up for us?"

Melba pondered, then meekly asked, "Macaroni?"

"*Bare* macaroni? Just *plain?*" he asked. "For the love of Christ stir a little somethin in with it, girl."

"Oh, sure!"

He gave her a whack on the fanny and she was off.

"Nude macaroni," Gordo said, shaking his head. "Well I guess you can damn well have your pussy and eat it, too, but you can't expect it to cook."

Gene had a hit off the Southern Comfort, wondering how long it would be till the day sure to come when Melba walked calmly into the living room holding a shiny new .38 revolver purchased after months of careful pilfering from the grocery fund and put a hole right between Gordo's beady little eyes. Gene would have liked to be there to see it, but he wouldn't want to stick around to wait.

They all ate warm macaroni with peas out of cereal bowls, washing it down with their respective brands of booze.

Melba was allowed to turn on the TV. She liked to watch reruns of "The Brady Bunch." It was in color but the wrong kind. The people had bright orange faces and purple bodies. Everything else was green.

What with the vivid orange, purple, and green from the TV screen, the macaroni and peas washed down with Southern Comfort, and Gordo's conversation, Gene was getting decidedly nauseous. He was going to suggest to Barnes they find a motel, when the door opened and a girl came in.

She lived in the rooming house next door and sometimes she came over to watch TV with Melba. She could look out her window and see if the set was on in Gordo's living room.

She had on a long plain green bathrobe, and a pair of big black galoshes with a lot of buckles that she took off when she got inside, and was barefoot then. Her chestnut hair was clean and thick, the bottom cut off straight across just below her shoulders. Her name was Lizzie.

Gene got out of his chair so she could have it but she thanked him and took a spot on the floor. Instead of going back to the chair, Gene sat down on the floor beside Lizzie. Not right next to her, just beside her.

He held the bottle toward her and smiled.

"I guess I can't offer you any of the niceties but here's the straight stuff if you'd like some."

She smiled, thanked him no.

Her upper teeth protruded very slightly, giving a lift to the lip, not like pouting but as if she were thinking of something and just about to speak.

But she didn't so he did.

"We just got in," he said, not knowing why.

"You missed the party."

"Yeh. I'm beginning to think it was just as well."

"It wasn't Iowa City's finest."

"Did you come? For long?"

"I dropped in every so often and had a beer or smoked a little. Just to be neighborly."

"Hey, Lizzie," yelled Gordo, "when ya gonna let your pants down for me? You're the only one of them girls next door I haven't had. You and that prissy one, what's her name?"

"Marge, I guess you mean."

"Yeh, she's a real priss. But what about you? You're no priss. I see you with other guys, what about ole Gordo?"

Gene felt his cheeks getting hot. He looked to see how Lizzie was taking it. Evidently she was used to it. Her skin was still pure as milk.

"You get enough," she said to Gordo. "You'll be all right."

"Goddam Lizzie," Gordo grumbled.

Lizzie took a pack of Camels out of the pocket of her robe, offered one to Gene, lit the one he took and then one for herself.

"Where were you," she asked, "before you got in?"

"Oh. Maine. I mean that's where we started from."

"You live there?"

"I worked there, sort of, this summer."

"I always liked it. I mean the sound of it. It sounds clean and cold."

Her voice was kind of high and tended to go up at the end of a sentence.

"It can be," he said. "Clean and cold."

Gordo told Melba they were running low on booze, she should get off her fanny and try to scare up some bottles from the neighbors. Lizzie volunteered to help, so Gene did, too. He realized it was kind of screwy, him going up to doors of strangers with two young women he'd just met, begging for booze. But he wanted to be sure Lizzie came back. He wanted to talk to her more. He didn't know what about.

The raiding party scared up a half bottle of brandy, some cooking sherry, and two quarts of Ballantine ale.

Everyone wanted brandy so the bottle was passed around. Lizzie reached in the pocket of her bathrobe, got out some grass and papers and rolled a joint.

She asked Gene more about Maine, sounding like she gave a damn what he thought.

He told her about it, leaving out the part about Stella the Divorcée.

She listened to what he said, not just in an offhand way, but like it mattered.

Gene was dog-tired but he didn't want to leave, he didn't want to move away from where Lizzie was. There was something about her, some quality that drew him, nothing that was said or seen on the surface, but something that seemed to infuse what she said and did, her look, her manner. It was a quality he hadn't encountered for a long time, it was something even Lou didn't have though he loved her anyway. As he watched Lizzie, listened to her, he realized what it was about her that drew him to her so powerfully, and how rare it was to find in someone. It was kindness. She was kind.

He had a terrific desire just to lay his head on her lap and close his eyes. Of course that wasn't the thing to do, but he did it anyway. It was not a calculated move, it was natural and felt, as simple and deep a kind of urge as being cold and wanting warm.

He put his head on her lap and she stroked it, gently. There was TV noise and people noise, Gordo and Barnes repeating tales of the old days, Melba giggling and making appropriate remarks of awe and wonder at the exploits of drinking and fucking and dope long gone, more glorious than now, all of it huge and heroic. Gene didn't listen. Lizzie's hand rubbed across his forehead. Soothing.

He woke with people saying g'night, see ya, yawns, yeh, man . . .

Lizzie leaned her mouth to his ear, whispered, "Come."

She took his hand and he followed. He didn't look at anyone else or say thanks or good night or see ya later, Barnes or anything at all, he just followed Lizzie out the door and over the cold yard to the rickety white frame rooming house next door and up the stairs. Maybe she did this all the time. Whatever, Gene didn't care.

In her room, she closed the door, drew a small bolt, lit a candle.

The room was old-fashioned. It had a big high brass bed with blankets and a quilt on it; old, tinted photographs in gilded frames, a faded print of a country landscape. Gene was glad it was that way. He was glad there weren't any posters of Jefferson Airplane or Jimi Hendrix, no signs with peace slogans or Viet Cong flags. This was another, quieter time and place, with candlelight. With Lizzie. She took off her robe with no drama nor shame. Simply. She was milky white all over as she went to him, her face calm and thoughtful.

What she and Gene did in the high bed was something he realized he hadn't done for a long time. He had fucked and sucked and humped and screwed, been blown and frenched and nibbled and bit, in old and new and unknown positions. But that night he and Lizzie did something different together than all those things.

What they did was, they made love.

Lizzie thought truck stops were the best places to eat, and she took Gene to one of her favorites for breakfast. Over her meal of waffles, sausage, milk, a piece of apple pie with ice cream, and a cup of coffee, Lizzie swore her passion for trucks was not just because of the wonderful food you got at the truck stops. She drove a beat-up old blue Ford pickup that was her proudest possession, and she said quite seriously after she got her B.A. she planned to go to truck-driving school.

"Do they have them?" Gene asked.

"Of course. It's something you have to learn, like a science. Well maybe it's not exactly a science, but a skill anyway."

Her major was American Lit and she loved to read it but she didn't want to write it or teach it so she couldn't make a living with it and therefore needed a trade. So why not something you love? Which in her case was trucks. She had always loved trucks, ever since as a kid she preferred toy trucks to dolls. Also, she felt she had the right personality for a long-distance truck driver.

"I'm basically lethargic," she explained, "but I like speed. I mean as in amphetamines, as well as going fast on the highway. Truck drivers take it to stay awake on long hauls, and that would give me a justification. I wouldn't just be taking it for pleasure, but to help me in my career. Also, since I'm basically lethargic anyway, speed doesn't really get me all nervous, it just sort of brings me up to normal. So I'd drive well with it. In fact I do. But I mean on the job, on long-distance driving."

Gene, having finished a comparatively modest breakfast of scrambled eggs and bacon, ordered another coffee. He wanted to prolong it, being there with Lizzie, listening to her plans for a future career in long-distance trucking. No one had said anything about what would happen when breakfast was over. Maybe she would drive him back to town in her pickup, drop him off, and wave good-bye.

"Where are you going?" she asked. "I mean from here?"

He wanted to say his plans had changed he wasn't going anywhere he wanted to move right in to her old-fashioned room. But he didn't want to scare her off.

"California," he said. "L.A."

"When do you have to be there?"

He thought a minute and laughed.

"I don't," he said. "In fact I don't have to be *any*where."

It was true, and the thought gave him kind of a floating feeling, a little scary, like he might just go up in the air like a balloon without a string, drift higher, and disappear.

With the same sort of blind impulse that last night had made him put his head in her lap he blurted out, "Lizzie, I like it here. A lot. I'd like to stay longer."

She nodded, slowly. There was a kind of gravity about her that showed through her youth.

"I know a place," she said, "you could stay awhile."

He hoped she meant her room, that would be fine.

No. She was thinking of a farmhouse out in West Branch some graduate student friends of hers had rented for the year. But the woman had run off to Canada and the husband had left to search for her.

"All over Canada?" Gene asked.

"Mainly the Northwest," she said. "She talked about Vancouver a lot."

"Well, that narrows it down."

Still, there was no way to know when or if both of them would be back. The guy had put Lizzie in charge of the house, which just meant checking it out and feeding the cat. There wasn't any reason why Gene couldn't stay there as long as they were gone. Maybe even after. Maybe the husband would need a roommate if he came back alone.

"What's it like?" he asked. "The farmhouse?"

She thought.

"It's the kind of place Bonnie and Clyde would have liked to hole up in after a job."

Exactly.

━━━━━━━━━

It was on a small road off Interstate 80 about fifteen miles from town. Battered gray frame with a peaked roof, a front porch with a swing suspended from rusty chains. The whole house looked tilting, but in opposing directions, so its angles seemed to be in lazy contradiction. It perched on a small hill, so from the road in front it had a kind of stark pride about it, set alone against the sky. Gene was in love with it even before he saw the inside, the iron wood stove in the kitchen or the pedal organ in the living room with a bench that opened up to a treasure trove of hymnals and songbooks and old-time sheet music.

"I'll take it," he said.

She smiled, nodding, and said, "It's special somehow."

Then the grave look came over her and she sat down. She got out a pouch and some papers and slowly, exactingly, rolled a joint. She lit it, had her hit, and passed it to Gene. For some time they sat not saying anything, smoking and passing the joint back and forth.

"You can live here," she finally said, "but I can't move in with you."

"Oh," he said.

He hadn't really thought of what was happening specifically, he was just going with it, staying with Lizzie.

"I have to have my room in town," she said.

"Because of the university?"

"Because of a guy."

"In town?"

"No. He's not in town."

"Where is he?"

"I can't tell you. See, the thing is, he has to hide out right now. There are people looking for him."

"People?"

"The FBI."

"Did he really do something?"

"Lots. About the war. You know. To stop it."

"Sure."

Gene was glad the guy wasn't some kind of thug.

"There'll be a time when I can go to him, and when he tells me I'll go but in the meantime he's alive and I'm alive and we do what we feel like, with who we feel like, and there's other guys in town I like, but that's different than moving in with somebody, really living with them. That would sort of—"

"Change things. Yes. I see."

He did see. It was a boundary she had to observe, a pact she had to keep with the guy hiding out. The guy she loves. No. Gene decided he would think of him as "the guy hiding out" instead of "the guy she loves."

"If you stay here," she said, "I could come out and spend the night, but not all the time. I'd come when I could, but I couldn't make a schedule. I guess you'd mainly have to trust me."

He felt dizzy with the grass and the revelations, him and the house and the guy hiding out. This time yesterday he was on his way to Los Angeles. Now he was making up his mind about staying in a house where the people who lived might return anytime and he'd have to leave, in order to be near a girl he just met who was waiting to hear from a guy hiding out from the FBI and would go to him when he said to come.

Suddenly Gene laughed.

"What?" Lizzie asked.

"It's time I put down roots," he said. "I'll stay."

Her grave look left and she smiled, big.

"Besides," he said, serious, "I trust you."

She nodded.

————

"It's hard to explain," Gene said.

Barnes said he understood.

They were having a beer in a booth at Donnelly's.

"All I know is, right now it feels good," Gene said. "It might be over tomorrow or next week or a couple of months, but in the meantime, if it's good, why not?"

"Sure. Sounds like good medicine."

"It kind of takes a lot of the bad taste out of me, from everything back to breaking with Lou."

Barnes said he didn't mind driving on the rest of the way to L.A. by himself, he'd look for Gene sooner or later. He gave him the phone and address of the producer who'd know where he was, and a check so Gene would have some bread to tide him over, he could pay him back when he got there and landed a job. He insisted. Gene said a couple hundred would be swell. Barnes made it three.

He ordered another round.

"This is the one for the road," he said.

Gene raised his glass.

"Go west, old man," he said. "Be well."

The house, worn by time and weather, well used, useful, personal, rumpled, safe seeming, surrounded by brown fields and guarding trees, going gold now, red, orange, falling, fall. Fall. October. Fires and fog.

Lizzie, bumping up in the beat blue pickup, work boots and corduroy, chestnut hair swinging thick, gravity and grace, then everything shed, warm and milk white and holding, held, instinctive, right, in bed.

The house and Lizzie.

His life.

He'd walked into it like walking up the aisle of a movie and melting into the screen and becoming a part of the picture, the story, finding out what happened as you went along, knowing from the beginning how it would end but not when. Then he'd be standing on the stage feeling silly and strange with the screen dark and the houselights on. Bright. He'd be blinking, trying to find his way out. In the meantime this was his life.

House.

Her.

Sometimes they just stayed in, spending long times in bed. Sometimes they got high and played Chinese checkers with an old set Gene had found stuck behind the organ.

Sometimes they sat on the organ bench while Lizzie
picked out hymns with one finger and they bellowed out
"Leaning on the Everlasting Arms," "Rock of Ages,"
"Abide With Me." Sometimes Gene cooked, most always
stews. Nothing fancy would do. Not the time or place or
person. This was stew country, stew weather, and Lizzie
a stew lover, hearty, fresh, full.

She took him to parties, nothing like the one he had seen
the remains of at Gordo's place. Gentler.

A turkey dinner one Sunday afternoon in town, a dozen
some people sitting on the bare board floor, white angles of
sun slanted in. Richie and Marian lived there, he used to
be in The Writers Workshop but started his own custom
furniture business, she designed and he carpentered and
they had two kids, twin towheads, playing through the
party. Marian did the turkey; other people brought things
to go with it: Brussels sprouts, glazed carrots, mashed
potatoes and gravy, mince and apple pies. "This is great,"
Gene said to Marian. "What's the occasion?" "None," she
smiled. "I think they're the best, don't you?" He agreed,
shifting along the floor till he got himself right in a shaft
of sun. Warm. They all were drinking a sweetish wine
called Wild Irish Rose. Fine. Just fine.

They were playing Carole King music, warm, friendly
things like "Song of Long Ago" and "You've Got a
Friend," and then someone put on a new Carly Simon
album, and its title song seemed like a personal message
to Gene. It was all about how we can't know what's coming, we ought to enjoy things now, while we're together,
because—and she belted the line, making him shiver, thrilling to it:

These are the good old days.

Yeh. Now. This moment. He looked at Lizzie, her head
back, her mouth slightly open, smiling, her hair lit in the
late sun. He wished he could have that moment, keep it,
save it, hold it. He squeezed his eyes shut, trying.

Sometimes they watched TV on the big color set in the

farmhouse, and always found funny stuff, no matter what was showing. Maybe because they were high. Who knew? Or cared? They watched the old black-and-white movie of *The Roaring Twenties* with James Cagney, guys machine-gunning one another all over the place, and there was one part where Jimmy and some of his Prohibition henchmen are pouring big jugs of alcohol into a bathtub. Lizzie tapped Gene's arm for attention.

"Hence the term 'bathtub gin,'" she said.

"Hence," said Gene.

It got them giggling, and they kind of adopted the word as their own, working it into the conversation whenever they could.

"Hence."

Sometimes when Lizzie stayed overnight Gene would ride into town with her the next morning. He'd perk some coffee for them to warm up with and then they'd have one of those knockout truck-stop breakfasts Lizzie loved so much and then she would drop him off on Main Street. He'd stand at the corner across from the Iowa National Bank till he caught the time and temperature, blinked in dull gold bulbs that formed the numbers, and then he set off on his ramble, feeling he had somehow oriented himself, that knowing the time and temperature showed he had his shit together, though it was rare that on these occasions he had any notion of what day of the week or date of the month it was, but what the fuck, you couldn't be on top of everything. Besides, as the temperature started getting down in the twenties he figured it must be about November.

The University of Iowa was there, of course, but Gene had seen enough of campuses to last him a lifetime, what he dug was the town itself. Of course, it was called Iowa

City but to Gene it was a town, that was what he liked
about it, the feeling it was small, slow, easygoing. It reminded him of those towns "the boys" came home to in
World War II movies. There were old-fashioned hardware
and dime stores with wooden floors, bars with billiard
tables, diners that served homemade chili, the Epstein
Brothers' homey bookstores where you could browse all
day without being hassled. Most of the downtown buildings were small, two and three stories, and after a couple
of blocks were the white frame houses with big front
porches, an occasional vacant lot, the streets wide, the trees
old. Sometimes you'd come upon something that would
jerk you back to the sense of the pressurized present, like
the anger-dripping red-lettered sign painted on a big
board fence that said "Smash Agri-Business Power!" But
at least it had the "Agri" in it that kind of gave it an Iowa
flavor. He doubted if they'd heard about "Agri-Business
Power" in Boston. Maybe Lou had. Oh, well.

Anytime he got depressed he headed straight for Donnelly's. There were lots of good bars in town but Donnelly's
was the oldest and to Gene's mind the best. It was dark,
with wooden booths, a billiard table at the back, a long
mirror that went the whole length behind the bar, like the
ones in movie Western saloons, and, to top everything off,
a big jar of liquid with some mysterious greenish-yellow
objects floating in it that Gene discovered were turkey
gizzards. For a quarter you could get a turkey gizzard to
munch with your beer! No fancy-pants cocktail dainties in
this place. Turkey gizzards. There weren't many fancy
cocktails ordered either, people came to Donnelly's for
serious drinking, mostly beer or shots.

One day in Donnelly's Gene was telling the bartender
how much he dug the place, the bar and the town both,
and he learned to his amazement and outrage that it
wouldn't be that way long. Urban renewal was coming.
They would even tear down Donnelly's. Tear it down! Shit,
Gene thought it should be a national monument, a fuckin

historic site. But it wouldn't. It would just be a memory. Instead of old wood there'd be plastic here, like anywhere. Gene figured if they could do it way out here in the middle of the country then finally there wouldn't be any towns left at all, just one big national strip of fast-food, quick-stop, Plexiglas and plastic, an Orange Julius on one end, a Taco Belle on the other, so you would know which coast it was. Along the way there'd be signs to tell you where the towns used to be.

He was glad there was still a Donnelly's to go to the day he hitched into town and happened to look at the pile of newspapers in the drugstore. He hadn't been buying or reading papers since he went to Maine, he figured it elimi-nated a lot of junk from the general accumulation in his head, but he sometimes glanced at a headline to see if anything big was up like the war or the world ending, something that made any difference. On this particular day when he looked down at a paper from Des Moines what caught his eye was not a headline but a picture of Janis Joplin. He figured maybe she was coming to give a con-cert somewhere around there so he picked up the paper to find the details. Maybe Lizzie would like to go. But the picture was not because of a concert. It was because Janis Joplin was dead. In a motel room in Los Angeles. Of an overdose.

He went to Donnelly's and drank straight whiskey at the bar. He felt like someone he knew had died. She'd been scary, yeh, but real, and special. You always heard about this or that writer or politician "speaking for" some group of people or other. That's what Gene thought Janis had done, besides make real good music. She spoke for a lot of people—not just young people or hip people or hippie people. She spoke for the people who hurt bad.

Even in a town like Iowa City you could find bad news. After finding out about Janis Joplin dying, Gene stayed out at the farm for a while. He went for long walks, some-times to a creek where he'd "dry-fish," just sit there and

concentrate the way he'd do if he had a pole and line and
bait. Sometimes he watched the weather. The fog was like
a whole other element, the way it came so quick, rolling
up over the hills and around the house, spreading across
the roads so thick that cars would have to pull over to
the side, waiting for it to pass. Gene chopped wood for the
iron stove in the kitchen, played records, read books—not
the grad students' books, but the ones that must belong
to the farmers who owned the place—*Mutiny on the
Bounty, Rebecca* by Daphne Du Maurier, *The Prisoner
of Zenda.* It wasn't lonely because he knew Lizzie would
be back. He didn't mind waiting. He trusted her. She
came.

One night she took him to a chili dinner at Mulligan's
house. Mulligan was this big red-bearded poet who lived
in a farmhouse a few miles from Gene's. He reminded
Gene more of a ballplayer than a poet, one who'd make
a good high-school coach. His teams wouldn't win a lot
but the kids would all dig him. As well as being a poet he
was a chili freak, and he had asked a bunch of people
over for a batch of his favorite, which he said was a recipe
he'd created from the best of Iowa and Mexican chili
methods and ingredients.

He must have leaned heavy on the Mexican. The chili
was so hot that only Mulligan could eat it. The rest of
the room looked like a Red Cross station for people who'd
just escaped a burning building and were suffering from
smoke inhalation. They were coughing and wheezing, calling for water, tears rolling down their cheeks. Gene had
taken one big bite and it nearly did him in. Mulligan was
enjoying the chili so much he didn't notice for a moment,
but then he looked around the room and said, "Oh, shit.
I guess I did it again."

Mulligan's wife got up and went to the kitchen. She
was tall, slim, with black hair and dark, lively eyes that
seemed as if they could penetrate walls. Gene thought her
incredibly beautiful, like some kind of Navajo princess or

something, and he found it hard to get used to matching her up with the name Mulligan called her by. Her real name was Melanie but he called her Mama. She was, of course, they had two kids.

When she came out of the kitchen she was carrying a big tray with cold chicken and potato salad. She was very quiet and solemn-looking but every once in a while the corners of her straight thin mouth would start wriggling in betrayal of some inner hilarity as they did now when she put down the food and said, "I made it just in case."

Mulligan loved to make chili but he couldn't help making it so hot that no one but him could eat it.

No one minded. Mama's dinner was swell, and Mulligan consumed most of the other chili, then leaned back and played from the fifties jazz records he collected, guys like Getz and Desmond and Monk and everyone listened and smoked some gentle grass.

That was nice and then someone asked one of the other poets there to recite some of his new poems. It was his girlfriend. Who asked him.

Mulligan turned the music off and this young guy, with a big swatch of blond hair that he kept brushing back off his eyes, recited some of his poems. When he recited, his voice changed, but then Gene found that all the poets' voices changed when they recited, even Mulligan's.

Besides his voice changing, this young guy stomped one foot as he recited, like he was playing the rhythm to it.

Gene didn't dig the poems. They seemed very angry, like the poet, and full of pictures that didn't go together. When the guy finished reciting he gave a little lecture about how all poetry written before the last five years was archaic, and that the poets who still wrote the way poems were written five years ago were dead.

"Did they all die at once?" Lizzie asked.

There were some snickers, but the young poet managed a sneer in return.

Lizzie asked Mulligan to say one of his poems, and named one she especially liked.

Mulligan had his poetry-reciting voice too, like they all did, but at least he didn't stomp his foot or keep brushing his hair back all the time he was saying it. He sat there like a regular person would, and even though his poetry voice was different it was quiet and perfectly pleasant.

Gene liked the way Mulligan said his poem, and he liked the poem a lot, too. It was about an ordinary day, at Mulligan's place that was formerly a farm but now a poet's house; it was about Mulligan trying to write a particular poem but being distracted by looking out the window and seeing his wife and children. Without saying so, it was about how he loved them. It was also about how he didn't want his poetry life and his family life to be separated, and the last line was:

"Mama, come into my poem."

Gene liked it a lot. He liked Mulligan and "Mama," and they visited back and forth. Gene called sometimes and if Mulligan wasn't wrapped up in a poem he might fall over and drink or get high with Gene.

At first Mulligan's setup struck Gene kind of funny— a farm with a poet on it instead of a farmer. But then he began to see others like it and see how it made sense around there.

Some of the farms still operated as working farms but a lot of them were rented out or the people had retired and sold the place, it was harder all the time to run a little farm and make it pay. But people from the cities liked the farmhouses and the land around them that provided space if not crops and that had become valuable now, the space itself. Poets seemed to prize it more than ordinary people. There were four or five poets anyway living on farms within a ten or so mile radius of Gene.

Instead of producing food anymore, the farms produced poems. Food production was mainly done now in huge scientific operations. Gene never saw one but felt the food in super markets didn't grow like it used to, that now lima beans and corn and spinach came out of the ground in cans with appropriate labels, or in giant freezing chambers the boxes of Brussels sprouts and broccoli and peas grew from tiny cardboard seeds, nourished by infrared rays till they got to be just the right size for scientific sealing and selling.

So what better use for the old small idle farms than to let the poets work on them, sowing their words out there in the necessary silence, nurturing rhymes with the help of nature and reaping at harvest whole sonnets, odes, ballads, *books* of poems?

Mulligan said it was happening not just here but in former farms in Michigan and Oregon, Vermont and New Hampshire. Poets were raising their rhymes and sending them off to market in New York, or some of the smaller new local markets. There wasn't too big a demand yet, that was the problem, the supply was so huge and the demand so small, but the poets hoped the public might develop more of a taste for their crop, get used to having this other kind of nourishment on their tables, find it good, and get hungry for more.

Gene liked the poets, and it was good he had some people he could be with if Lizzie wasn't around, sometimes she liked to be with people her own age, that was cool too. Sometimes she probably went out with those other guys in town she mentioned she liked, and that was fine with Gene. He just didn't think about it.

Only once did she mention the other guy, the one she was waiting for.

━━━━━━━━━

Staring out the window at the farmhouse, the fog rolling up, she looked suddenly sad. Her eyes got a little moist, but she didn't cry.

"Why?" he asked.

"Him," she said. "Wherever he is now. Things."

"Cry," he said.

She shook her head. Blew her nose. Took a tiny white pill from a little tin she kept in her pocket. Swallowed.

"What was it?" he asked.

"A White Cross."

"What's that?"

She shrugged.

"Just your ordinary garden-variety speed."

In a little while she was fine.

That was the only time she ever mentioned him. Except for the last time, when she had to.

Till then it was beautiful.

Headlights of Lizzie's truck on the rutted roads going back in the black nights from Mulligan's farmhouse, the bumping up and down part of the pleasure, the giggling and gasps, then up the hill to Gene's, getting out and looking up to see a brilliance of stars, the same old patterns since childhood but closer seeming, more part of the landscape, the land, the personal weather. Cracking up wood for a fire in the kitchen stove, and then to burrow under the old piled quilts and blankets of the ancient bed.

Him and Lizzie up till dawn talking to Mulligan and Mama, all the old tired stuff new in this new place these new people, sex and childraising, religion and politics. And no one getting mad!

Gene was surprised to learn about 4:00 A.M. one fine high morning that Mulligan and Mama were both Catholics even though they didn't go anymore, that in fact there were lots of Catholics in Iowa, unlike most of the rest of the Midwest.

"Hell, Iowa was started by Catholics," Mulligan said.

"Not started, darling, settled," Mama corrected him.

"OK, I guess the Indians started it, if you wanna get technical. Anyway they both blew it. The Indians and the Catholics."

Mulligan said he and Mama didn't go to mass anymore since they started having it in English instead of Latin.

Gene asked why.

"The last time we went to mass," Mulligan said, "they sang folk songs. Might as well have gone to a Joan Baez concert. The hell of it is they wanted to appeal to the young. and they did just the wrong thing."

Mama nodded.

"They took the magic out," she said.

A new kind of magic had come to town. It was all over Iowa City, posters announcing lectures about it, training programs, initiations.

The new magic was TM.

Transcendental Meditation.

As taught by the Maharishi. Or his Iowa disciples who had learned the magic from him in India and taken it back to spread among the magic-hungry youth of America.

Some people said it was just another rip-off. Some people said it had changed their whole lives for the better, that because of how they taught you to meditate just twice a day for three or four minutes apiece, you breathed easier, thought more clearly, digestion improved, and you just felt better all around. They even said when you got into doing the meditation you could stop drinking or doing any drugs. The meditating didn't *make* you stop, it just made you feel so damned terrific all the time you didn't have any desire to get high.

Gene found it hard to imagine such a state unless there was some hitch to it. Maybe they hypnotized you or the meditating itself was a sort of hypnosis that whacked out your mind and made it placid.

Still, for thirty-five bucks, learning how to whack out your mind like that was a bargain. If you got yourself in some spot where you couldn't get a hold of any booze or dope you could just squat down and blow your mind through meditation.

He was tempted, but he didn't want to do it alone, the initiation and all. He wasn't scared, just embarrassed. He asked Lizzie if she'd do it with him. But Lizzie had already done it. Last year.

"What happened?" he asked.

"I wasn't very good at meditating," she said. "I kept seeing trucks when I closed my eyes."

She told him he ought to try it, though, she knew some people who still were doing it and thought it was swell.

Gene went to a lecture about it. The lecturer told all the wonderful things it did for you, but he said there was no way to explain how to learn it without being initiated, it was one of those experiences that couldn't be described by words. But he swore it was strictly scientific, there wasn't any mystical religious stuff to it.

What the hell. Gene figured it couldn't hurt.

The hard part was that even though the lecturer said there wasn't anything religious about it, that the whole thing was purely scientific, when you went to get initiated you had to bring with you six fresh-cut flowers, a piece of fresh fruit, and a white handkerchief.

Gene slunk around Iowa City trying to get the stuff real casual-like so no one would know what he was up to. He hoped to hell he didn't run into Mulligan, or anyone else he knew. He bought a package of three white handkerchiefs at the dime store, opened the package, and blew his nose on one so the salesgirl would figure he was buying them for ordinary purposes, not for anything weird. He got an orange at a little market without any trouble and tossed it a little way up in the air, just like a guy who felt like having himself an orange to eat later on. In the flower shop he pointed to a bunch of some rather anonymous-looking flowers and said to the lady, "I think I'll have some of those. Make it about six of those."

"Oh," she said, "I see. Getting initiated."

"What?" Gene said, feeling the blush come.

"Oh, we've had a stream of people in all morning getting their six flowers. We always know when there's an initiation coming up, we sell ever so many bunches of six flowers."

Gene mumbled something and got out of there as quick as he could, looking at the floor.

The initiation was held at an ordinary-looking white frame house on a little street in Iowa City.

When you went inside you had to take your shoes off. Gene hoped that was because it was raining, but it was because of the initiation rites. He wondered if the lecturer was on the level about it not being religious.

He wondered even more when he went into a little bedroom where a teacher was to give him his mantra, the word he would meditate with. On a dressing table was a little shrine sort of thing with a picture of the Maharishi. The teacher, a regular-looking guy in a tweed suit and tie —but no shoes—knelt down in front of the little shrine and said Gene had to do the same.

"I thought it wasn't religious," Gene said.

"It's not," the teacher said, folding his hands in the attitude of prayer and launching into a chant or prayer or something in Swahili or some damn thing. Gene was kind of pissed, for all he knew, the guy was selling his soul to some foreign devil. He could have just got up and left but then he'd have blown the thirty-five bucks.

Sha-bas.

That was his mantra, specially designed for his personal needs. That's how you got it on with the meditation, concentrating everything on your mantra.

Gene tried like hell, he did it just like you were supposed to, twice a day.

He wasn't any good at it. Instead of concentrating on
the mantra, after twenty seconds or so he'd think of all
kinds of stuff he didn't want to think about. Lou. His old
man. Dying. He pictured primitive tribesmen in awful-
looking masks. He came out of the three-minute meditation periods sweating and needing a stiff drink. After about
a week or so he gave it up. He wasn't pissed at the meditation people, he figured this just wasn't his kind of magic.

He asked Lizzie what *her* mantra had been, the one
suited specially for her own psychic needs.

"Sha-bas," she said.

"Shit, that was mine. Maybe they recycled the dude."

"No. I think there's just two. That and one other one.
I think they alternate them, as the people come in. But I
guess people like to think their mantra is just made for
them special, so they tell em that."

"Maybe that's how come I couldn't get it on," said Gene.
"Maybe they gave me the wrong fuckin mantra. Maybe if
they gave me 'Shazam' I'd have blown my mind by now
and been a regular guru."

"Maybe," said Lizzie. She rolled them a joint.

After a great Thanksgiving dinner at the Mulligans', Gene and Lizzie back at the farm groaning fondly with glazed ham, succotash, sweet potatoes, pumpkin pie, and knowing the whole thing was done with Food Stamps somehow made it even more of a marvel, an extra magical feast. Gene said they'd been to such great parties they ought to have one of their own, not just the Mulligans but others, too, Richie and Marian, some of the regulars from Donnelly's, people from the other poetry farms around. Gene would construct a giant stew with a beef and apple base, and provide plenty of Wild Irish Rose. You always should go with the wine of the country. Lizzie would buy some good hash and whip up a batch of Fruit-N-Crunch specials, a ready-mix she'd found that hash worked best in of all the ones she'd tried.

Mulligan brought some of his fifties jazz which was good with dinner, sitting on the living room floor with the bowls of stew and then the brownies, but then Gene put "Anticipation" on and they danced with it, everyone, on the slanting farmhouse living room floor, warm, well-fed, friends, flying everyone feeling it, no one denying *These are the good old days.*

Gene thought, this is what Home should be like. But it isn't. Or anyway this one. Isn't mine.

The next morning Lizzie had to get in for a class and Gene was still drinking tomato juice with Worcestershire sauce and popping Excedrins when all of the sudden she was back, her eyes large and shocked.

"You forget something?" Gene asked.

"He called," she said.

Him.

The He.

Gene was suddenly sober. They sat down on the swayback living room couch. His first impulse was take her upstairs, at least once more. But he knew it would be no good, she was sitting there still but she was already gone.

She rolled a joint and said, "Don't say anything."

He nodded.

They smoked, looking straight ahead.

Gene's ribs hurt.

When the joint was done she put her arms around him and they hugged. Then she stood up and he went to the door with her.

"Hey, Lizzie," he said, "it was good."

She nodded, gravely, then turned away, going to the truck.

He stood on the porch in just his jeans and a half-buttoned shirt, barefoot, not noticing the five-above-zero wind, watching the battered blue pickup start, back out, roar off, to the highway, leaving a cloud.

Aloud, Gene said, "There went the good old days."

He shivered, hurried inside, and retched.

That night he stayed at Mulligan's house, and Mulligan said of course he'd drive him to the highway tomorrow if he really was sure . . .

"This part is over now," Gene explained. "Not just Lizzie. Living here."

They got drunk on Wild Irish Rose and Gene told Mulligan he had to keep moving now he knew it was right but he sure hoped sometime he'd find a place to light.

Mulligan cleared his throat and in his poetry voice said:

> We shall not cease from exploring
> And the end of all our exploring
> Will be to arrive where we started
> And know the place for the first time . . .

They both were quiet for a while and then Gene said, "Heavy, man. Did you make that up?"

"No," said Mulligan. "T. S. Eliot made it up."

"Far out," said Gene.

V

Mulligan gave him an old suitcase, the kind with straps around it, a hug, and a ride to Interstate 80. The sky was flat gray, snowflakes stirring. Gene grinned and stuck out his thumb. He thought of the Nilsson traveling song and started singing it, loud, his cold breath coming out in puffs with the words:

> *"Goin where the sun keeps shinin*
> *Through the fallin rain,*
> *Goin where the weather suits my clo-othes . . ."*

Only a few minutes later a pale blue Chevy skidded to a stop on the gravel bank of the road ahead, raising a halo of dust. Gene ran to it, lugging the big strapped suitcase.

He crossed the Rockies with a frail-looking girl behind the wheel of a battered Jag, smoking a flat green hash pipe she kept passing to Gene to light again. On high hairpin curves she'd be fiddling with the pipe and a match, sort of steering with her elbows, saying, "That's the hang-up with hash. Keeping the damn stuff lit." Gene did not allow himself to look at the speedometer. When they came down out of the mountains he figured he might make the Coast after all.

At a truck stop in Nevada he picked up a newspaper someone had left on the counter and looked for the date. It was December 2. Hot damn. He would make California for Christmas.

If they had it there.

They did.

There were already big tall Christmas trees lined along Sunset Boulevard. The only difference was, they weren't green. They were colored a kind of peroxide blonde. A Hollywood Christmas! Gene dug it.

He also dug the place where Barnes was living. The Château Marmont. Gene had never seen a château before, but this dude looked like a regular castle. Even so, at first he couldn't find it. It wasn't on the street, it was stuck in this hillside up above Sunset Boulevard. A sure-as-hell castle with cone-topped towers, like right out of Snow White or Robin Hood. There was even a swimming pool beside it invisible from the street, trees all around so people couldn't peep in. Barnes was livin.

His apartment looked out on the hillside in back, so you wouldn't have any idea you were right above Sunset Boulevard. You might be in fuckin Spain for all you could tell. The main room had a couch and a bed and a table where Barnes had his typewriter and shit laid out. Off it was a kitchenette with a little refrigerator. Barnes got em a couple cold Mexican beers out of it.

Gene was impressed. But even more than by the place by fuckin Barnes. That was the shocker. Gene had to look at him twice. This was not the sallow old slump of a guy who wore what looked like secondhand threads from another decade. His hair was long but neat and stylish, sort of cupped around his head. His face had a definite trace of a tan. He wore zip boots whose expensive-looking leather was recently shined, a pair of light blue denim pants with all kinds of unexpected pockets and silver buttons, a broad black belt with a big silver buckle, and a white muslin shirt, semicowboy. —

"Hey, man," Gene said, "you writin the movie or playin the lead?"

"The God's truth is, in this business, it's hard to know."

"How's it goin?"

"Give you an example. First night here the director takes me to dinner, wants to assure me he knows what my book is *really* about. I ask. He says, 'Illusion and reality.' "

"Your mystery? *Death of a Deb?*"

"Yep."

"Shitman," Gene said, "maybe he was puttin ya on."

"I wish. That'd make it easier. I wouldn't have to sit around in meetings talking about illusion and reality. Fuck it. I just keep writin the thing, feedin em pages. Best not to think about it, otherwise your head gets all screwed up."

"Illusion and reality. That's a heavy number."

"Fuck it," Barnes said. "Let's have lunch."

They went across the street to the famous Schwab's drugstore of Hollywood, Barnes acting real cool about it, calling the waitress by name and all, ordering himself a bacon and avocado sandwich on toast.

He's really getting into it, Gene thought.

Barnes said Gene could sleep in his room at the Marmont, since he just used it as a place to write in the daytime now. He was sort of living with this girl and he stayed over at her place every night.

Gene thanked him about the room and asked what his new woman was like.

Barnes scratched his head.

"It's kind of hard to describe her."

Gene wondered if she was missing an arm or something. He didn't want to press it.

"She's unique," Barnes added.

Jesus, Gene thought, *maybe both arms are gone.*

"Oh," is all he said.

"Yeh. You'll see. Just don't say anything to her about plastic."

"Plastic? What kind of plastic?"

"You know, about L.A. being 'plastic,' " Barnes said. "A lot of people when they first get out here put it down for being too 'plastic.' "

"Sure, man. No plastic."

Barnes was gazing off in the distance, over Gene's shoulder somewhere, far. He absently rubbed his paper napkin at his mouth.

"Belle is very loyal," he said.

"To you, you mean?"

"Huh? Oh. No. I mean to Los Angeles."

――――――――

Belle had nothing missing.

To put it mildly. In fact she was one of the most abundantly endowed women Gene had ever laid eyes on, and the abundance was all in the proper proportions. When people complimented her about the marvelous condition of her body she said, "I work at it," the implication being that she, as opposed to God, should get the credit, which was certainly true in part but Belle didn't deal in compromises. All or nothing. Her hair was dark brown and straight, cut short, and her eyes deep brown. The first time you saw her they were likely to seem menacing. Her habitual stances were either with arms folded firmly across her chest, or fists planted on waist, as if ready to bawl someone out if the occasion arose, or even if she thought it arose. She liked to wear long, old-fashioned dresses with lace trimmings, and big hats, all of which she got at thrift stores but which looked very classy when Belle wore them, as probably anything would have. Later Gene learned she was just the same age as he, but in comparison he always kind of felt like a kid.

She lived on a quiet little street off Sunset in a renovated guest cottage behind a big house. It was basically one room with kitchen and bath. She had fixed it up to be comfortable and cozy, but still it seemed too small a place to hold her properly. Gene thought she was the one should live in a castle, not just a part of it, the whole operation.

"Nice to meet you, Belle," said Gene, smiling, making an affirming nod of his head.

"My God!" said Belle. "He's so *pale*. Is he all *right?*"

"He's fine," Barnes said quickly. "Just be nice to him, OK?"

"Be *nice* to him? Well, of course, I'll be nice to him. He's your friend, and besides, he doesn't look well. Can I *get* him anything?"

Gene hoped she wasn't going to give him any medicine.

"A drink," said Barnes. "You can get him a drink. Me, too. Please."

She hurried from the room; the kitchen suddenly burst into a clatter of glasses, bottles, and ice. Gene felt slightly in shock, as if someone had hit him from behind with a two-by-four. He supposed this was what Barnes meant when he said his girl was "unique" and "hard to describe."

He looked at Barnes, who was trying to wink at him, no doubt for reassurance. But Barnes was one of those people who did not have the capacity to wink; both his eyes moved at once in a kind of squint, as if he had just got sand in them.

Belle came out bearing a tray with three cocktails.

"These are old-fashioneds," she said. "Some people don't like them. But they *should*."

"Love em," Gene said.

"Hers are great," said Barnes.

Belle raised her glass and said, "Well, here's to your friend's *health!*"

"Goddam it, Belle, he's not sick!"

"That's a *toast*, for heaven sake. 'To your health.'"

Barnes took a belt of his drink, grumbling.

Gene started giggling.

He was on the verge of getting really pissed when it suddenly seemed funny.

"Belle," he said, "the fact is you're right. I'm run down and I'm done in. I've come out here to get cured. I figure California's my last hope."

"Well it's certainly your *best* one," she said, suddenly brightening.

"And I think this drink is a sign, a good sign I'm on the right track. I've been a bartender, Belle, and I've mixed these myself, and I've never had a better one."

She had an absolutely radiant smile, and it was now on full.

"Well, thank you, Gene, I can see you're a person of *standards*. That's so rare nowadays."

At last, she'd addressed him directly, using his name. Barnes looked drained but relieved, like a man in a car that just swerved barely in time to avoid a head-on collision. From there on in, the evening was a joy.

After avocado vinaigrette, chicken Marengo, asparagus with hollandaise, new potatoes with parsley, and strawberries with cream, accompanied by two bottles of Inglenook Chablis, Belle brought out snifters and brandy, and rolled a couple of joints.

Gene finished his ravings over the meal, which in fact was splendid, by telling Belle he could see now why Barnes was in the best shape he'd ever seen him.

Belle agreed, explaining, "The potential was there, it just had to be brought out."

"But it's not just good cooking," Gene said, "it's the hair, the clothes. He's a new man."

"I know," Belle said. "I did him over."

She made a sudden little giggle and covered her mouth with the tips of her fingers for a moment, gesture of a naughty child.

"Shee-it," said Barnes, turning his snifter around, embarrassed and pleased.

Belle turned to Gene, put her fists on her hips.

"Now, what about *you?*" she demanded. "What're we going to *do* about you?"

"He's gonna use my room at the Marmont," Barnes said. "To sleep in."

"Well, thank goodness someone's going to get some good out of it with you paying all that money for it when we *could* rent a nice little house somewhere."

"We've been through that, Belle, I know all about it."

"Well, Gene doesn't, maybe *he* wants to know."

"No, he doesn't. Let's get back to *him.*"

That had the ring of a running battle, and Gene was anxious to help them get off it.

"I need to make some bread, Belle. I owe Barnes, and I want to buy some clothes, get myself together."

"Are you an artist?" she asked.

"No."

"Good. That makes it easier. Artists are so sensitive, there's a lot of things they can't do. I know because that's what *I* am. An artist."

"She's good," said Barnes.

"I'm sure," said Gene. "I'd like to see—"

"Someday I'll show you my studio," she said, "but the immediate problem is you."

"I often am," Gene said.

"No, no, we'll have none of that self-pity business, we can't have any of *that.* This is just a logistical problem."

"OK."

"Do you know anything about the horrid swindle called 'rock music'?"

"Well, I listen to it, kind of keep up, if that's what you mean."

"That sounds about right. You see it's in my opinion the

easiest way of making money without knowing much, the whole 'rock music' business. I use the term 'music' loosely, it's really just noise for children, but it is a *business*, I'll grant you that, and shrewd men make piles of money in it by taking advantage of innocent children who have no taste. Well, when I was naive and impressionable I got to know a lot of those people, in the Groups and the record companies and all the rest of it, but eventually I couldn't stand to hear the 'music' anymore, it was absolutely upsetting my equilibrium. But I'm still friends with a lot of those people unless they've done something horrible, because basically I'm a loyal person. Some of them might be able to hire you for something, and I can start calling tomorrow."

"Hey, Belle, that's terrific, but I'm just a fan, I don't really know anything about—"

She waved the objection away like a pesky mosquito.

"That's the beauty of it, you see, you don't have to *know* anything. You're slim and kind of cute, even though at present a little anemic-looking, but you have a nice way about you. I think you might fit in. It's sort of an instinct. You look very much like someone I know in Black Oak Arkansas."

"I've never been there," Gene said.

"Not the place, the Group."

"See, I'm just a hick," Gene said.

"They'll think that's refreshing," Belle said. "Take my word. I always know about these things."

"She does," Barnes affirmed.

Belle seemed relieved about having settled Gene's future, and went to put a record on her battered old portable phonograph. When she turned it on, static came out. Then she put the record on, and if you strained you could hear the thin sound of the music over the static. It was the old Broadway musical *Finian's Rainbow*. That was the only record she played anymore.

"It's pretty, I think, don't you?"

No one dreamed of disagreeing.

The next morning Gene woke to the phone ringing. It was Belle. She had already set up an appointment for him.

"Have you ever heard of Muller, Behr and Starkie?" she asked him.

He hesitated.

"Is it a Group?"

Her giggle escaped.

"No, it's a business."

"I'm sorry."

"Don't be. *They're* not. They're not even ashamed, for heaven sake. They are what is alleged to be a public relations firm, which means they take a lot of money from the rock stars and those who want to be stars who are taking money or trying to from the innocent youth who have no taste, in return for getting their names mentioned places and having people talk about them. Ray Behr is a friend of mine and he said he'd see you about doing something for them."

"At least I could sweep the office."

"I don't think they do that."

"Well, thanks. I'll talk to this guy."

"Don't mind him, now. He's very cynical. Of course you'd have to be, to make a living like that. But he's very good-hearted, even though he doesn't act like it. He's very sleek-looking. Starkie is the fat one. Muller left the firm. After a year he couldn't take it anymore. He's a forest ranger in Oregon now. I can't say as I blame him."

She gave him an address on Sunset and said to go by after lunch.

Gene didn't know what to wear to the interview, so

Barnes looked through the stuff in his suitcase and picked out some faded jeans and an Iowa Hawkeye T-shirt. It had a picture of an enraged gold hawk on a bright blue background.

"Why that?" Gene asked.

"It looks crazy," Barnes explained. "Besides, they won't have seen one before. It'll be something new."

The office was on the fourteenth floor of a tall, anonymous-looking building on Sunset. Going up in the elevator with a man in a dark blue business suit and tie, and a woman wearing a medium-length dress, with stockings and standard heels, Gene wondered if Barnes had steered him right. Maybe it would be an ordinary business office.

His fears were unfounded.

The only furniture in the big main room was water beds. One yellow, one red, one blue. On one of them a young guy wearing a motorcycle jacket was tickling the bare tan tummy of a girl wearing a handkerchief halter top and tight denim shorts with assorted patches. On another one was a big fat guy in white pants and T-shirt sitting in a Buddha pose. That must be Starkie. Beside him on the floor was a pink princess telephone and a bottle of Wild Turkey.

There was a small room off of this where a woman with big shades was working an electric typewriter. Gene found the typewriter kind of reassuring.

"Do for ya?" Starkie said.

"Spose to see Behr," Gene said.

Starkie nodded and patted the place beside him on the water bed. Gene guessed he meant for him to sit down there so he did. Starkie handed him a red balloon that hadn't been inflated yet. Gene didn't know what the fuck he was supposed to do with it.

"Blow it up?" he asked.

"Right."

Gene took a deep breath and started to blow up the balloon.

Starkie tapped him on the shoulder.

"No, man," he said. "That way."

He pointed across the room to a big red tank that looked like a fire extinguisher. The leather jacket guy was standing by it filling a balloon from it. When it was filled, the guy put the end in his mouth and let go, so whatever was in the balloon shot into him. Then he started to giggle.

Gene felt like a real hick. Blowing up the goddam balloon himself. This was the latest high. Laughing gas. The kind dentists use.

Gene got his own balloon of laughing gas, took it in, all in one rush, blinked, and looked out the window. Los Angeles was gray and giggly. Towers tipped. The freeway crawlers looked funny.

"Huh?" asked Starkie, smiling.

"High," said Gene. "I mean up. We're high up. Here."

It sounded hilarious. He laughed. Starkie nodded.

In another moment it was gone, the tipping buildings and the fun. It was a short high but it was new, it was all the rage just then. Gene saw a number of big red tanks in the weeks ahead. He was glad he'd learned right off they weren't fire extinguishers.

Starkie patted the water bed again and when Gene sat down he gave him a glass of Wild Turkey. That was better. Steady, sure, down and in. He knew about that.

The phone rang, Starkie yelled, "Patty, turn that shit down." The girl who'd been having her tummy tickled, and most recently, licked, jumped and turned the switch and the speakers went off. Starkie picked up the phone.

"Starkie," he said.

He nodded, grunting.

"Sure ya can come. Oversight. Laurel Canyon, above the Deebs place. After five.

"Look for tents. Not pup, Arabian. Yeh. Hey—got a photographer? Bring em."

He put the phone back and had a slug of Wild Turkey.

"Sound again?" Patty asked.

"Noise," said Starkie. "Turn it on."

She did.

Starkie grimaced.

"Stone Hinge," he said.

"What's that?" Gene asked, sipping faster.

"New client. Just took em on. Ball buster, gettin anyone to listen to em, much less talk to em."

Several joints and several Wild Turkeys later a slim, cool-looking guy came in, handed something to the typist, took some message notes she gave to him, riffled through them, slipped one in his pocket, crumpled the others, and dropped them on the floor beside him. He came out to the other room, poured a Wild Turkey, but just before he brought it to his mouth grimaced, looked around the room, then at Starkie, asked, "What kind of shit is that you're playing?"

"Stone Hinge," Starkie said.

The guy shook his head, then sighed.

"Well," he said, "at least it's a challenge."

He closed his eyes and knocked down the shot of Wild Turkey.

Starkie said, "Gene's here to see ya."

Gene stood up.

"Belle sent me."

Ray Behr gave a small grin, looking him over, taking him in.

"Of course," he said.

He was brisk again, occupied.

"See you out there," he said to Starkie. "Gene, come with me."

Ray Behr drove a vintage silver Oldsmobile sedan, probably 1940. It was high up off the ground, and the engine sounded like the motor of a small airplane. It was hard to talk, which Gene was just as glad of. He didn't know what to say to Ray Behr, though he already thought that he liked him. He was one of those guys who you might miss his age by ten years. You looked at him one way, he might be a very hard-living thirty. From another angle, you'd swear he was a well-kept forty. He was always moving, even standing still—tossing a key ring or fiddling with coins. He wore tight jeans, ankle-high boots, an expensive buckskin jacket, slightly fringed. Brown hair razor cut, face on the ashen side. His laugh was not funny. Amused maybe, in a distant kind of way.

They were booming around these curving roads, high up, and turned onto a dirt job, almost a path, with bumps that were jolting them around like pinballs. On a hillside, Gene saw tents. Definitely not pup. Ray Behr skidded the car up alongside some other cars and vans and a truck in a sloping meadow. They got out and Gene looked across at the tents on the hillside. There was one huge one and three or four smaller ones ringed around it. The tents were of multicolored stripes. Flags flew from them, trim little pennant jobs, whipping in the wind.

Gene looked and said, "Wow."

"Well," said Behr, "it's not Camelot, but it's better than somebody's living room. C'mon."

The party was to get publicity for the first album of a Group called Epidemic. Half the musicians in it looked like they'd been in one. There were six of them, playing on a raised platform in the main tent. Their own appearance didn't match the party motif. They looked scruffy and dazed, like a juvenile gang apprehended in the heist of a truck full of Ripple. Gene figured the exotic tone of the party was maybe to take people's attention off the Group. The tent was strewn with gaily colored pillows and long divans. A woman with dark hair, a gold headband, and a gold belt around the waist of her short white dress reclined on a purple divan, sipping champagne and examining her outstretched toes. The nails were painted gold. Every so often a man wearing a cloak, a monocle, and a top hat came to the divan and fed her a grape. She ate it, not seeming to notice the man in the cloak. Gene wondered if they were just guests, or part of the rented decor. It was hard

to tell—not just about them, about anyone. He had never
seen so many people in costume outside of Halloween,
but this was different. Except for the hired harem serving
girls, the costumes people had on were real. That is, it was
what they would wear to a party, or maybe to lunch.
With friends, or in public anywhere. There was an Indian
princess, a pair of turbaned twenties flappers with strings
of pearls and long cigarette holders, a paratrooper, motor-
cyclists, beachboys, swamis, and more cowboys than you'd
care to count. And even real stars, famous people Gene
recognized. Mama Cass! Right there, walking right by
him, the real Mama Cass, in the abundant flesh. Some he
didn't recognize till he was told. A tall, pleasant-looking
fellow who seemed out of place, wearing only an ordinary
sport jacket, open-neck shirt, slacks, waved to Ray Behr.
That was Paul Morrisey, Andy Warhol's movie director.
Gene figured looking ordinary must be *his* costume.

Ray Behr had to get moving now, he set Gene loose
amid the marvels of the tent. Young girls in harem costumes passed silver trays with hot hors d'oeuvres, some
with cold, some with neatly rolled joints, carefully arranged
in patterns that harmonized with the shape of the tray.
Gene took a tiny grape leaf stuffed with lamb, and a glass
of champagne. After he did the grape leaf he took a joint,
settled on a purple pillow, lit up, enjoyed, all of it swimming around him in the noise, the blare of Epidemic,
which, if nothing else, added to the sense of disorientation.
He dug it.

Every so often he caught a glimpse of Ray Behr nodding and bobbing through the crowd, giving his wry grin,
laughing but looking somewhere else, then he was coming
right toward Gene, a woman beside him shaking her
finger, lecture fashion. Unlike most of the other women she
looked quite ordinary, wearing a plain kind of baggy
brown pants suit, serious black-rimmed glasses, carrying
a bulky straw bag. Maybe the anonymous outfit was just

her costume, maybe she worked for Warhol, too, maybe
his latest star, who knew?

"Edie, this is Gene," Ray Behr said. "Gene, will you
look after Edie a moment while I attend to some matters?"

"My pleasure," said Gene, uncurling from his pillow to
stand. The woman plopped down on a gold pillow. Gene
sat down again beside her.

"I'm tired," she said. "And I don't want any more
double-talk from you people. This whole thing, it's ridiculous, and if you call this a buffet dinner, I don't. And
what's the point of a *tent*, for Godsake? It's hot in here.
And the smoke. You can hardly breathe."

Gene didn't know what her problem was or what he
had to do with it, but he knew she was feeling lousy and
mad at the world and since he was in a marvelous high
feeling wonderful and at peace with the world he thought
everyone else should feel that way, too. It seemed a shame
if anyone didn't feel just as good as he did, and anything
he could do to help them he would.

He offered her a toke from his joint but she screwed up
her face like he'd offered her a rancid prune.

"Hate that stuff," she said.

"Then may I suggest the champagne. It's quite excellent,
and very cool."

She looked at him suspiciously, like he was trying to
trick her, but he just smiled and got her a glass of champagne.

"I noticed you before," he said.

That part was true.

"Oh?" she asked.

He had her interest.

"You looked real. Like a real person. Not like one of these
cartoon people, pretending to be something else."

"You mean you're not taken in by this cheap display of
glitter and half nudity?"

"It's not my scene," he said.

That was true, too. He only *wished* it was.

"It's really kind of—childish," he said.

"Well, that's a refreshing point of view."

He kept feeding her. Champagne and flattery. He fed himself champagne and grass along with it. It was easy.

Suddenly a man in a French Foreign Legion uniform ran up to Gene and said Ray Behr wanted him right away.

He was put with some others in the back of Ray Behr's mighty Olds. He didn't know where he was going or why. He closed his eyes, smiling.

He woke on a living room couch. There was pleasant soft music, a few people talking. He sat up and rubbed his eyes. The girl he'd watched being tickled in the office came over and asked if there was anything he'd like.

"There was," he said, "but I can't remember what."

She smiled.

"How about a sandwich and a glass of milk?"

"Right," he said. "That was it."

There was a plate-glass window looking down at sweeps and sprinklings of lights. Belle had told him how pretty it was. This was the living room of Ray Behr's house in the Hollywood Hills. Gene blinked, got different lights. An authentic Wurlitzer jukebox from the forties. A pinball machine. Starkie was sitting in a green leather barber's chair in the center of the room, cranking himself up, then down, slowly. A painting of a palm tree at sunrise. A blown-up black-and-white photograph of the entrance to Ralph's Market in Hollywood, covering a whole wall.

The tickle girl brought him a plate with a large ham and cheese on rye with a pickle and a napkin laid beside it and a tall glass of cold milk.

"You must be the guardian angel," he said.

She winked.

"Just Patty."

He wolfed down the food and just as he was wiping some mustard from the corner of his mouth with the nap-

kin, Ray Behr sat down beside him. He was holding a can
of beer.

"You did good," he said.

"How?"

"Getting that bitch out of her funk."

"Edie?" he asked. "Easy."

"Not for most people."

"What's her problem?"

"She thinks she has power. In a little way, she does."

"Who the hell is she?"

"Edith Ast. She writes a rock column out of San Francisco. The trouble is, it's syndicated. That's where the
little power comes in."

"Well, I'm glad if I helped or anything. It was fun. It
was quite a party."

"I'm glad you enjoyed it. That means you'll like working
for me. Would a hundred and ten a week be OK to start?"

It was almost twice what he'd made at Adams House,
Publishers.

"When do I start?"

"You already did."

"I did? When?"

Ray Behr gave it his famous sardonic smile.

"When you got the first glass of champagne for Edie
Ast."

Electric.

Electric guitars, electric bass, electric organ, twang and boom and trill of everything turned on, turned up, and the lights, beating and slashing, electric sight and sound, together. Gene began to feel *he* was electric. Wired. Turned on, plugged in, pulsing.

Parties. His company had them for clients. The record companies had them for Groups they were pushing, singles, albums, new stars; promoters had them before or after concerts, everyone going back and forth to each other's parties, part of the business, keeping up, keeping in, staying with it, on top of it, being there, seen, the scene.

Ray Behr was always on top of it, magnetic and enigmatic. Some said he'd been a serious musician who had played under Ormandy in Philadelphia and for no apparent reason in the midst of a concert had thrown down his oboe (some said flute) and said fuck it, and had come to L.A. Others believed he had been a hot young executive at Chrysler and one day walked out of a board meeting, said fuck it, and had come to L.A. Of course he had all the women he wanted, they couldn't resist the sardonic smile, but some said he'd never got over his first wife, who was either, depending on whom you heard it from, a dazzling product of Scandinavian royalty (she slipped away to elope by crossing some fjord in a boat with muffled oars) or an octoroon beauty descended from Sieur de Bienville, founder of the city of New Orleans. Whatever the case, it did not prevent successive waves of other women from trying to make him forget.

"Chicken wings!"

Ray Behr stopped his pacing to exclaim this latest stroke of genius.

Mouths hung open and heads shook in sheer wonder, breath sucked in and let out in low whistles of admiration.

Ray Behr had put his foot down an hour before saying how sick he was of these same cocktail weenies and rubbery shrimp and half-dollar-size slices of bread with some anonymous gunk spread over them and crummy crackers that you stuck in some sort of goo that looked and tasted like paste—no! The end of that. People were sick of it. Give em something new for Godsake. Original. Something to munch on and drink with that hadn't been used before just because everyone was stuck in the same old rut.

Starkie had moved his great bulk forward from his Buddha squat and said, "Cracker Jack! Boxes of Cracker Jack. You'd get a prize to take home. Novelty item."

Ray Behr wrinkled his nose, showing how wrong it was.

"Sweets?" he asked.

That's all he had to say. Everyone knew the idea was a bummer.

Starkie grunted, his head falling back on his chest in renewed contemplation.

Joints had been passed, a few uppers taken, Wild Turkey was sipped, and still for more than an hour Ray Behr had paced in silence, his associates mute, except for one desperate cry of "Sardines?" which he didn't even acknowledge. And then, out of nowhere, just like that, he had pulled the answer right out of the air.

Chicken wings.

Of course.

And then he went himself one better, he took the basic idea and put the finishing touch on it, the one thing that would make it even more of a hit.

They wouldn't just be any old chicken wings, they would be *Colonel Sanders Chicken* wings! And they would be served in the regular Colonel Sanders cardboard chicken buckets! It was too much. It was perfect. Camp. Hip. And yet functional. Couldn't you just picture the goddam cardboard chicken buckets sitting around on cocktail tables at this posh estate in Beverly Hills?

Hell, it was art.

It was Gene's job to arrange for the procurement and delivery of chicken wings for two hundred people, an assignment he handled with the efficiency and dispatch that Ray Behr was coming to expect from him.

"No sweat," Gene had said when the chicken-wing assignment was delegated to him, even though he realized at once that part of the tricky logistics of the thing involved accurately estimating how many chicken wings a guest would be likely to consume at a cocktail party for a rock group.

"No sweat," was what he always said. He had learned to handle the company car, a hearse painted red white and blue by one of the hip young Los Angeles artists. He made pickups and deliveries: food, liquor, record albums, promo materials, dope, bodies. Not dead. Just out of it. Smashed. Fried. Booze or dope or uppers or downers or combinations thereof or all of the above. He was adept at administering the tickle in the throat, the steaming black coffee, the random bandage, and if necessary, the deposit of the body at Emergency. But, of course, he tried to avoid that. He kept a first aid kit in the glove compartment.

He had to be up, not only in his head, but at all hours, till dawn off and on, and Starkie got tired of doling out his own Ritalin pills to Gene and gave him the name of a nearby Dr. Feelgood who serviced many in the music industry.

"You don't have to make up any symptoms or shit," Starkie explained, "just tell him what makes you feel good."

"Dexamyl," Gene said.

He said that because he and Lou used to take it when they had to stay up late or get up out of some downer and it hadn't made him near as nervous as this Ritalin that Starkie had.

"No!" the doctor shouted.

Had he got the right doctor?

This one was pasty-faced with patches of black left from careless shaving. He had black hair slicked back over a shiny dome. He sure as hell looked the part. Later Gene learned this doctor offered free prescriptions to selected women in return for the opportunity to suck their tits. There were rarely any takers.

Right now he was giving Gene a lecture on the evils of Dexamyl and how the U.S. Government had just issued a warning to doctors that this dangerous substance was being abused and should henceforth only be prescribed to hyperactive children and adults who suffered from some disease Gene never heard of that was some kind of sleeping sickness.

Dr. Feelgood asked with a sneer if he could qualify in either of those categories and Gene said no, was there anything else the guy could give him, his work required his staying up late a lot.

Dr. Feelgood gave him a prescription for Ritalin.

Evidently that drug was newer and hadn't been officially abused yet so Dr. Feelgood wouldn't get in any trouble giving it out, even though it affected Gene a lot more powerfully than Dexamyl and made him more edgy and jangled.

Well hell, it got him up, that was the main thing.

Everyone agreed the party with the chicken wings was
something else, but the party at the Busch Beer Garden
was the one Gene would never forget. That was another
of Ray Behr's astounding inspirations. Even harder than
dreaming up things to serve at parties was thinking of new
places to have them in. Offbeat, camp, surprising, but most
important *new*. And it seemed every place in the greater
Los Angeles area had been used. The old dance pavilion
at the deserted Santa Monica amusement park. Everybody's beach house in Malibu. The ballroom of the old Am-
bassador Hotel in downtown L.A. The pool at the Marmont. Yawn. Ho hum. Jesus. Every place had been done.
Short of an airlift, where could you find a new place for
a party?

"Is there any way of doing something underwater?"
Starkie wondered.

"No acoustics," Ray Behr said in quick dismissal.

And then it came to him.

The Busch Beer Garden. They really had beautiful
grounds and gardens, pretty little artificial lakes, and tours
of the actual brewery in these jazzy little monorail cars
that went up in the air beside the building so you could
look down through the windows and actually see the beer
being made! Not only something new but something to do
in the likely event you got tired of hearing whatever
Group it was perform.

The crowd was in such a good mood, what with the
monorail tours and the artificial lakes to walk around and
the free hot dogs and beer in big cardboard cups that
said Budweiser, hardly anyone complained about the
band, an undistinguished English Group called "Fly."
They hoped to be the new Beatles or Stones. Who didn't?

Belle had come so Barnes could go to still another rock

party, he couldn't seem to tire of them. He had discovered early on there weren't any "movie parties," at least not of any kind of scale and interest like the music events. Movie parties were proper little sit-down dinners at married people's houses where you talked about shit like Vietnam and the Panthers and Antonioni. Very heavy, responsible. The new Hollywood. You mentioned the word "starlets" they looked at you like you had farted. That was the *old* Hollywood. Bad old sex-ridden fun-filled crazy erotic old Hollywood! Shit, Barnes said, born too late again. But at least he had the luck to meet Belle, whose array of advantages included being invited to all the good music parties.

She went for his sake, and the chance to complain about the music. If "hardly anyone complained about the band" at the Busch Garden bash, Belle was the hardly. She stood there shaking her head, scornfully staring at the musicians banging and blowing away at their trade.

"Look at them. Do you realize those are *grown men?*"

"Don't mind her," Barnes told Gene, "she's prejudiced."

"Worse yet," Belle said, "I can *hear.*"

Barnes led her off to look at the pretty little artificial lakes.

Gene just milled for a while stopping to light up or light up someone else, seeing if anyone wanted anything, alert, looking, listening.

Two tall, statuesque women sharing a joint, one wearing a long gown with a slit to the waist on one side, the other in an old Girl Scout uniform and brown leather boots.

"Grace Slick has some nerve, naming her baby God."

"I know. It's so damn San Francisco."

A man in a white jump suit and crash helmet, a girl in satin hot pants and halter.

"How about a hit of the coke, Roger?"

"We promised we wouldn't have any more till we got back home."

"We can always break our promise."

In a break between sets a girl in a cowgirl outfit rushing to the Budweiser keg.

"Gimme a beer, gotta wash it down."

"Bad frank?" the concession man asked as he drew her a beer.

"No. I just gave head to the drummer."

Gene went up to a bored-looking woman wearing Levi's and a "Mr. Natural" T-shirt and asked if there was anything he could do for her.

"Yeh," she said, "bring back the polka."

"I'll do all I can," he said.

He wandered on, seeing if there might be anyone he knew at one of the round metal tables scattered around the outdoor pavilion.

He didn't see anyone he knew but he saw someone he wished he knew.

She was alone, eating a hot dog.

She was small and dainty, with the perfect blond hair and blue eyes of a doll. She was wearing a pink angora sweater, a pleated white skirt that came just above her knees, and blue suede boots.

He wanted to eat her up. As he went toward her, he hoped she was overage. He couldn't tell.

"May I?" he asked, pointing to an empty chair across from her.

Her mouth was full of hot dog but she nodded, her blue eyes friendly, playful.

After she swallowed she smiled and said, "Please."

He wanted to say something clever, astounding, some bombshell of a line she'd never forget.

"You with Xanadu?" he said.

That was the company that recorded tonight's Group.

She shook her head.

He scratched his.

"Well, I'm glad you're here," he said, "but how'd it happen?"

"I know Ray Behr," she said.

"Really? How?"

"Doesn't everyone?"

Of course. Jesus. He was coming on like some kind of FBI jerk.

But all he could think of were these dumb questions. The thing was, he wanted to know about her, anything, he was enthralled, he couldn't stop asking things. Her voice was lovely, high and clear, with a kind of lilt, and what sounded a little like an accent.

"Are you from England?" he asked.

She laughed.

"Encino," she said.

Gene told himself to stop asking these jerk questions that made him look like an ass. Let it happen. So what if her presence here, like her accent, went unexplained for a while, or forever?

"Can I get you a beer?" he asked.

Her cute little nose wrinkled.

"Can't stand the stuff," she said.

Jesus. Maybe she was too young to drink. He could feel himself blushing.

"Isn't it a gorgeous evening?" she said.

"Incredible," Gene said. "Beyond belief, really."

"I'm glad we don't have snow."

"No! I mean I am, too, Jesus. I spent a couple of winters back East. In Boston, actually. Terrible! Snow everywhere, you have to walk through it to get anywhere. Real bummer."

She asked him to tell her more. About the snow. He really got into it. Once he had a subject he loosened up a little, relaxed. Actually she really was easy to talk to, friendly. She laughed easily, and her eyes were incredibly bright, alive.

They just chit-chatted along for a while, Gene trying to keep her amused, sometimes feeling guilty he might be trying to seduce some innocent teenybopper, but not guilty enough to stop. While he was rambling on she took a small white purse from her lap, almost like a little girl's play-grown-up purse Gene thought. She took a small piece of folded Kleenex from it, and then snapped the purse shut and put it back on her lap. He didn't ask about it, not wanting to look like an ass again, so he just kept on talking. He'd exhausted snow as a subject and moved on to fog. She unfolded the tissue, picked up an almost transparent little tab from it, and split it in half with her fingernail. She took one of the halves, put it on her tongue, and swallowed. She pushed the tissue with the other half on it toward Gene.

"Care to join me?" she asked in that little girl lilt.

He cared to join her in anything, but he felt it would be best if he knew what it was, even though the question sounded so damn stupid.

"What is it?" he asked.

"Clear Light."

"What's that?"

"Acid, of course."

"Acid?"

"The very best."

He had sworn long ago he'd never do it. He figured he had just the right kind of a head for a bad trip. Only a couple days ago he had begged off dropping some acid with Ray Behr, who said it would be good for their business relationship as well as their friendship to do it together. Drop acid. He had turned down Ray Behr and now here he was sorely tempted to do it with this little girl he'd known for fifteen or twenty minutes. And knew nothing about her except she had come to the party because she knew Ray Behr. Shit! It might be a trap! Maybe Ray Behr commissioned her to come to the party and lure Gene into taking acid with her. The trouble with that was she hadn't lured him. She had just sat there. Nor had she tried to persuade him. All she said was, "Care to join me?" That was hardly a powerful sales pitch.

Now she said with only the slightest hint of disappointment in her voice, "Don't, if you don't want."

But he did want. He wanted to get all mixed up with her, no matter how.

"I do," he said.

He put the little thing on the tip of his tongue, swallowed, and washed it down with some Bud.

She smiled.

Her name was Laura.

Nothing happened.

They kept on chatting and then after a while they got up and walked around the pretty little lakes. Gene even made so bold as to hold her hand. It gave him a tiny, thrilling little squeeze.

He wondered when the acid was supposed to start but he didn't want to ask, he didn't want to start sounding square again.

She wanted to ride back to town in the back of a pickup some friends of hers had so they could see the stars.

Gene said that was wonderful.

When they got to the parking lot he suddenly, without thinking about it, broke into an imitation Groucho Marx walk, doing it very fast, going around in circles. Laura laughed and clapped her hands together. Like a child, delighted.

Gene didn't know if he did it because he was trying to keep her amused or whether it was the acid starting up.

The important thing was she came up to the room at the Marmont with him. He got her a glass of milk and him a beer.

"Are you all right?" she asked.

He realized he wasn't talking.

He realized he couldn't.

But that was all right. He felt just fine. Nothing bad was happening, he just knew he couldn't talk.

He wanted to reassure her, so he went to Barnes's writing table and got a pencil and a piece of paper. He drew a

large letter R on the piece of paper. He smiled and showed
it to Laura.

"R?" she asked.

He nodded and smiled.

The R meant "I am all right." See, the R was the first
letter of "right" and it stood for the whole thing.

She smiled back at him. She stood up and walked
around the room, slowly, picking up things, looking at
them—pencil, pillow, paperback—putting them back
down, laughing every once in a while. Then she came
over and kissed him on the forehead.

"I'll come back," she said.

Gene was still smiling.

He woke up on the floor, his head resting on a large
dishpan. He didn't remember going to sleep, or getting a
dishpan to put his head on. He ached like crazy. But so
would anyone who'd spent the night on the floor with their
head resting on a dishpan. He saw the R and remembered
what it meant. That he was all right.

Evidently he'd had a good trip. At least he could think
of nothing bad about it. Except he hadn't felt like trying
to do anything about Laura, and he hadn't even bothered
to ask her last name or how to get ahold of her.

Then he remembered she said she'd be back.

She didn't say when, though.

———————————

"Joshua Tree," Ray Behr said thoughtfully.

"Who?" Gene asked.

"It's a place. In the desert. I'll take you sometime. It's
the best place in the world for dropping acid."

"Why?"

Ray Behr looked at Gene intently and asked, speaking
slowly and meaningfully, "Have you ever seen the sunrise
in the desert?"

"No."

Ray Behr smiled and walked from the room. Evidently his question was the answer.

Gene had told him about losing his cherry, acid-wise, and Ray Behr had been terrifically relieved, looking forward now to him and Gene doing it together so Gene would know him in a deeper way, find out where his head was really at.

But Ray Behr claimed he was unable to place this little girl Laura, he just drew a blank. He told Gene not to worry, there was plenty more where that came from. Gene started to explain how that wasn't so, how fresh and incredible and wonderful this girl was, but he realized he'd only sound like a dreamy-eyed adolescent jerk. Which is exactly how he felt.

Belle said she didn't know her either, and when Gene tried to describe Laura he evidently got too carried away and Belle turned up her nose.

"I know that type," she said.

But not Laura.

No one seemed to know her.

A week went by. Gene went to all the parties but couldn't find her.

———————

But out of the blue, or the past, or both, came someone Gene had forgotten awhile, hadn't really expected to see in this scene, and in fact he wasn't quite in it. He was trying to crash it.

Flash.

Arguing with a security man at a party after a concert at the Santa Monica Civic. Flash had got into the concert by buying a ticket like anybody else could but anybody else couldn't buy an invitation to the party, and that included Flash. He was trying to persuade the guard he was somebody. Gene could understand the guard's skepticism.

Flash was wearing white buck loafers, gray flannel slacks, a Jefferson Airplane T-shirt, a red button-down sweater, and love beads. His hair was long and brushed down over his forehead in a bangs effect. He looked like he'd got his decades mixed up.

Gene got him in but after much clapping of backs and just one drink he wanted out again. He said he had just hit the Coast and he didn't feel at home yet. He said a guy didn't know "which way to go out here, hip or straight or God knows what else." That explained the getup he was wearing. He was trying to go in all directions at once, just to cover himself. He kept looking nervously around the room and finally said, "Fuckin phonies. C'mon, man, let's hit the Strip."

Hit the Strip?

Flash had heard the Sunset Strip was something else (Gene figured he got that word somewhere around Sunapee, New Hampshire) and he was anxious to check out the famous go-go strip joint bars like the Pink Pussycat, the whole big gaudy neon strobe nude nooky but only for lookin at scene, so Gene went along though he told him it wasn't much different than the Combat Zone in Boston and Flash just laughed and said, "Still a hick at heart, huh, man, defendin the old town."

Gene just smiled, sat back telling Flash where to turn and which way, thinking how funny it was for him and Flash to be tooling along in L.A. in the night, who'd have thought it a year ago, and yet everyone was getting here, over the humps of the country like they showed on the geologic maps, over the humps and down into Southern California, Los Angeles, into the final slot of the American machine, the map of its playing board tilted southwest, to L.A., far out, the farthest finest final clink, the slot. Blinkers, buzzers, lights.

The Strip.

Strobes throwing jumpy stripes through the room, drums beating the ancient rhythm for bump and grind, so old it must have started on the Sodom Strip, a middle-aged woman wearing only blond wig and silver high heels, looks at row of hushed hypnotized faces upturned to her tits as she cups them, tantalizing, sweat on the foreheads of the middle-aged men mostly in suits and ties some sport shirts one a bull-necked crew-cut head of a brawny construction worker tanned and tattooed he holds up a folded bill and the woman nears, stops, mocks a question whether to come nearer, does, stands so her silver heels are close enough for him to stick the folded five-dollar bill into one, while his head is melting in perspiration, she turns, still moving to the ancient music, kneels, so she is squatting on the heels, moving the rump back and forth so near he can kiss it and does, his tongue flicks hungry out on the strobe-lit ass, gets a hint of it before she stands, moving back along the runway, the five secure in her shoe, looking for another, who?

When the next entertainer comes on, bored, standard, clad in pink bikini Flash knocked back his little four-dollar highball and said, "Shitman, is this all there is?"

"Wha'd ya expect?" asked Gene. "Gorillas humping?"

"Shit. Let's go to my place and rap."

Gene offered the room at the Marmont to have smoke and drink but Flash insisted they go to his motel on Hollywood Boulevard, he wanted to check on his Group.

"You got a Group again?" Gene asked.

"Yeh, man. Managin again."

"What's the Group?"

"Rasputin and the Dreamers."

"The *Dreamers?*"

"Yeh, these new chicks didn't go for being Schemers. They're a little young to dig it."

Gene could understand when he saw the girls. They

both had on shorts and halters, and looked about fifteen. They were pouting because Flash didn't leave em any bread for dinner and the TV was no good.

"What's wrong with it?" Flash said. "I see the picture OK."

"It's only in black and white," one complained.

"It's more realistic," said Flash.

He peeled off a five and told them to go out and get them some burgers and shakes, but don't go far and come right back.

When they left, Flash pulled a fifth of tequila from his suitcase and poured a glass for him and Gene. There wasn't any ice in the place. In fact, there wasn't much of anything. Gene spotted a couple cockroaches, though.

"Where'd ya find the girls?" Gene asked.

"Here and there."

"Runaways?"

"Aren't we all?"

"Yeh, but we're overage."

"Well, they will be, too, eventually."

"Where's your Rasputin?"

"We rendezvous with him up at Oxnard. Got a gig at a roadhouse there couple miles out of town."

Gene offered to help him, maybe get Ray Behr to introduce him to some people.

"Nah, thanks, man, but I wanna see us make it on our own. Don't want to owe nothin to nobody. Then when we're ready to go to a record company we can make our own deal, we won't have our hands tied."

"Sure, man," Gene said.

He drank to the success of Rasputin and the Dreamers, told Flash to keep in touch, and said he'd better split, he needed some sack time.

Flash said to look for his group in *Rolling Stone.*

Gene said he'd keep an eye out.

Where the hell was she?

One night he came in and found something stuck in his door. A napkin. It had "Hi" written on it. The *i* was dotted with a circle. It was her. Laura. She had been there and he had been gone. Shit.

In spite of some Mexican beers and a couple of joints, Gene couldn't get to sleep that night. Or the next.

He went back to Dr. Feelgood and got a prescription for thirty 25-mg. Seconals, and a harsh lecture on drug abuse.

He took one of the Seconals when he went to bed that night and went right to sleep.

He woke up an hour later, so wide awake he knew he might as well get dressed. Shit. Maybe he really should go down to Joshua Tree and drop some acid with Ray Behr. Maybe he'd have one of those trips where you suddenly had some blinding flash of insight and knew what the fuck it was all about. Life and everything.

Sunday afternoon he was sitting in the room sipping a Carta Blanca and reading another John D. MacDonald. Violence and lust on the Florida Coast. Gin and mosquitoes. Bones crunching, beautiful broads. The sombitch was almost as good as dope. Kept your mind off itself.

He almost didn't hear the little knock at the door.

It was faint, small, like it might have been a mistake. He got up anyway to look.

Laura.

A little navy blue silk dress, white cardigan over her shoulders, white short-heeled sandals, little white vinyl purse.

He kissed her, hard, and she met it, opened to it, and then pulled away, smiling.

"Come along now," she said, in that little girl lilt, and he followed, as she danced so lightly down the stairs, out

to a waiting VW bug, black, with beaten fenders. Laura
slipped in the back and Gene sat next to the driver, whom
Laura introduced as her friend Sue. Sue worked for
Xanadu records. They were going to a Xanadu party at
somebody's swanky estate up in the Hills. Sue had a lot of
tan makeup on her face, which was pitted here and there.
Her black hair was short, with bangs, and she had on a
black leather miniskirt and those thong sandals that tie
around the legs all the way to the knee. When Gene got
in beside her she looked him up and down, kind of an
amused appraisal, and let out the clutch.

A pool shaped like a teardrop, and underwater lights
coming on after sunset. The Group played out on the hill-
top, the music brought back to the veranda and pool with
big portable speakers for those who didn't want to join the
crowd on the hillside. White-jacketed waiters, shrimp rolls,
champagne, the joints on silver trays.

Gene and Laura sat on the grass, away from the hill
crowd, facing the veranda and the pool. Laura slipped
off her sandals, curled her toes into the dewy grass.

"Yummmmmm," she said.

He had planned to ask her where she'd been and why
she didn't come sooner and how could he find her when he
wanted to but all that seemed sort of silly now, square
even, like he was some kind of truant officer. All that fac-
tual shit might take the magic out of it.

They passed the neatly wrapped joint between them.

"Your hair is not yellow," he said. "I had thought of it
as yellow but it's not. It is gold. It is definitely gold."

"Nnnnnnnn," she said, nestling her head against him.

A white jacket lowered a tray of champagne glasses in
front of them and Gene plucked one off it. They shared.

Laura opened her little girl purse and took out a tissue.
She unfolded it carefully on her knee. There was a tiny
piece of purple, like a flake of something. She carefully
broke it in half and gave one part to Gene. Each of them
swallowed their part, and had a sip of champagne.

"What is it?" Gene asked.

It didn't matter now, but he was curious. He liked to know the names of things.

"Acid," she said.

"But I mean does it have its own name, like the other was Clear Light?"

"Blue Sea" she said.

"It was purple."

"Sometimes it is."

She kissed his neck.

"Let's go somewhere," he said.

"In a while, little while . . ."

Don't press. Don't lean. Lay back. Way back. Sway. Let it be. That's the way.

Bodies fall, diving, water splashing, lights on the pool, veranda, not white but gold, not gold like Laura's hair, not so pure, but golden anyway, not harsh or spotlike. Bikinied bodies. A top taken off. Natural. Naturally. "Leeeeeee. . . . Loooooook. . . . Meeeee." Party play, pretty people, playing. Boom! Final boom of band and crowd comes down from hill, and band, all in purple velvet, lean, tall, bless em all, over the long green lawn. Laughing. What about the Blue Sea? We'll see. Let it happen, cap'n. Thongs. Sue standing over them, smiling, not seeming happy though, smoking regular cigarette, looking down on them, summons Laura just wants to borrow for a while well be sure you bring her back, Laura blows him a kiss, skips across lawn, onto into veranda, house, one of the many doors. Staying, swaying, Gene watches the water, how it pops open and spits with bodies falling in, and after a while he stands up, swaying, and seems to see it coming toward him. The water. Is this Blue Sea? Recede. It recedes. He is safe again for now but better find Laura find out how this sea thing works is the sea supposed to come out at you, she'll know how to put it back, see, yes, she has control of the sea, goldchildgodchildgoldenhair find her, blind flash just for a second then back to light everything fine all right,

laughter, shrieks, giggly tickly squeals, people come out
a door, Gene tries another door, locked, but the next knob
turns, opens, a guest room, double bed and table with
lamp beside it, lamp on the overhead light, bright, a white
vivid, door-framed photograph, lit in Gene's mind like a
blown-up color photograph in graphic detail:

One of the band, his shirt and velvet jacket still on him,
his velvet pants tangled down around the ankle-high black
buckle boots on his feet, his white body writhing on the
bed his tongue licking up at the black fur of Sue the girl
from Xanadu her leather skirt pulled up around her waist
as she rides up and down on his mouth while his cock high
and swollen is leaping and turning to the lick of the small
pink tongue of the other one her mouth goes down as the
spastic spurt begins so she swallows some and some goes
over her cheeks her long gold hair falling over his hips he
arches with a scream and she looks up, licking some of it
off her pink delicate lips, smiling, looks at Gene, says in
her high little girl lilt:

"We were going to do you later."

Insides coming out, spilling on his shoes, the blue and
white Mexican tiles of the veranda, spoiled, lumpy pink,
stinking, sinking, the sea, stop it, go, run, get to the room
where the sea can't get you she can't get you nothing can
get you again ever never no

White.

Ceiling. Walls. Room.

Faces.

Swimming.

Blink, they stop.

Barnes.

Belle.

Barnes is scared.

Belle starts talking.

"People shouldn't try to commit suicide. They should read Trollope. Especially the Palliser novels. How can you go around trying to commit suicide when you haven't even read the Palliser novels? You probably read these disgusting modern novels that don't have any stories in them, and words put in queer places all over the page and rotten things like that."

"No," he said, a feeble croak.

"Then you go to these horrible modern movies, that's what you do. You go to see Bergman and those foreign people and these modern Hollywood jerk directors who don't have any plots and no *wonder* you get depressed and want to kill yourself. And on top of it all listening to that disgusting rock noise, it's enough to make *anyone* de-ranged."

Belle didn't put any blame on Laura or the acid because she didn't know about Laura and as for the acid she en-joyed doing some from time to time and didn't like to believe those lurid scare stories about the dangerous kind of bad trips people could have. She believed her bedside lecture, and also blamed the rotten influence of Ray Behr and blamed herself for getting Gene mixed up with him and his depraved associates. She was determined now to aid in Gene's rehabilitation.

That was fine with Gene. He figured he'd need all the help he could get.

His hand was bandaged. Two fingers broken. His body was cut, scratched, and burned in a couple of places. Had someone beaten and tortured him? Yes. Himself. How?

The Sea. The Blue Sea. The seal that came out of it. He had always been fond of seals, had loved to watch them slip through the water at the Aquarium in Boston. But back in the room that night at the Marmont when the Sea re-ceded it let out the seal, it was there with one blink, a black, slimy, snarling beast with blood coming out of its mouth. Coming at him. He hit, hit it, hit it. Then it stopped coming at him and he was it. The seal. A black slimy thing, ugly and sick. He tried to scratch the slime off him-self, then tried to burn it off with matches. Then he got the pills, tried to kill it with the pills, poison it to death. Almost did. Barnes came early to work on his script and found him.

Laura. That last night of her bright in his mind still made him nauseous. But that one would fade, in time the colors would dim and the shapes would come unfocused. The one that freaked him was the seal, the blood-fanged ghoul from the great blue acid sea. That was no mental snapshot fixed in place, that was a real monster that had already made another flash appearance in his head. He didn't know how he'd kill it off without getting himself in the process. Maybe he'd learn, maybe it would leave if he got himself together, started living better.

He spent another night in the hospital and after a little talk with a tired shrink, he was released.

'Twas the night before Christmas.

God knew what all was stirring through the Marmont.

Not Gene.

He read a MacDonald, sipped a beer, slept.

━━━━━━━━━

Christmas at the Marmont. Telephone operator nipping from a guest's gift bottle of holiday cheer. Rock stars dripping in the pool, assortment of groupies in brief bikinis draped around it, an actor from England with wife, kids, nanny, stretched on a lounge chair reading the Trades. No Santa Claus here—too fat to get in. Too old. Wrong clothes.

Gene was glad Belle picked him up to go with her and Barnes to her parents' house for dinner at noon. Scrambled eggs with chorizo, the sweet Mexican sausage, champagne Barnes brought, then gourmet gumbo, made and served by Belle's mother, most gracious welcomer Gene had ever been welcomed by in any new place. She and Belle's father took polite puffs off the joint that was passed, wanting to make Belle and friends feel at home, then, in the somnolence ensuing, Mother said, "Well, shall we all just lie around aimlessly awhile?" and they did, till sometime later Belle took Barnes and Gene on a walk to see how beautiful it was and it was, the curving streets and lanes, silence, the whiteness of houses instead of snow, just as good, and the soft warmth of the winter sun, in Hollywood, not the imaginary place of movies but the one where people lived.

Walking back Gene feared that Barnes would blow the whole peaceful scene when he said, "Belle, why can't you be more like your mother?"

Gene braced himself for an onslaught, but Belle just sighed and said, "Why can't everyone?"

Her mother gave Gene a jar of preserves that he didn't want to eat but preserve, like the day, the calm and soft of it, quiet relief from the jittery electric life he'd been into, the jangle and the din.

God rest us merry gentlemen.

VI

The first step in Belle's plan to cheer up Gene and give him a better outlook on life was to show him her artwork.

She drove him out to her studio in Venice in the beat-up red Triumph given to her by a former boyfriend who was an actor. When he got his first big part he bought an XKE and took up with a woman whom Belle described as "one of those starlet hussies." At any rate he gave his old Triumph to Belle "sort of as a going-away present," she said.

Belle propelled the car in a series of fits and starts, bucking and snorting, squealing and backfiring. She refused to drive on the freeways, for which Gene was thankful. She knew her beloved native city by heart and darted through all kinds of shortcut alleys and plunged along avenues, pointing out little-known stores or shops or restaurants that had earned her favor, explaining that avoiding freeways was not only safer but more educational, since you got to see more of the actual city. When Barnes that first day had spoken of Belle's "loyalty" to Los Angeles, Gene could not have imagined its depth and ferocity, not yet having met Belle. When Barnes warned Gene about calling L.A. "plastic" in Belle's presence, he hadn't mentioned that Belle had lost all patience with

people who mouthed that cliché, and instead of trying to
"reason" with them anymore she simply kicked them in the
shins. Hard.

Belle's studio was in a large sort of loft above a garage
on a funky street four blocks back of the beach. It was
rented by a hot young sculptor named Donley who had
given Belle the use of an ample-sized corner for her own
work. She had partitioned off her section with bookcases
she had painted bright colors, to make it more her own.
The main space of course, was given over to Donley, who
worked exclusively in automobile tires.

He piled them on top of one another, he cut them in
halves and quarters, he tied them with ropes, he hung
them from ceilings with chains, he painted them in vivid
Day-Glo colors or covered them with velvet or leather or
silk. He was regarded as one of the bright young men of
the L.A. art scene, and had one-man shows about twice
a year at the very chic galleries. Rich people bought his
tires and hung them in their living rooms in Beverly Hills.
Then they weren't tires anymore, they were "Donleys."
That, Belle explained, was how the art world worked.

Belle thought Donley was wonderful and admired his
ingenuity at what she called "hornswoggling the public,"
though Donley never admitted to that, he stood by his
work as genuine Art. And who could tell? A hundred
years from now? Anyway he was nice to Belle and gave
her the free space in his loft.

"Was Donley one of your boyfriends?" Gene asked,
beginning to be genuinely impressed with the number,
variety, and talent of that category.

"Well, not what I mean by a boyfriend he wasn't, he's
not ever really anyone's boyfriend, like living together or
doing things with you. Donley just fucks people, and then
he goes on and fucks other people. He isn't a cad or anything, it's just his way."

That was enough about Donley, now they would get
to see Belle's work.

Gene was not prepared. He was speechless. Belle helped him out.

"Aren't they wonderful?" she said.

The Palm Trees.

Belle had more palm trees than Donley had tires. That was her art. Everything was palm trees. Paintings of palm trees of all shapes and sizes, in different places at different times of night and day: palm trees at sunset, palm trees by moonlight, palm trees by the ocean, palm trees on the street, individual palm trees, and rows of palm trees. In addition to the paintings there were ceramic palm trees and palm trees cut from beer cans, palm trees made of pipe cleaners and palm trees carved from wood.

"They really are something!" Gene said.

"Don't you love them?"

"Yes, I really do. I just hadn't expected—all of them."

"Well, you can't have too much of a good thing. Of a wonderful thing. To me, they're just wonderful. Not only because they're beautiful but because they mainly grow *here* as far as this country, so if you see a palm tree you think of Southern California. Or if you don't you *should.*"

"I see what you mean. Absolutely."

Belle sighed.

"What gets my goat," she said, looking at the other part of the loft, "is that Donley can sell all his tires to people for exorbitant sums and I can't sell my palm trees. It isn't fair."

"I agree."

He really did. He thought many of the palm trees were perfectly swell, and he would have far preferred one of those to a velvet-covered automobile tire. He found out, though, when he asked people, that Belle's problem was not so much one of "art" but to put it gently of "public relations." Friends had got gallery owners to look at her work, but fearing they might not like it Belle always attacked them before they could criticize her palm trees first. One wealthy gentleman of the L.A. art world who looked at

her work had started to say something about the difficulty
of introducing new artists, even very talented ones, and
before he could finish Belle had called him a "gutless fag"
and kicked him in the shins. She had also kicked in the
shins of an influential lady gallery owner who had simply
asked if Belle ever painted anything else but palm trees.
So most of Belle's paintings were sold to friends, or friends
of friends. Her boyfriends all bought at least one palm
tree during the course of the affair, sometimes at prices
that demonstrated an appreciation of Belle as well as her
art. But aside from such personal patrons there were
genuine nonpartisan supporters of her work, there were
palm trees hanging in distinguished homes from Beverly
Hills to Malibu, and one as far north as Santa Barbara.
That's about as far north as she'd want one to go unless it
was a special unusual person who lived up there. She considered San Francisco and its citizens *almost* as unredeem-
able as New York and the poor souls who didn't know any
better than to live in it.

━━━━━━━━━

After Belle showed Gene her Art she showed him a little
of Venice. The nicer part, around Washington Street and
the pier. It wasn't fancy by any means but there were
some nice little bars and informal places to eat, a good fish
joint, a new wine and cheese shop with tables where you
could have a light lunch, a bar with sawdust on the floor,
and a popcorn machine with bowls beside it so you could
just scoop some out free to go with your beer. Ocean
Front Walk was a straight little sidewalk that went along
in front of the houses facing the beach. The houses were
mostly one- or two-story, stucco and frame and fieldstone,
pleasant-looking, individual, and unpretentious. They
weren't "beach houses," they were just ordinary houses

that happened to be on a beach. The beach was long and white and there were hardly any people on it. Gene asked if it got crowded in the spring and summer and Belle said no.

"How come?" Gene asked. "It looks real nice."

"People don't come to this beach," Belle explained. "They go to the beach at Santa Monica."

"Oh."

They went out on the Venice pier, looking down at the ocean lapping at the posts, looking at the people, some strolling, some staring out to sea, some fishing. There were little kids and old men and a couple of young black guys, fishing with long rods, buckets beside them, cans of bait. At the end of the pier was a round wooden concession stand where you could buy hot dogs and coffee and pop. Everything was windy, and fresh. Gene even liked the strong fishy smell of things. They walked back and had salads and glasses of white wine at the wine and cheese place. Belle said this Venice was started in the twenties by some man or group of men who wanted to build a town that would be a California version of the other Venice. The one in Italy. They even dug the canals. Then the Depression came and the whole thing went bust and never really recovered. That's why you still saw these ditches running through the place, some completely dry, some with a little stagnant green water, they were supposed to have been canals. Some artists and writers lived here and other people who liked it because it was cheap and funky and the beach was so pretty.

"It's different," Gene said. "The feel of it. It's kind of like a resort."

Belle giggled.

"The *last* resort!" she said.

Maybe so. Maybe that's part of what he liked about it. Whatever it was, he was drawn to the place.

He rode out to Venice with Belle again the next day, figuring he'd nose around a little, play it by ear, see what came along.

Belle invited him to join in a search for Donley, who hadn't been at the studio for over a week and had promised to take some of her palm trees to a gallery owner he knew in Ojai. Gene didn't have anything definite he was going to do, and said he'd be glad to help her track down Donley.

The ingenious tire sculptor lived in a little ramshackle house the next street over from the loft-garage. A sleepy-looking girl in a man's bathrobe opened the door and said Donley wasn't home, she had no idea, where or when or if ever.

"That was no lie," Belle said as they walked away.

"Where do we go now?" Gene asked, following Belle's swift stride.

"Uncle Phil's."

"Donley's uncle?"

"Everyone's."

Uncle Phil lived in a large red-brick apartment building shaped around a courtyard, facing right onto the ocean. A kid was playing with a toy train in the courtyard while a young woman wearing shorts and a tie-dye T-shirt looked on, smoking a cigarette. Belle looked around her and said Uncle Phil's apartment was right on the ground floor but she could never remember what door it was, they all looked alike. None had numbers.

Belle looked at the young woman and said, "Which one's Uncle Phil's door?"

The woman shook her head, stood up, took the kid inside.

Belle sighed.

"That's Venice for you."

"What's wrong?"

"They all protect each other. It's nice, but it's kind of paranoid. They think if you're looking for someone you must be fuzz or a bill collector or a hit man. They're very loyal, though, especially if you've committed a crime."

"A real neighborhood, huh?"

"That's the idea. At least here in the funky part. Some parts are just dull and ordinary and people go to work every day and don't talk to each other just like everywhere else."

She turned around again, looking at each of the ground-floor apartment doors.

"I know it's got a window on the ocean," she said, "cause he always brags about the view. Let's try *this* one."

They went to one of the end apartments, nearest the beach.

Gene said, "The name on the bell says 'Ramirez.'"

"Oh. That doesn't mean anything. Except that probably no one named Ramirez lives here."

She pushed the bell.

Gene noticed curtains move, but he didn't see anyone.

"Yes?" came a voice.

"Uncle Phil? It's me, Belle. And a friend. My friend Gene."

There were voices in the background and then the door opened. Uncle Phil was buttoning up a pair of old Levi's. He didn't have anything else on, including underwear.

"God," said Belle sweeping in, "don't you ever get tired of doing that?"

"Sometimes," he said.

He had the wry, battered look of someone who's been through a war but is tolerant of civilian innocence; not condescending, tolerant.

A girl, yawning, came out of the other room. The bedroom, evidently. She was wearing a man's unironed shirt over orange bikini panties. She was tall and had long dark hair and gave the impression of being rather regal until you heard her voice, which was high and had a childlike lisp.

"This is Pepper," Uncle Phil said.

"Hi, Pepper," said Gene. "I'm Gene."

"Listen, Pepper," Belle said, "you know you can go blind doing that stuff all the time."

Pepper looked at Uncle Phil, her eyes wide.

"No, honey," he said. "Why don't you roll us some joints?"

"I was looking for Donley," Belle said, "but I guess he's not here, unless he's still in that other room and the three of you have been doing unspeakable things to each other."

Uncle Phil pointed to the bedroom.

"Search," he said.

"My God, I wouldn't go into that den of unnatural practices for all the tea in China!"

The apartment was small but cozy. Burlap curtains of a warm, goldish color. Wicker furniture. Battered TV, good stereo, lots of books, paperbacks, and some large weighty-looking tomes.

"Nice pad," said Gene.

Phil nodded.

"Courtesy of our benefactors, the great State of California."

"Phil is a Welfare artist," Belle said.

"True. And I'm about to bring off my masterpiece."

"You mean you can get even more money out of those poor innocent Welfare people?"

Phil lit a joint and started it around.

"This, my dear, goes far beyond mere Welfare. It is a step up, a much richer step up, a whole new category."

"Does it have a name?"

"Affectionately known among its recipients and aspirants by its initials, ATD, it is, in formal terminology, Aid to the Totally Dependent."

"My God!" said Belle. "Are you going to saw off your legs?"

"No, no," said Phil.

"Well, he would," Belle said to Gene, "if it meant he could gouge more money out of the state."

"Fortunately," Phil said, "such measures are not necessary. It is possible to be graded 'totally dependent' due to psychological as well as physical problems."

"Won't they stick you in the nuthouse?" Belle asked.

"They're overcrowded," Phil pointed out. "Besides, if I study symptoms well enough and get them down pat, I will be officially 'totally dependent' on the society and yet of no threat or danger to it."

"Except to its pocketbook, you mean," said Belle.

"Where do you get the symptoms, man?" Gene asked. "I mean where do you find out what they are? For what you want to have?"

Phil pointed to the weighty tomes Gene had noticed. "Medical dictionaries of pathology," he said. "I am studying in consultation with a new neighbor who was recently departed from UCLA medical school when it was learned that he had a way of making certain pain-killing drugs seem to vanish into thin air. They judged him wrong. He is not a thief, he is a humanitarian."

"If you pull the wool over their eyes," asked Belle, "will you buy one of my palm trees?"

"Of course. And we'll hang it proudly and prominently in the living room of our new apartment."

"For heaven sake," said Belle, "will you move to Beverly Hills or something?"

"No, no, Same place. Same building. But just a larger apartment, higher up. Better view. Although I must say the view from here is quite splendid. Especially at sunset."

He pulled back the curtain, showing a dramatic stretch of beach and ocean.

"Wow," said Gene. "You really got it made."

Uncle Phil grinned, took the joint that Pepper was handing to him, and said proudly, "Don't tell *me* the System doesn't work."

There was an A&W Root Beer stand on Ocean Front Walk near the pier and Gene got a job there. They had a small grill and served burgers and hot dogs and tacos along with the root beer. It was sort of like working outdoors because there was a window at the front where people could come up and order and then sit down at one of two little tables in front of the place, and the window was always open. It hardly paid anything but Gene hardly wanted anything. He found a room on Speedway, the sort of little paved alleyway that ran behind Ocean Front Walk. He had asked about an apartment in a little white cement four-apartment unit there but it was $110 which was more than he wanted to pay and so the owner showed him a little room beside the garage. It had one small window, and there was a hot water heater in it that serviced the apartment above; it was all unpainted concrete, but Gene could have it for fifteen bucks a week. He took it. There was a toilet and a washbasin but no tub or shower. He figured he could bathe in the ocean.

It felt strange going back into town, to Hollywood, now that he was out in Venice. He'd only been there a few days but already he felt it was home, and Hollywood, especially Sunset and Hollywood boulevards, the business and restaurant and nightclub areas, were weird, unfamiliar, frantic places, supercitified, souped-up, garish.

The office of Muller, Behr and Starkie was a whole other planet. It felt like stepping back in a dream that maybe didn't happen at all. Gene didn't want to go there but felt he should see Ray Behr in person and tell him what he'd decided to do. Ray Behr had been a bit abrupt on the phone, but he knew what had gone down and told Gene to take his time about coming back.

Ray Behr was nodding and pacing and snapping his fingers behind his back while Gene tried to thank him for the job, for everything he'd done, but that Gene had decided he was going to live out in Venice.

Ray Behr nodded, as if he had known this was what would happen all along, from the very beginning.

"Venice is the last stop," he said.

Gene didn't want to ask "for what" and besides, Ray Behr had given it his enigmatic smile with the quick turn on the heel and disappearance from the room.

Over.

The rains came.

Since Gene hit L.A. in early December it had never rained once but just before New Year's it started and still was going now a week later, unceasing, drumming, pouring, blowing, winds making the palm trees bow, winds shaking the houses, rain seeping in everywhere, under doors, in cracks of windows, flooding the streets, stalling cars, this was not a thunderstorm it was like a monsoon, or what Gene supposed one to be, where the rain was all, was everything, ruled, was constant, king.

Gene was glad he wasn't in town when the rain came, he figured it would just be depressing there but out by the

beach it was beautiful as well as terrible, it was raw and
elemental, real and cleansing. He walked in it, soaked in it,
wandered in it, held up his face to it, took off his shoes
and socks and waded in it, rolled up his pants and walked
along the beach in it, slept through it, woke to it, felt he
was in it and wanted to be, wanted to feel rained on rained
out drenched clean of the crud in and on him.

But not even the great torrential rain dispelled the horrible blood-dripping seal. It would come before him in a
flash, while drinking beer or walking down the street and
he would stop and squeeze his eyes shut, holding his
breath, clenching his fists, trying to will it away and it
would go then leaving him exhausted, spent, but he knew
it was not gone for good it could flash back anytime and
would. And he couldn't talk about it. Who could you tell
you were frightened by a seal? Maybe someone else who'd
had a bad acid trip, maybe Uncle Phil, but the hitch was
talking about it brought it back and so it was best to try
to keep it at bay, do battle with it each time, try as well as
you could to forget till it wouldn't let you.

One of the first days after the rain stopped, leaving the
whole place bright and dripping, fresh and new, Belle
dropped by the A&W. She wanted to invite Gene to come
and have dinner with her and Barnes. She picked him up
after work, seeming unnaturally subdued. Even the trip
into town in her red Triumph was prosaic, lacking the cus-
tomary spirit of adventure and sense of narrowly escaping
danger by bizarre maneuvers and a benevolent fate. When
they got to her place she pulled up next to the curb and
said, "Let's take a walk."

"It's nice out," she said, as if in explanation. But it
usually was.

"See these houses?" she said.

"Yes?"

They were the small, one-story frame or brick or stucco
houses that lined so many of the streets in this area of

Hollywood, between Santa Monica and Hollywood boulevards, between La Cienega and Doheny. Quiet little streets
with quiet little houses, none of them grand or opulent,
their charm of a modest kind, coming from trim lawns and
trellises, well-tended shrubs and flower-bordered porches.

"Don't you think they're wonderful?"

"Well, yes. I like them a lot."

Belle giggled.

"See that one?"

It was one of the frame ones with a pointed roof, a front
porch with trellises, the sort of house you could find in any
quiet street in the Midwest, like Iowa City.

"See, the people who built these came from *Ohio* and
places like that, and they thought you always had to have
those pointed roofs because of the snow, and so when
they came to live here they built them the same way even
though they didn't *have* to. Anyway I think it's kind of
nice, all these people from those places like *Ohio* coming
out here and building their little houses because they knew
it was *better* out here."

She pronounced the word "Ohio" as if it were something
outlandish, as if it were a wonder such a place as that even
existed.

"I dunno," Gene said, "I kind of like the Spanish-style
jobs. The stucco ones with the red tile roofs."

"Oh, they're wonderful, *too*," Belle said. "I sort of prefer
the little wooden *Ohio* ones but all the ones on these streets
around here are wonderful. I'd love to live in almost *any*
of them."

Gene understood now.

"But Barnes wouldn't," he said.

Belle sighed and put her fists on her hips.

"That *fool*. See, he *says* he would like to live in one of
those houses but then he gets all these excuses."

"Like what?"

"Well, the stupidest one of all is, he says he wants to

wait to see if his movie gets made and then he could
actually *buy* a house."

"You don't think the movie'll happen?"

"I don't know. All I know is he shouldn't *count* on it
happening. I've lived here all my life and I've seen all
these people come out here, writers and actors and people
who want to direct, and they believe what everyone tells
them and then they're heartbroken. I said to Barnes with
my utmost sincerity, I said, 'Please,' I said, *'Don't believe
in Hollywood!'* I meant the movie part, of course, not the
wonderful little streets and houses."

They had strolled back to Belle's, and sat down on the
little slope of lawn in front of the big house she lived
behind. It was dusk, quiet, you could see the Hollywood
Hills in the distance, green and blue, unexpected, too
steep to be all built up, leaving lots of wild unsettled space,
a frontier feeling. He understood Belle's loving it here.

"Maybe Barnes is afraid," he said.

"Well, he shouldn't be afraid. He's too old for that."

"In Boston he never took his books out of the boxes."

"What boxes?"

"You know, cardboard boxes he had packed his books in
when he moved there. He was afraid if he put the books
up on shelves he'd be there permanent."

"Well, I can understand feeling that way in *Boston*. It's
too cold there. But now he should *want* to be permanent."

"Sounds like a good deal to me, anyway."

"Well, you should tell him that. It's for his own good."
Gene said he'd try.

At dinner Barnes seemed grumpy, and Belle banged the
dishes and silverware around a lot. Afterward they sat
around smoking grass and listening to *Finian's Rainbow*.
Gene said he ought to be heading back and Belle said why
didn't he spend the night in Barnes's room at the Marmont,
then she'd drive him out to Venice in the morning when
she went to her studio.

"Besides," she said, "somebody might as well get some

money's worth out of that expensive room nobody sleeps in."

Barnes pretended not to hear.

Belle suggested Barnes walk over to the Marmont with Gene while she cleaned up the dinner.

Barnes stopped at a liquor store on Sunset and bought a bottle of Courvoisier.

"We'll have a nightcap," he said.

The nightcap turned out to be the whole bottle. Barnes killed most of it.

"How come you keep it, man?" Gene said. "The room here?"

"I like it. It's great to work in."

"Isn't it kind of steep, just for that?"

"Then if anything happened, I'd still have my own place."

"If what happened?"

"If me and Belle split."

"You want to?"

"No."

"Does she?"

"She wants a little house. For us to live in together."

"What's wrong with that?"

"How do you get out of it?"

"Of the house?"

"Of the whole thing."

"Somebody leaves."

"Yeh, but then it's a mess. It hurts more then. Everybody. Besides, it makes me nervous. Living in houses. You can't just up and walk out of a house. It's more of a permanent type thing. Here, I could leave any day, any time of night or day. Or I can stay. I like knowing that. It's the way things are. Things change. People move on. Nothing stays the same. That's what life is."

"A hotel."

"Yeh. So you might as well stay in one. Isn't that how it is?"

"I guess," Gene said.

He was sorry though. About Belle. And Barnes. About himself. About the way it all was.

The Life Hotel.

Gene was glad to get back to Venice. Not just to get away from Barnes and Belle's troubles. He felt at ease there, like he blended in. It was funny. He wouldn't have felt that way at all in Marina del Rey or Santa Monica, the communities bordering Venice to the north and south. If you just walked south across Washington Street you were in Marina del Rey, a whole other scene, streets with cutesy nautical names like Buccaneer and Outrigger, fancy expensive new houses that Gene thought of as phony Spanish-modern with lots of glass, swinging singles apartment settlements for thirty-five-year-olds trying to live a perpetual college life of beer blasts and water polo, sleek expensive restaurants serving lobster and candlelight. People said Marina del Rey was the future, the affluent leisure life of the smiling upward mobile, and to Gene the idea was so awful he figured it might be true.

If you walked north clear across Venice you came to Santa Monica, and Gene liked that a lot better but it wasn't his thing. He liked to go to the shopping mall there and hit one of the health food stores for a celery shake and raisin on rye, natural nutbread or whatever special was featured. But that was about it. Santa Monica was stolid, secure, sleepy, established, Establishment. You saw a lot of middle-aged men wearing suits and ties, pale and serious, like they might have been accountants in Akron. Santa Monica was nice, with the beach and pier and palm-lined avenue that ran along the ocean, but Gene could never feel part of it, like he did in Venice.

It wasn't that Venice was all hippie or all funky, it was a mix of that with middle-class and working people but there wasn't any rich part, no fancy or pretentious stuff, and people of one kind didn't seem to take much notice of people who were different, or care. Gene went to a little fair in a vacant lot by one of the canals—they had a little water now from the annual big rains—and there were some watercolors for sale, hot dogs, homemade cakes and pies, a local rock group, a girl selling pots she made. It was to raise money for some kind of Free School they had there. Little kids played in the dust, teenagers walked with arms around each other's waist, ringlet-haired housewives, sun-burned bald men, intense young guys with beards, a black man in a dashiki, another in slacks and a polo shirt, thirtyish long-haired women wearing leather sandals and minidresses. It was Sunday. It was Venice.

The idea of it Gene dug, too, of a dude trying to build a whole city that would be like the one in Italy. The one Belle called "The Other Venice." Canals that never got used. They reminded Gene of the line in "American Pie" about driving to the levee but the levee was dry. Right on.

They played that at Uncle Phil's a lot, the whole record by Don McLean, and it seemed to Gene like the perfect theme song for Venice, at least for his life and time in it. Everyone would always clap or shout approval at the part that said:

> ". . . They took the last train to the Coast,
> The day the music died."

This was it, the Coast, the edge, the last stop, make it here or fall off the edge, and Venice was the perfect head-

quarters. Especially Uncle Phil's place, where Gene had
taken to hanging out a lot. There were always people
coming and going, always some smoke, music, talk, or you
could just sit and look out the window, that was cool, too,
you never had to pretend or fake anything. Phil got named
Uncle because everyone felt that way about him, like he
was some kind of wise uncle who'd help you out, you
could lay anything on him, he never got uptight about
anything.

Uncle Phil wasn't really all that older than most of the
people who passed in and out of his pad, he just seemed
like it, in a way he looked like it. His body was hard and
youthfully lean, it was the face where the age was, the
grooved lines and wrinkles, the pounded eyes. And he had
a kind of rattling laugh, as if something was loose inside,
and it often led to coughing spells. Gene had the sense of
him sort of dying on the hoof. Of course we all are, he
knew, but Uncle Phil seemed to be going about it faster,
more relentlessly, not caring, much less worrying about it.

There were all kinds of different stories about him,
Gene never knew which if any were true. Some said he
once had killed a man. Or a woman. Or a woman had
killed herself on account of him. Or a woman took a kid
she had by him and went back to live with her wealthy
parents in Pasadena and got a court order so he couldn't
even come and visit the kid. Some said he had killed a man
but it was in a war, either Korea or Vietnam, and he got
a big medal for it but then got sick of the whole scene and
deserted. Some said he was the illegitimate son of Errol
Flynn. It was certain he had grown up around Los Angeles,
so it was possible. Those who held to this theory supported
it by pointing out that he never went to the movies. He
wouldn't talk about it he just wouldn't go, which to the
Errol Flynn theorists suggested there was some terrible
thing in his past connected with the movies or with someone who was important in them which embittered him to
the extent that it created this peculiar aberration.

He was not a real pusher. He just used a lot of dope and he bought it in large quantities for economy's sake and then sold what he couldn't use himself right away. There was always somebody coming in or out who wanted to buy something. And Uncle Phil usually had it to sell. That's all. It was all on a casual basis, rather than a business-type operation. More or less what you might call a community sort of thing. A service.

One day when Gene dropped by Uncle Phil's he found him in the midst of snorting some white lines off a mirror. Gene figured it was coke, and wondered why he hadn't been offered any. When Phil finished, laid the mirror down, and turned to Gene with a beatific smile, Gene asked, "Coke?"

"No," Uncle Phil said. "Skag."

"Oh."

Phil didn't offer any and Gene didn't ask for any.

Another time, out of curiosity, Gene asked him:

"What's it like? Heroin? I don't mean what it does to you if you're hooked, I mean how does it make you feel?"

Phil thought awhile and said, "Are you familiar with the term 'peace of mind'?"

"I've heard it mentioned," Gene said.

"That's how it makes you feel," Phil said. "Like you have that. Peace of mind."

"Wow."

Maybe he'd try it sometime. Peace of mind. That would be a new trip all right. He knew of people who'd just had a snort or so and never got hooked, and every once in a while he heard of some guy who supposedly was able to shoot up regular maybe once a week and still be able to take it or leave it. He'd never actually met the guy, though. But he figured with Uncle Phil, if he only snorted from time to time he probably wouldn't get hooked because his body must be so confused by this time from all the different shit he put in it, heroin might not have the same effect it did on everyone else.

Well.

It was something to think about.

―――――――

One afternoon at Uncle Phil's he met a woman named Lottie. She bought a lid of grass and stayed to share a joint with Uncle Phil and Pepper and Gene. She was small and tan and angular with high cheekbones that gave a kind of Indian cast to her face. Her hair was short and she wore big hoop earrings, her only jewelry, a neat blouse and skirt and sandals. She sat very straight. *Prim* was how she seemed to Gene.

He was surprised when she stood up to go and asked him if he'd like to get a beer.

Why not?

They went to the bar on Washington Street with the free popcorn.

She told him she had been a housewife in Toledo and one day when she was taking out the garbage she realized someday she was going to die and nothing would have happened to her, so she packed one suitcase, took the $2000 some dollars out of her personal savings account and split. Now she collected unemployment, made pottery, and lived in a nice funky house with two other women, one who sold vitamins from door to door and the other a student at an unaccredited law school in Santa Monica.

"Why would anyone go to an unaccredited law school?" Gene asked.

"They can't get in the other kind," she explained.

There was something kind of flat about her, weary and

drained. What the hell, she probably thought the same
about him. Maybe they were well matched.

They went to his place and balled, perfunctorily, he felt.
Which was OK, too.

Afterward, smoking a cigarette, she told him for a while
she had a filing job in an office in Santa Monica, but one
day when some strange man came up like men sometimes
did and asked to buy her a cup of coffee, instead of just
telling him to get lost she told him she didn't have time
for the coffee but if he wanted to spend some money they
could go to a motel. They did. She charged him $25.
After that she quit the filing job.

Gene asked if she dug the hooking.

"Better hours," she said, "than the filing."

More time for doing her ceramics. What with unemployment and a trick now and then, she got along fine.

He liked her attitude. Which was more or less Fuck It.

Thinking of her getting $25 a trick turned him on a
little, and the next time they made it it was better.

She was just the kind of woman for him, the way he felt
now. He wouldn't hurt or get hurt. He wouldn't have to
feel anything. There would be no entanglement. If they
wanted to do something they would. If they didn't they
wouldn't. They saw each other two or three times a week.
They didn't have a whole lot to say to each other. That
was all right, too. The whole thing between them was
bland but safe. It was sort of like cottage cheese. Sometimes that's all you want.

———————

Gene answered the phone at the A&W one afternoon
and it was Barnes.

"Hey, old buddy!" he said with what sounded to Gene
like too much heartiness. "Guess what?"

"I can't."

"I'm your neighbor now!"

"In *Venice?*"

"No, no. The Marina. I got a place over in the Marina."

"Where? What street?"

He knew some of the phony-named nautical streets next to Venice. Near the border.

He could hear Barnes clearing his throat.

"Well, actually, I'm staying here at Single Shores."

"You shittin me, man?"

"Listen, it's not for that, the whole thing is I had to find a place real fast and this thing is all completely furnished. All you have to do is get your suitcase and walk in the door. In that way it's like the Marmont. It's convenient and saved a lot of hassle."

"Sure, man."

"Fuck you."

"OK, man, I'm sorry. Couldn't resist. What's up?"

Barnes had split with Belle, for real, it was all over, the movie thing had been shelved but they paid him for the script, he was going to forget about all the movie shit now and get down to work on a new mystery novel. He might even set it there, have it take place in one of these huge singles apartment complexes. Anyway he was making a new start, he wasn't just drinking and mooning over Belle, it had to end sooner or later so it really was better to have done now, he had already met a cute chick there at Single Shores and he wanted Gene to come over with a girl and the four of them would all go for dinner. Gene said yes. For old-times' sake.

It loomed ahead of him, an ordeal. He would have to try to explain it all to Lottie, they would have to get dressed, Barnes would take them to one of those lobster and candlelight joints. Dinner and dates. Thinking about it was like preparing his head for an expedition to the Yucatán.

Lottie was appalled. She couldn't believe that Gene had a friend who would actually live in a middle-class, fra-

ternity house, organized fun and games, Miss American,
nineteen fifties Cutesy-pie infamous supersquare place like
the Single Shores.

Gene tried to explain. About Barnes. The background of
the thing. Lottie looked suspicious. He told her to just
relax and enjoy it, pretend you're looking at a movie, think
of getting the free booze and food.

She said she'd try.

When she came by his place that night to pick him up
he at first didn't recognize her.

She was wearing a platinum wig, a sheer see-through
white minidress with black bikini underwear, and black
vinyl boots.

"Like it?" she asked.

"What's the idea?" Gene said.

"You said to try to think of it like a movie."

"To *see* it that way," I said, "not *be* in it."

"Well, at least I'll be a 'conversation piece.' "

He figured it was no use to argue.

"Mymy," she said, "aren't *you* the hip young stud."

He was wearing a jean-jacket outfit from his days working for Ray Behr. He was trying. Anything for a friend.

The Single Shores apartment complex was as big as a
miniature town, and Gene had to stop and study the map
to figure out how the hell to get to Barnes's apartment. He
was in building F-2, Hall 6L, Room 127J. While Gene
was trying to trace this fucker on the huge map at the
entryway, Lottie was reading announcements from the
large, lighted bulletin board with cynical relish:

"Hey, you bridge nuts! Remember the C-block tourney
is coming Wednesday in Low Tide Lounge"

"Single Shores victorious water-volleyball club takes on
Bali-Hey Club Saturday at nine. Turn out poolside to cheer
'our boys'!"

"OK," said Gene, "OK, enough."

He took her by the hand toward what he hoped was the
correct building.

"There's a luau Thursday night," she said. "Don't you think we should come to the luau? Maybe your friend will invite us."

Just before they rang the bell to Barnes's apartment Gene said softly, "Please. OK?"

She sighed, nodded.

Gene for a moment forgot to worry about Lottie behaving when he got a load of Barnes. He was wearing the exact same clothes he was wearing the first day Gene got to town and saw him at the Marmont, but they looked wrong now. Barnes had already lost what little tan he had, and was fast getting back the flab, the jowly look. There were deep circles under his eyes, and a lot of little red tracks in the white of the eyeballs. Gene had the distressing sense that the new clothes were on the old Barnes. The two didn't go together.

Barnes only blanched slightly at the sight of Lottie, and got drinks for them. His date would be along in ten minutes or so.

"So how you doin, man?" Gene asked.

"Terrific. Got out of that Belle business just in time. Next thing you knew I'd have owned some damn house in Hollywood. What the hell business have I got owning a house? Anywhere. Much less Hollywood. The movie stuff is all crap. I'm back to books for good now . . ."

He went on explaining, justifying, endorsing what he had done and was going to do.

Lottie kept looking around the room, a little smirk on her face.

It had a Spanish motif. The lamps were supposed to look like lanterns. The wallpaper had bullfight scenes. Gene hoped Lottie didn't comment.

Barnes's date was named Bitsy.

Gene didn't know people had that name anymore.

She was curly blond, bouncy, and full of enthusiasm.

Just the thing to drive Lottie up the wall, Gene figured. He started drinking faster.

They went to dinner at Charlie Brown's, one of the
fashionable steak-or-lobster and candlelight places.

Bitsy was thrilled.

She was from Indianapolis, had attended Butler University in that same city, had eventually moved to Los Angeles
because she had gone to Disneyland on her vacation and
fell in love with it so much she wanted to live here. Of
course she didn't mean she only fell in love with Disneyland although that was certainly wonderful beyond words,
but it was all of Southern California she loved, everything
about it, the weather, the people, the food, the water, the
freeway. Everything.

She clapped her little hands together.

Even Barnes looked glum.

Lottie had been totally silent, every once in a while
staring at Bitsy with a mixture of venom and disbelief, but
holding her tongue. Gene was grateful. He threw in little
comments as best he could, agreeing with and admiring
Bitsy's views. He wasn't proud. Peace at any price. But
Bitsy, no doubt worried about her own social responsibili-
ties, thought perhaps she should try to draw Lottie into
the conversation. Bitsy apologized about how she'd been
going on and on about how wonderful her work was as
secretary and assistant to the social director of indoor
sports at Single Shores.

"What do you do?" she asked Lottie.

"I'm collecting."

"Oh! Antiques?"

"Unemployment."

"Oh. Well, I'm sure you'll find something soon."

"I'm not looking."

"Oh?"

"I get along."

"On unemployment?"

"I do a little hooking on the side. Not rugs, darling. You
know. Hooking as in hooker, prostitute, one of those chicks
who open their legs and let men stick their pricks in for

money. My own fee, unless there are extenuating circumstances—"

Everything came apart at once. Gene yelled, "Shut up, goddam you!" at the same time Bitsy, whose mouth had already been open in astonishment, let out a scream through it, Barnes dropped the carafe he was trying to pour more wine with, a waitress and the hostess came rushing to the scene. Lottie stood up and Gene stood up to grab her, knocking against the table and propelling Bitsy's lobster into her lap.

From then on Gene just tried to keep hold of Lottie's wrist, and tried not to see all the people staring at them.

Somewhere in there with Barnes trying to soothe Bitsy out of her hysterics Gene made some signal to him with his hand or expression or both that he and Lottie were splitting, he knew there wouldn't be any argument.

The argument was him and Lottie back at his place. He had never seen or heard her like that. Yelling. Transformed.

"Just like I thought, you gutless little prick, you're ashamed of me, ashamed of me and how I live because of some birdbrained little piece of fluff who will never know her ass from her elbow and your stupid friend trying to cop a little young blond pussy that's why he's living there in that ridiculous playpen that kindergarten for grown-ups that Republican right-wing Chamber of Commerce bunch of pigs in their pen all that's what I left what I split from spit on and I'll spit on it again anytime I see it hear it look at it feel it touch it you're one of them yourself goddam you the only way you ball me's on top like it says in the Boy Scout manual I've had boring lays in my time but nothing to—"

"Goddam you, how the hell *you* ever got paid twenty-five dollars for a trick is something the goddam Better Business Bureau oughta look into, any poor john who—"

"Why you poor pathetic excuse for a cock you'll never touch me again unless you pay and I'll charge you extra for being such a goddam lousy lay goddam I'm bored no wonder I'm bored with you as an excuse for a lover who wouldn't—"

He left, quick. He had to get out before he hit her. He saw it, he saw he would hit her and she would hit back and God knows where it would end and how bad.

He left quick and walked quickly, straight down Ocean Front Walk to Uncle Phil's.

"What's a matter?" Uncle Phil asked when he looked at him.

"I need some peace of mind," Gene said.

"You sure?"

"Yeh. Just a snort, you know."

"Sure."

Gene sat down. Phil went to the kitchen. When he came back he had the mirror and a little packet.

"First one's always free," he said.

"I know," said Gene.

Uncle Phil started tamping out the little mound of white stuff.

"I know you know," he said, "but I have to say it."

"How come?"

Uncle Phil looked up at Gene and grinned.

"Tradition," he said.

━━━━━━━

Gene thought about it. How after he snorted the skag he went back to his pad and found Lottie still there. She wanted to fight some more. But she couldn't because there was no one to fight with. Gene wouldn't, couldn't. He wasn't mad at her. At anyone. Ever. He was a man of peace. A man of peace of mind. He sat down on the floor against the wall, smiling. She tried to goad him but nothing worked. He only smiled, beatifically. He told her how he had gained peace of mind and first she looked shocked and then sort of interested, admiring even. Maybe it made her think he wasn't one of those Republican Chamber of Commerce type freaks after all. He giggled a lot, everything seemed funny to him. Not hilarious, just funny. Gently funny. Smily. Smile. Soon she was doing it. Smiling. She said she was sorry. He said it didn't matter. It didn't. Nothing did.

"Really," she said, "how do you feel? What does it feel like?"

"Peace," he said, smiling like the Buddha.

Then he said he had to sleep.

The next day he woke with a terrible hunger. That, and an aching feeling through his whole body, an exhaustion that felt like all his vital juices had been depleted. Lottie was still there. There was only a hot plate in Gene's place but she said she'd go get him something, make him some eggs or something. He said to get everything she could. He couldn't move very fast. She put on a pair of his jeans and one of his shirts and went to the grocery. She came back with two big bags of groceries and started cooking. It was like feeding a maw. He had two quarts of milk and one of orange juice, eight scrambled eggs, four peanut-butter-and-jelly sandwiches, a wedge of Monterey Jack cheese, and a quart of chocolate ice cream. Eating it, every once in a while he giggled.

By night, except for the huge tired he felt, he was back to more or less normal.

No more peace of mind.

All gone.

He felt completely at home at Uncle Phil's now. He liked the people who came there. He felt like he was one of them. There was one particular song on the *American Pie* album that seemed to be about them all. It was called "Crossroads." One of the things Don McLean said in this song was how Gene felt.

> ". . . I'm all tied up on the inside
> No one knows quite what I've got . . ."

That's how everyone seemed at Uncle Phil's. They didn't complain about their condition they just accepted it, they did whatever they could to make it feel better. They were in fact far out in a literal way, out along the edge of their own minds, of their own survival. With Uncle Phil farther out, farther along than anyone else. Once when he was offering a batch of some crazy goofballs he'd just concocted to anyone who wanted to try one, the black guy known as Ace shook his head and said, "I'm not like you, Uncle Phil. I don't wanna obliterate reality. I just wanna *modify* the sombitch."

There was a big swarthy guy named Rodney who'd been

offered a graduate assistantship in anthropology at Berkeley and he had to decide whether to take that or go into the family business. The family business happened to be the Mafia.

"At least it's good bread," Uncle Phil said.

"Yeh, but there isn't any future in it anymore. Another few years it may not be able to function efficiently."

"How come?" Gene asked.

"Because the whole thing is based on the ultimate threat—they can kill you."

"So? They still can, can't they?"

"Sure. But fewer people care anymore."

"That's heavy," Gene said.

Rodney sighed.

"It's sure as hell bad for business," he said.

The people around Uncle Phil's represented a wide variety of businesses.

Pepper, who was Uncle Phil's old lady, was in show business. That's what Uncle Phil called it, anyway.

She worked at a place called the Nutrient Center. It was on the second floor of a run-down office building about four blocks away. The center got its customers by placing an ad in the *L.A. Free Press* every week that said simply "The Nutrient Center. Consultation by Rhonda." Enough readers figured it was some kind of kinky sex trip that they went out to Venice and had a consultation. It went like this. When a customer came, Herb, who ran the Nutrient Center, called up Pepper, who hopped on her bike and went over. She would sit on a chair in the back of the room partitioned off by a curtain. If the customer wanted a $5 consultation, Pepper sat there and read a chapter from a book called *Nutrition and the Inner Mind*. If the customer popped for a $15 consultation, she did the same thing only with her clothes off. That was it. Herb was always on the other side of the curtain so the customer couldn't get any other ideas about further types of consul-

tation. Pepper said none of the customers yet complained.
Some even returned for more consultations, even though
they all were the same.

"Isn't that show biz?" Uncle Phil asked.

Gene had to admit he wouldn't know what else to call
it.

———

Sometimes outsiders dropped in. Not outsiders in the
head sense, but like they lived somewhere else. Not the
Marina of course, but Hollywood or Beverly Hills or
Laurel Canyon. One time Belle came, with her new boyfriend. His name was Jack. He was a comic, and had just
done a gig in Honolulu. His agent had promised him a bit
in a new movie. Belle had told him not to believe in
Hollywood.

"Do you ever see that Barnes person?" Belle asked Gene.

"No," Gene said, figuring that was easiest.

"Well, I guess he can't help the way he is," she said.
"But I hope he burns in hell."

The comic gave Gene a big slapstick sort of wink.

Gene nodded. He sent his love to Belle's mother.

———

He didn't want to leave his people, his world, but he
still felt some kind of loyalty to the old one, to the people
from before, so when Barnes called and told him Flash was
living somewhere in the Valley and wanted them to come
to dinner he said OK he would. At least he didn't have
to take a date.

Barnes picked him up and Gene asked what the hell
Flash was doing living in the fuckin San Fernando Valley
and Barnes didn't know, Flash had only said he wanted

them to come out and see "what a real sweet little setup"
he had there.

"Maybe it's a nightclub," Gene said. "Maybe he decided
the only way he could get any gigs for that group of his
was to own the nightclub."

It wasn't, though.

The Valley seemed to Gene like the flattest largest most
monotonous stretch of civilized earth anywhere on the
planet. The straight flat streets went forever, mile upon
mile, an endless repetition of houses or businesses, restaurants and bars and TV repair and Laundromats, Jesus,
nowhere on earth were there so many Laundromats.

Flash was living in a tiny house much like the countless
other tiny houses extending to infinity on either side of
his and across from his. Flash didn't own this particular
tiny house, nor did the woman whom he lived in it with.
She just rented.

Her name was Mildred.

She was a manicurist and Flash had met her when she
did his nails at a hair-styling salon in Hollywood. After the
gig in Oxnard, Flash's Group had broken up, one of the
teenyboppers running off with the new Rasputin, the other
returning home to Topeka, so Flash had come back down
to Hollywood to see what he could get moving. He was
down to his last fourteen bucks so he figured to cheer himself and to show how confident he was no matter how dim
things looked at the moment he'd go and get himself a
manicure. And as long as he was going to do it he'd get
him the best. That's how he met Mildred. She was the best.
The manicure cost ten bucks and he gave her a two-buck
tip.

"What the hell," Flash said out of the side of his mouth,
"the way I figure, we pass this way but once."

Flash had then asked Mildred if she knew of any nice
quiet sort of homey place a lonely man could have dinner
and sort of on an impulse she invited him to her place,
and he'd been here ever since.

As he proudly told the tale Mildred looked on beaming, obviously adoring her dashing knight. She had curly dyed red hair, a too-perfect set of dentures, and was probably clipping her way toward fifty.

"Show your friends the new watch I got you, hon," said Mildred.

Flash held up his wrist, looking rather critically at the watch.

"It's silver," he said. "It's a good timepiece, but gold is my color."

Mildred said maybe she could exchange it.

They sat around a small kitchen table for their dinner, which was beef Stroganoff. Flash was very proud of that.

"Is this beef Stroganoff," he asked, "or is this beef Stroganoff?"

"This is beef Stroganoff, all right," said Barnes.

"Gene?" Flash asked.

He had to say it, too.

"This sure is beef Stroganoff, man," he said.

Flash was satisfied. Gene remembered him like that, the satisfied look, the napkin tucked into his sport shirt, eating his beef Stroganoff lovingly made by Mildred the manicurist in a little house in the San Fernando Valley.

He remembered Barnes, driving back, in the dark of the car, telling him there was hope again for his movie getting made. There was a chance that they could get Diana Ross to play the Deb, and if they could then the picture was a sure thing.

"A Black Deb?" Gene asked.

"Sure, man. They have em now. Anyway the important thing is to get a star if you want a studio to back you. Doesn't matter what the hell color they are."

Because of this new development Barnes had put aside his new mystery set in the Single Shores. If Diana Ross *did* sign, then he'd have to do a lot of rewriting on that part.

"Well, I wish you luck, man," Gene said.

Barnes looked dim and shaky.

Gene remembered just how Barnes and Flash had looked that night because he had a feeling he might not ever see them again. Not that any of them was going to die, it was just that Gene felt too uncomfortable now going out of Venice, out of the circle of Uncle Phil and his friends. That's where he was at ease now, that's where he felt he belonged, and he wanted to be even more a part of it, get into it deeper.

He and Barnes and Flash had simply gone off in different directions. He thought of them, himself, too, listening to Don McLean singing "Crossroads" at Uncle Phil's:

> "You know I've heard about people like me
> But I never made the connection.
> They walk one road to set them free
> And find they took the wrong direction."

Had they? Had he?
Who knew?

He thought a lot about the peace of mind. The heroin. Everything gentle. No freak shows like with acid, no jumpiness that speed made, not over so quick as coke and more than any of them it brought the famous "peace of mind," the cessation of interior hostilities, the calming of the mind's confusion, the easing of the pain.

He knew, of course, the ultimate price. Your life. One way or other. Quick, with an overdose, or slow, as more of it gave you less peace and there was no peace in between but doing whatever you could to get the bread to buy the skag that you needed by then just to get back feeling like you were before you started.

Well.

He understood all that.

He tried not to dwell on it.

He walked a lot. He often woke at dawn with the fog-horns and he walked the beach, looking at shells, watching the birds, formations of sandpipers, diving of gulls. He tried to focus on very small things. A single pebble. Turn it in your hand. Examine. Commune. A strand of seaweed. A footprint. His own big toe. Sometimes he'd sit cross-legged in the sand, trying to hold his mind still. Sometimes he kept it blank for a while. Not long though. Sometimes the seal came, always leaving Gene wrung out and shaky from willing him away. Sometimes Lou would appear, bright as life. Sometimes Laura, frozen in the door-framed snapshot that last time he saw her. He didn't want to think of these things, these people or anything, he just wanted to be there. But they kept creeping in, the thoughts. Lizzie. Mulligan. Chicken wings.

One specially warm day he went out on the pier to feed the sea gulls. He laid out a row of pieces of stale bread on the wooden railing, and stood at the end of it. A gull came down and padded toward the first piece. His yellow beak banged down and got it and then the next, advancing along the row. Suddenly there was an angry *caw* from above and a beating of wings. Gene ducked but this new gull wasn't after him, it attacked the one that was eating, gave it a terrible blow just under the eye with its beak, knocking it off the rail. The attack was quick, fero-cious, frightening, from out of nowhere. Gene dropped the rest of the bread in the water.

At work that afternoon a guy in a loud sport shirt came in and ordered a taco. He had a lot of black hairs coming out of his nostrils. Gene prepared the taco, put it on a paper plate and placed it on the counter in front of the man. The man took a couple of bites and said, "You call this a taco?"

Gene didn't answer. He took off his apron, folded it neatly, and placed it on one of the stools at the counter.

He walked out the door and down Ocean Front Walk, neither fast nor slow, his hands in his pockets.

"Hey, you!" the customer called after him.

Uncle Phil offered Gene a Carlings, and they sat around talking about George Allen's handling of the Rams for a while.

Then Gene said, "I want some."

He didn't have to say what.

Phil nodded and went to the kitchen. It was not for him to make moral or medical judgments. He was not a doctor or a priest. He would never have urged anyone to try it, but if they asked him and he had it he'd provide it for them. But of course he couldn't keep giving it away. Before he got to the kitchen he turned and looked gently at Gene.

"You understand, it's not free," he said.

Gene nodded.

"Nothing ever is," he said.

Dell Bestsellers

"WE ONLY HAVE ONE TEXAS"

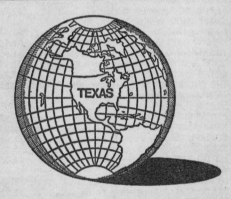

People ask if there is really an energy crisis. Look at it this way. World oil consumption is 60 million barrels per day and is growing 5 percent each year. This means the world must find three million barrels of new oil production each day. Three million barrels per day is the amount of oil produced in Texas as its peak was 5 years ago. The problem is that it is not going to be easy to find a Texas-sized new oil supply every year, year after year. In just a few years, it may be impossible to balance demand and supply of oil unless we start conserving oil today. So next time someone asks: "is there really an energy crisis?" Tell them: "yes, we only have one Texas."

ENERGY CONSERVATION - IT'S YOUR CHANCE TO SAVE, AMERICA

Department of Energy, Washington, D.C.